Death on Deck

by

Courtny Bradley

The Cruising Crew

Dedication

Thank you to all of the feisty older ladies in my life. This book wouldn't have been possible without my Nonnie, Nannie, and Grandma Janet. I love you all.

Acknowledgements

To say that I'm an author is something that I never thought I would be able to say about myself. As someone who has been an avid reader since I was a child, I never thought in a million years that a story of mine would reach someone else's hands. I truly hope you love The Cruising Crew as much as I do. This book would never have made it to shelves without the following people being my cheerleaders.

First, I have to thank Ellie Alexander. You have been my rock through this process, and your Mystery Series Master Class is the foundation for my writing. As a reader, I fangirled when you would repost my review on Instagram, and now I can call you my dear friend and mentor. I truly adore you to bits.

To Aaron, my love, my best friend, and the person who started me on this journey of being wholeheartedly myself. If it hadn't been for you pushing me to create my YouTube channel and talk about my love for cozies and finding my 'people' I don't think this book would have happened. I wouldn't have had the confidence to write my own story. I love you and the boys so much. Thank you for supporting me every step of the way.

To my sister, Miss Priss, Aimee McFarland, I love you more than words express. And while you've never read a cozy, you love the punny titles I send you! Thank you for letting me brainstorm my story conundrums and red herrings. You have no idea what it means to me that you listen. Muh!

To Mom & Dad, thank you for always believing that I can do anything I set my mind to. Thank you for taking me to the bookstore every payday and buying me the newest Mary-Kate and Ashley Olsen Adventure novels. Those books are what sparked my love for reading and mysteries.

To the best mother-in-law in the world. Thank you so much for helping me edit my book. Your eye for detail is unmatched, and I love that you also have so much love for my ladies. You are an absolute gem; I'm so lucky to have you!

To Victoria Gilbert, you are one of my favorite people. I love the stories you weave and hope to write as descriptively as you do one day. Thank you for reading the ROUGHEST version of this book and not laughing at me. Your feedback was invaluable and helped set me on a course for success. I hope you love it.

To my work besties, my work wives, Rachel Doty and Jordan Dunkerson-Hurst, I don't think I've ever met better hype people in my life. Your belief in me and my writing means so much to me. Thank you for reading my book's first draft and thinking it had potential. Thank you for constantly asking me for updates and when you can preorder. You both are beautiful humans.

To The Cozy Engagement Group- Anna Ross, Blake Langrehr, Jasi Lowe, Kyla Dietz, Rebecca Guyer, Spencer Calquhoun, and Susan Smith. Cozy Mysteries brought us together. We are scattered all over the country, yet I can call you if I need anything. The friendship we have cultivated over the past few years has made me believe that friendships can be found in the most unlikely places. A special thanks to Spencer, Anna, and Susan for reading different versions of Death on Deck. I hope you love this final form.

Thank you to Najla Mahis. You took a chance on

me, a brand-new baby author. Your love for these feisty ladies and their adventuring gave me faith that you were the perfect editor for this book. Your patience and understanding through my constant emails of questions about editing, cover art, and the whole publishing process have been amazing. Thank you!

To The Wild Rose Press, thank you for being so open and caring about your authors. I knew the moment I signed with you that this was going to be the start of an amazing adventure. I've loved being a part of The Garden, which is The Wild Rose Press.

Finally, to you, my cozy mystery reader. If this is the first time you've heard of me or if you have been following my whole journey through my YouTube channel, Book Club, or Instagram, thank you. Thank you for all of the messages asking me when my own book would be coming out. This book is in your hands because of your support and belief in me. I hope it is everything you thought it could be.

Chapter One

"Knock, knock! Bev! Are you ready?!" I hollered as I opened the front door and walked into the cozy living room of Beverly Aft's four-bedroom suburban house. I rolled my suitcase to the living room entrance and observed what could only be described as the quintessential grandmother's house. Everything was in its place.

"Lisa, you're here! I will be down soon! I'm just packing a few more essentials. Are Charlotte and Wilma here yet?" Beverly shouted from her bathroom in the hallway.

"Not yet. But I am sure they will be soon." I walked into the living room, which had dark walnut flooring aged with scuffs and scratches from being lived in and loved for many years. In the wood flooring, I read a story of children running around, toy cars rolling on the floor, furniture moving over the years, and happiness soaking into the walls. The throw pillows on the couches gave "grandma vibes," as my daughter, Veronica, would say. All are hand-embroidered with wildflowers and bold and colorful designs. Knowing Beverly, she made or thrifted them from local vendors or secondhand shops.

The seating all faced each other to encourage conversations and enjoy the beautifully restored fireplace that Beverly and Ryan had brought back to its original red brick, flanked by floor-to-ceiling bookshelves. I walked towards the shelves, taking a journey to the past. I could always tell who a person was by the items they displayed on their bookshelves. If the bookshelves look like they had come out of a magazine, that person might hold their feelings tight to their chest, not wanting to let others into their world. Other shelves might hold only self-help, dieting, or spiritual books, telling of a person who is open and ready to grow, wanting to be more than what they are.

Then there were shelves like those before me, full of books of all genres. Agatha Christie, Jane Austen, Douglas Adams, and more cozy mysteries than one could count. Surrounding these very well-loved books, judging from the broken spines and the post-it notes sticking out of them, were shelf enhancers. All genres were bracketed by thrifted bookends of playful cats lying on books, sculptures of hands holding candles, and pictures of Beverly's life throughout the years. People with shelves like these tended to be open books. Those who wore their hearts on their sleeves, who would give you the shirt off their back to keep you sheltered and safe.

I noticed a picture in a vintage frame depicting all of us during our final summer at Camp Cimarron by Oklahoma's man-made Grand Lake. I looked slightly different now, fifty years later. I had kept my girlish figure, though things were no longer as perky as they once were. Streaks of silver ran through my blonde hair, and my face bore a few extra wrinkles, evidence of spending more time in the sun than doctors would recommend nowadays. Overall, I was happy with how I aged. Tears filled my eyes with longing and sadness, and a good dose of love filled my heart as I looked at the picture. We hadn't a care in the world. We meant everything to each other back then, and we still did.

"You girls had no idea what was coming for you. The whole wide world was waiting for you," I whispered as I shook my head, a feeling of almost regret washing over me as the front door creaked open. No knocking. Charlotte and Wilma were just letting themselves in as they always have.

"Ladies! The party has arrived!" Wilma hollered. She was followed by Charlotte, reading a map with a crease on her brow, glasses on her nose, and biting her lip.

I turned from the fireplace to take in two of the most influential people in my life and couldn't help the smile cresting my lips. Wilma looked like a geriatric advertisement for Lululemon. She was medium height, slightly built, and toned from all the yoga retreats she had participated in since her retirement. Her skin appeared pale, given how much time she spent outside in her garden and meditation area in the backyard of her house. She wore athleisure clothing more expensive than some people's monthly car payments and looked relatively comfortable for the nine-hour drive we were about to partake in.

"I told you, Char, the car has navigation. Why are you reading a map? You can't be that antiquated. Get with the times!" Wilma exclaimed as she took one of her ear pods from her ears, gesturing to me. "Meditation class. Utterly useless once Charlotte picked me up and wouldn't stop squawking about needing a map and having to stop at a QuikTrip before heading this way, or we'd already be here."

Charlotte rolled her eyes and sighed as she carefully

folded her map of Oklahoma and inserted it into her floral leather fanny pack.

Charlotte hadn't changed too much since the pictures on the mantel were taken. She had filled out and was curvier than when we were younger. Charlotte grew up with her head in a book; her only true friends were the girls and me. A stack of books, a notepad, and a pen was always within arm's length. While her parents were always worried, she wouldn't make it in the real world with her head always in a book or writing stories, Charlotte proved them wrong.

She held an air of pride that lifted her and made you want to strike up a conversation with her. Char's years as a librarian and national best-selling author brought in more money than she could handle, but you wouldn't know it by looking at her. Her previously dark brown curls, now white with streaks of silver, had a personality of their own, like Medusa's. She wore the quintessential librarian cardigan tied around her neck, a Peter-Pan-collared white shirt, and slim-fit trousers.

"Listen, when we run into a service outage and no longer have Siri, Alexa, or whoever is navigating us through a hailstorm, you'll be happy I brought my antiquated map!" Charlotte snapped back as she took in the house and breathed a sigh of relief as she plopped onto the ottoman. The tension she had been carrying melted off her shoulders, almost tangible in its release, leaving her visibly relieved.

My brow creased with worry, and I opened my mouth to comment on it when Wilma rushed up to me and knocked her hip with mine. She grabbed my hips and started making me sway and dance to music only she could hear.

"Hey sugar, what's cooking? Are you doing all right?" Wilma's concerned hazel eyes looked into mine with love and compassion.

"I'm fine, Wil. Charlotte's map isn't the only thing that has become antiquated," I stated matter-of-factly as my green eyes threatened to spill over with tears.

Chapter Two

"Oh, honey! Come here!" Wilma exclaimed as she opened her arms for me to cry into if I needed it.

I sighed, wanting to fall into her caring arms but not wanting to pull down the vibe of this trip. "Not right now, dear. I need a glass of wine to mellow out before the drive to Galveston. Do you think Beverly has any good stuff? Or is it just grocery-store stovetop wine?"

I looked down my nose at wines I didn't consider quality. I wanted to know the grape, the temperature it was picked at, the age of the wine, and even the soil it was grown in. That is very bougie, as the Gen Z kids would say, of me, but I liked what I liked. I understood I was being ridiculous, but at my age, I wouldn't settle for the cheap stuff when I could afford, at least for now, the good stuff.

I caught Charlotte and Wilma catching each other's glances and rolling their eyes, and I couldn't help noticing the smiles tugging at the corners of their mouths. Now wasn't the time to think about how I'd been taken to the cleaners. It was time for our girls' trip to get started. Just then, the sound of wheels on the floor caught our attention, and we turned to see Beverly entering the living room with her bright yellow rolling suitcase.

"As a matter of fact, I have a perfect bottle of wine for this occasion. Though ladies, we can only have one glass each! Follow me!" Beverly looked like the classic grandma. She was five foot two, cuddly and curvy with wavy stark-white bob-length hair and wearing the most outlandish floral prints a person could want to find; losing her in a crowd wouldn't happen. As she came closer, the scent of cookies and coffee enveloped me as she hugged me tightly. It was a delightful combination that could easily evoke a smile and an irresistible urge to reciprocate her embrace.

As we followed Beverly, Wilma reached for her phone. She started playing music, taking all of us back to summers at Camp Cimarron and Grand Lake. "Turn! Turn! Turn!" by The Byrds started playing, and we all squealed like we were in high school again and no time had passed.

"Just you wait, ladies! I made a playlist of the best songs. We are going to be rocking out the whole trip down!" Wilma shook her phone and sashayed toward the kitchen to follow Beverly.

We entered the kitchen through an arched entryway. Beverly got out her step stool. Judging by the tiny painted handprints and fingerprint petals of flowers, this was either a gift from Beverly's kids when they were younger or a gift from her grandchildren. She strode over to the handcrafted mahogany bar cabinet she and Ryan— her recently passed husband—had purchased in Europe decades ago. Reaching out toward the beautifully crafted cabinet, Bev ceremoniously presented us with a dusty bottle of 1967 Kopke Port.

We all looked at her with dropped jaws and wide-eyed stares.

"Where did you find this?!" Wilma rushed forward and grabbed the bottle to inspect it closer. We all huddled around Wilma to better view the bottle and label.

It couldn't be, disbelief creeping into my mind.

"How did you get your hands on it?!" Charlotte asked, taking the bottle from Wilma's protective hands and adjusting her glasses on the tip of her nose in typical librarian form to take a closer look.

"Yes, dear! Do tell us! You haven't been keeping secrets, have you?" I inquired as I took the bottle carefully from Charlotte's not-so-careful grasp on the bottle's neck. Sure enough, it proved to be exactly what we suspected. But how?

"I was able to bid on it at the last auction Ryan and I attended about eight years ago. It came up, and I told Ryan we would have to get it no matter the cost," Beverly caught the surprised look on my face and winked, "What, Lisa? You think I didn't remember?" Beverly asked with a smug and uncharacteristically uncouth expression from sweet Beverly Aft.

"I just didn't think you would recall its brand or year. We stole it in the middle of the night on our last day at Summer Camp as cabin leaders," I reminisced as the memory surfaced. I could feel time slowly fade away and take us all back to that night, the last day of Summer Camp in 1972.

We had been going to Camp Cimarron since we were fifteen years old. We all started in the same cabin, number four. I remember how we were so scared to talk to each other the first night. Most of us were dropped off and had no say in what we wanted. Still, we became quick companions as shared feelings of abandonment from our adults emerged. That closeness grew—especially after the incident when the fifth member of our cabin, Diane, went missing.

8

Chapter Three

"All right, girls, let's have two fingers of this port and then get the heck out of Dodge," Wilma declared as she took the bottle from me, grabbed four tumblers from the middle of the butcher block island, and started pouring for everyone. A heavy silence enveloped us as we all took sips of the port. So many unspoken words filled the spaces between us, almost suffocating in their weight.

Charlotte took a second sip and cleared her throat. "You want to talk about it, Lisa?"

I could feel three pairs of eyes fall on me and heard everyone take a small breath and hold it in. I knew they were waiting for a Lisa-May Mide type of tantrum with colorful words, stomping, and plate smashing. Instead, I was oddly cold and distant from any significant feelings. Almost numb.

I took a small sip from my tumbler and sighed. "What is there to say? I have been traded in for a younger and cheaper model. They went with prim, proper, and inexperienced Poppy Harold. My research assistant. 'Budget cuts,' they said." I finished with air quotes.

I cleared my throat and continued. "But it was because they didn't want to pay my salary anymore or deal with me bucking against policies that interfered with my work." I snorted as I took a bigger swig out of my glass, finishing off the port without savoring it as I would normally.

"Surely you were ready to retire and settle down? Spend more time with Veronica and maybe even meet someone new," Beverly asked with the warmth and love of a caring friend. She was always the one to find the silver lining when things went south until Ryan passed. She almost didn't see the light at the end of the tunnel then.

I put my drinking glass down harder on the counter than intended. "Hell no! I wasn't ready to roll over and die. I have so much more left to give. Being sixty-four doesn't mean I must be taken out to pasture. But now I need to find something else to work toward."

This can't be it for me, I promised myself, as everyone else gave a moment of silence before I changed the subject. I didn't want the conversation to be on me anymore. So, I did what I always did: put someone else in the limelight.

"How's your next work in progress going, Charlotte? Kill anyone else off yet?" I quipped to take their gazes off me.

Seeing the hurt flash on Charlotte's face, I had taken it too far. But I was too prideful to apologize at that moment. I wasn't the only one who had a backslide in my career, but Charlotte was the one who murdered her own.

Chapter Four

"I just don't understand! The woman at the phone store told me this app would give us directions to Galveston! We could even program it as a man's voice in an Australian accent! Why won't it work?" Wilma grumbled, closing her phone with a snap and throwing it into the Mary Poppins tote bag she called a purse as she walked towards the front door and opened it for everyone to follow.

"It is not as though we will need a map," Beverly stated as she rolled her luggage to the front door. "I remember exactly how to get there from the last time we went on a cruise." She pointed to her temple.

Beverly has a photographic memory and remembers everything she sees, having total recall of memories. Ryan's map was meticulously made during their first cruise in 1976. Once he had completed the route, including rest stops, cute boutiques, and the best inns to stay at, Beverly never needed to look at it again. But that didn't stop her from carrying it in her hand right now. It had markings in Ryan's handwriting, explaining why she brought the map on this trip. She wanted a little piece of him with her on this journey. They had been serial cruisers; this would be her first cruise since he'd passed unexpectedly. I needed to talk to the other girls about making sure we kept a close eye on Beverly on this trip. We couldn't afford to have her go back down the dark path she was on for the year after he passed.

"Beverly, you can't still remember how to get from Broken Arrow, Oklahoma, to Galveston, Texas," Charlotte commented as she checked her fanny pack for the tenth time to ensure she had everything she needed for the ride down. Charlotte often got car sick and needed special glasses with four lens-like circles filled with fluid to read and annotate her current read. I would make a solid bet with anyone that Charlotte packed more books with her than clothes to wear for this trip.

"I sure as heck can! You watch! I will be better than any artificial Australian man! I'm far more entertaining and a lot sexier, too!" Beverly winked, stopped to put her hands on her hips, and took in all of us in the same room for the first time in eons.

We were all retired now, looking for guidance and wanting to spend quality time with each other. What better way to do this than to be locked on a ship for a week soaking up the ocean breeze with mojitos in our hands and excellent company to enjoy?

"All right, y'all! Are you ready to head out?" I announced with the heaviest Oklahoman accent I could muster, putting my aviator sunglasses on and rolling my suitcases toward the door.

"Shotgun!" Wilma shouted as we all made our way to Beverly's Honda CRV.

"That isn't fair, Wil!" Charlotte whined. "You always shove the chair as far back as possible, leaving no room for Lisa or me!"

We all laughed as this familiar argument that took us back to the road trips to the convenience store down the road from the camp came to mind.

"I need room for all of my things! I must have my

neck pillow, weighted lavender blanket, and snack bag!" Wilma yelled over her shoulder as she threw the seat back to the full extent and stuffed her items onto the front seat floorboard. There was barely enough room for her to fit in the front seat.

"Rock, paper, scissors, Charlotte. You know the rules," I said with a smirk, knowing full well what the outcome would be.

Since we were teenagers, Charlotte always lost to Wilma in this game. She always threw down paper, and Wilma cut right through with scissors.

As if I could tell the future, Charlotte brought her hand down on three with paper and sulked to the back passenger seat, her knees pressed as close to her chest as she could make them. You would think she would have learned this in the past fifty years, but alas, she was stuck in the back with me again.

"It is just like old times! Isn't it, girls?" Wilma grinned as she plugged her phone into Beverly's radio and started a playlist she had made just for the road trip.

As Beverly backed the car out from her driveway, Ray Charles' "Hit the Road Jack" started belting out of the speakers.

We had no idea our lives were about to change significantly, and we would not come back the same.

Chapter Five

Beverly dropped Wilma and me at the front of the drop-off zone with all of the luggage while she and Charlotte took the car to long-term parking.

"We are going to be late!" I screamed at Wilma behind me as I ran to the luggage check-in. I could feel my breath hitching in my throat and hear my heart pounding in my ears. *I need to work out more*, I scolded myself as I made it closer to the baggage drop-off.

We had overslept at the Sink 'n' Swim Motel. Or, as Wilma called it, 'Where Dreams Dive and Laughter Floats.' We found it at three in the morning when we finally reached Houston. Usually, this would have been an easy nine-hour drive, but our bladders and attention spans were weaker and shorter as we had gotten older.

We stopped at antique shops for Beverly, book shops for Charlotte, and even made stretching stops for Wilma with pit stops for all between roadside excursions.

I was the only one who could sit in a car for any length without making a pit stop. This might be because I have traveled my whole life for both work and pleasure and am used to the inconveniences of a full bladder and boredom.

"Lisa, they aren't leaving the dock for another two hours. They aren't going to leave without us. Slow down!" Wilma panted as she gained ground by running a little faster. It wasn't as though I was in better shape than her. She was trailing behind with five pieces of luggage while I only carried mine. When I offered to grab some of the luggage, Wilma shooed me away grumbling something about not being a wimp and being perfectly capable of getting the bags. I wasn't going to force my help on someone so determined not to take it. Plus, I kind of liked the fact I was beating her in a race if only in my mind.

Wilma and I finally arrived at the port luggage drop-off and got in line to release our bags. While waiting, we observed the crew grab and tag the luggage for the different areas of the ship. They were a well-honed assembly line. They all wore vests with the ship's name, *Oceanic Odyssey*, and wore headphones, jamming out to music by the dance moves we saw as they rolled luggage to each other. This was going to be a fun ship.

We followed the line as it moved up when a man slammed into me, knocking my luggage from my hand and spiraling it onto the concrete. The man was so rushed he didn't even look back to check if I was okay. My shoulder already felt tender, and I knew a bruise would likely form within a few hours.

My face flushed in anger when I shouted, "Hey, buddy! Watch where you are going! We are standing right here!" The man with dark shaggy hair and beard didn't turn to acknowledge, let alone apologize to me.

A young woman trailed behind him. She looked exhausted, with dark circles under her eyes, but that didn't take away from her beauty. She looked about five foot three with waist-length blonde hair and deep brown eyes. She turned back to me and mouthed, "I'm so sorry!" and ran after the man who seemed oblivious to her.

"It's okay, Lisa. It is a big boat. The likelihood of us running into him again is very slim. Let's drop these off and wait for Beverly and Charlotte to meet us at check-in. I am pretty sure we have four margaritas with our names on them."

Wilma and I made our way onto the boat, crossing the big ramp over the water and talking about the fun things we found on the ship's app itinerary. There were trivia nights, dance nights, formal dinners, and more. I could feel my energy starting to renew as I took a big breath of the clean, salty air as we crossed the threshold into the boat's foyer.

Cruise liners had changed a lot since I last was on a ship. The entrance was grand. We walked up to the railing, looking up and down. We could see multiple levels of the ship from this position. There was a dance floor two levels below us and a live band playing bluegrass. The bar was at least two people deep as people entering the boat lined up to start their vacation on a boozy level. The bar was nautical-themed, with fishing nets, sailor's clothing, and fake fish hanging from the rafters above the bartender. At least, I hoped they were manufactured.

I glanced up, and my breath caught in my throat as I took in the stunning chandelier. Created using a jellyfish as inspiration, what appeared to be the central part of the jellyfish was intricately blown bubbled glass about five feet long and fifteen feet across. Globes of pink, blue, and green coloring fell like bubbles in the water. The tentacles were well-placed LED string lights that played with gravity and made the chandelier feel like it was floating in the ocean but in the ship's middle.

I saw Wilma was just as enchanted as me. I could feel whatever stress she'd been holding roll off her. This was just what the girls and I needed to get the oomph back into our steps and take on the world. I didn't want to think about home and all the troubles waiting for me after vacation. That was Future Me's problem.

Wilma and I turned the corner to get onto the buffet floor; two were on this ship. Seating was scattered all around this level of the ship. Some tables were set for two, and others had extended family-style seating for guests with a big group. There were big, beautiful windows overlooking the water with tables set for four, allowing for the view to be seen from any chair at the table.

Charlotte and Beverly walked toward us with their plates stacked high with all the goodies a person could want. Cakes, pie, and ice cream. I motioned to our table by the panoramic view of the water, and they followed over. Wilma and I relieved them of the plates they had acquired for us, and we all sat down with big sighs of contentment.

"We didn't know what you girls were in the mood for, so we got a bit of everything," Beverly said with a little bit of ice cream on her nose.

"Already sampling the goods, are you, Bev?" I asked with humor in my voice.

Beverly wiped off her nose. "I was just saving it for later. Besides, this is a judgy-free zone, and if I gain ten pounds on this trip, it just means more of me for my grandbabies to cuddle."

Beverly was the first of the group to become a grandma. She took her role as the doting grandmother very seriously. I envied her a bit. Her grandchildren were obsessed with her cuddles, cooking, and baking. They always fight over who gets to help her with the cooking and cleaning. I've been over when they have big family meals, and Beverly is undoubtedly rich with love. There were always enough freshly baked treats for midnight snacks and the road when the sleepover ended.

"Of course, my dear. But make sure to take care of yourself or your grandbabies won't have someone to cuddle with," Wilma retorted hypocritically after taking a big bite out of a chocolate cookie. The cookie crumbled onto her shirt as she pointed it at Beverly for emphasis. She quickly licked her finger, picked up the crumbs on her shirt, and put them in her mouth. Wilma was an avid yogi and burned what ordinary people ate in calories daily. She still mainly ate whatever she wanted but didn't look like she did. She had a wicked sweet tooth.

"Well, that is morbid, Wilma. We don't need to have negativity on this trip. This is all about relaxation and becoming who we are truly meant to be in the new chapter of our lives. Let us eat what we want. Drink what we want. And be merry!" I pronounced while holding my cookie up in the air, causing the others to grab a sweet of their own and toast.

Our table was a perfect viewpoint for people-watching. People-watching on a cruise ship was better than people-watching at a Walmart. People of all shapes and sizes were wearing the best, most high-dollar outfits, showing as much as society would allow them in front of families and children.

As we started talking about what classes or spa treatments we wanted to partake in, the dining attendant for the buffet approached our table.

"Hello, ladies! My name is Rachelle, and I work in

the buffet in the mornings and the dining hall in the evenings. Is there anything I can get you or any plates I can take for you?"

Rachelle was a beautiful young lady with dark almond-colored eyes and wavy brown hair. Her cocoa-colored skin glowed from the kiss of the sun. She was very calm in her mannerisms and graceful in her movements. I would have pegged her as a dancer in childhood. Her smile was sweet and welcoming.

Since everyone else's mouth was full of food or drink, Charlotte looked up from her guidebook and answered, "No, dear, I think we are fine. We can get our plates and put them up. No need for us to be waited on hand and foot. Could you point us to the disposal and the plate drop-off?"

Rachelle waved her off. "It's ship policy for our team to clean up after guests. You are here on vacation. We will handle the dirty work."

Charlotte pursed her lips. "Well, if you say so. We can at least stack our cups and plates for Rachelle and make her job a little easier. Don't you think girls?"

We nodded in agreement and cleaned up some of the plates that magically became empty with nothing but crumbs to indicate they had been used.

"Why, thank you all so much! It is a rare thing to find such thoughtful people! If you all need anything at all, just let me know." Rachelle picked up all the soiled dishes and smiled at us as she walked away.

"Alright, girls, are you ready to go to our rooms? We should all freshen ourselves up, unpack our bags, and prepare for the safety briefing happening in about an hour," Beverly suggested as she looked at the itinerary on her phone.

"Yes, we shouldn't miss the safety briefing. We don't want to miss any important information and go down with the ship like Jack and what's her name in Titanic. You know both of them could have fit on that damn door," I replied with a roll of my eyes, causing everyone else to giggle, and started a passionate discussion about whether they really could have fit on the door. Little did we know what we would find below the deck.

Chapter Six

We walked out of the buffet area to find ourselves in a massive crowd as everyone waited on the elevators to get to their rooms. It looked like a long wait, which I was more than willing to do. Wilma, however, was not the most patient of people.

"Come on, ladies, let us work off some of those sweets we just devoured. It's only a couple of flights down to our rooms. We will have enough time to get ready and relax before the briefing." Wilma tugged a very pouty Beverly toward the empty stairwell.

I couldn't hide my grin. Charlotte and I caught each other's glances. We shared a laugh while shaking our heads and followed the bulldozing Wilma towards the stairs. This wasn't a hill we were willing to die on. We weaved through everyone else waiting for the elevators and started toward our rooms.

We all finally made it to our rooms on the eighth floor, two floors down from the Lido Deck and the buffet. Beverly panted a little. I hated to admit it, but my heart rate was also elevated. Wilma may be right…I needed to exercise more. I quickly shook my head to knock loose those rambling thoughts. We were on vacation, and I wasn't about to waste precious time sweating through exercising when I could engage in other activities.

Lisa, what is wrong with you? I chided myself. *I'm*

here to be with my lifelong friends, not to find a companion of the male persuasion.

"Our rooms are the perfect distance from the Lido Deck to use the stairs the whole week!" Wilma stated matter-of-factly and clapped her hands in joy. "We won't have to use the elevator at all!"

She turned back to face us with the biggest smile, which quickly fell when she saw the state the rest of us were in. Beverly was wheezing, I was wiping my damp forehead with my shirt and Charlotte looked like she ate something sour with the pursing of her lips.

"You don't have to use the elevator, Wil. But I'm on vacation. I will use the elevator as many times as I possibly can!" Beverly said with a grin as a little drop of sweat fell down her forehead.

Beverly loved to get under Wilma's skin when it came to health and happiness. They both had completely opposite points of view. They loved pressing each other's buttons, but we all knew they loved each other very much and wanted to take care of each other. Beverly would try her hardest to use the stairs, and Wilma would eventually bend her rigid rules regarding healthy food and exercise regimens. Having them both in our circle of friends created a healthy balance.

The hallway was a long, endless row of doors on either side of the carpeted floor. Some entries had beach-themed decorations and banners like "Seas the Day!", "Beach please, I'm on vacay mode!", and my favorite, "Shell-abrate good times and tan lines!"

Many people go on cruises to celebrate their honeymoon, an anniversary, or birthdays. We weren't celebrating anything specific except finally being able to spend time together. Decorations on other doors made me wish we had put something on ours. This was a celebration! Something like: "Age is just a number, and these ladies are Beach-tiful!" Okay, I'll work on it.

We noticed our bags had been delivered and were waiting just outside the door for us to take them in and begin unpacking. Everyone's luggage *except* for mine.

"What the hell? Where are my bags?" I asked in an aggravated tone. I looked up and down the hall to see if there had been a mistake and maybe my bags were put in front of someone else's room, but they were nowhere to be seen.

A room attendant walked past us, and Charlotte stopped him. "Excuse me, my friend's baggage is missing. Any idea where it might be?"

The young man's name tag read 'Arba.' He was small in stature, young with a look of playfulness on his face. "Yes, ma'am. Any lost or misplaced luggage will be at Guest Services on the tenth floor. Do you have the cruise ship's app?"

Charlotte got her phone out and handed it to the young man. He opened the app and tapped a few buttons before loading up a ship's map. He pointed her to where the service desk was located.

"How could my bags have been misplaced in the first place? I had them all together with tags on them." I sighed with frustration.

At that moment, the man Wilma and I hoped we wouldn't see again emerged from the room next door. He oozed confidence, his undeniable handsomeness turning heads wherever he went. His smug smile and the coldness in his gaze washed away any charm he may have possessed, leaving a bitter aftertaste in his wake.

Having overheard the end of the conversation in

passing, the rude man snorted and responded, "Maybe you need to get your memory tested, Grandma. Are you sure you should even be on this trip unsupervised?" He laughed at his joke while gripping the wrist of the young girl we had seen with him earlier. She gave a quick, annoyed glance at him before sending a look of apology my way.

"Come on," the girl said, pulling her wrist a little to get the man to follow her. "We need to go get something to eat before the safety presentation."

The man completely ignored her, though I could see his grip tightening on her wrist before he continued talking. The girl's look of discomfort and pain made me want to curl my hand into a fist and teach this young man a thing or two.

"Oh, really? And Arnold, my man? What's up with this place? No complimentary goodies on the beds for us to snag? And seriously, where on earth did you acquire your towel-folding skills? Aren't you a tad old for that?" He chuckled at his jest once more, striding down the hallway toward the elevator with the young woman reluctantly trailing behind, her face contorted in a pained expression.

A flash of anger sparked in Arba's eyes as he watched the man and his girlfriend disappear around the corner. "I am so sorry, ma'am, but you will have to wait until after dinner to get your bags. That is when all missing luggage is carried up to be claimed." He gave Charlotte her phone and told us he was our room attendant if we needed anything.

"What I need is a drink," I mumbled as I got my phone out to download the ship's app before we set sail and I lost my phone signal and access to the internet.

"That would be the Below Deck Pub on deck ten," Arba replied, pointing to the map still on Charlotte's screen.

"Come on, girls, I'd kill for a drink," I said as I placed my purse up higher on my arm.

"It's either go get a drink or we will have to get Lisa a lawyer because she murdered someone for losing her Louis Vuitton baggage," Charlotte retorted.

Chapter Seven

I surveyed our surroundings as we walked into the pub. The pub looked like what I expected a cruise bar to look like. It was a more elaborate version of the bar we saw when we boarded. Fish nets hung down from the ceiling with fake fish caught in the nets and old life vests, life preservers, and different tools of the trade for fishermen on the walls. The pumping music was a fascinating combo of Spanish salsa and bluegrass. I wouldn't mind finding out who the artist was.

The likelihood the decorative items had ever actually been used was very slim. Even the *vintage* items had a shine of newness on them. There was no doubt in my mind that everything on this ship, decoration-wise, was purchased in bulk.

I walked to the bar while the others found a prime table in the back corner. The bar was classier in design. The barstools were red pleather with chrome legs, and the bar was made from weathered dark oak. The craftsmanship looked impressive close-up. There were carved captain wheels, life preservers, and even different types of sea life edging the counter. Maybe not everything on this ship was purchased wholesale from a catalog named "Hooked on Decor."

I gaped at the bartender in awe as she handled the crowd at the bar with the ease of a pro. She looked to be in her mid to late twenties. She had gorgeous, curly, dark, almost onyx-in-color hair. Her mocha-colored skin made her green eyes gleam almost iridescently.

When she laughed, she threw her head back and gave it her all. I automatically liked her. A woman who isn't afraid of being her true self is something to behold. This new generation of women made me proud. They were coming out of their shells, becoming the mighty and strong women they were meant to be.

The bartender made her way to me, grabbing beers and filling up glasses as she approached. "What can I get ya, darling?" she asked in a husky Australian accent.

I nodded at the ever-growing line of people at the bar and smiled up at her. "You are talented at your job. You make it almost an art form."

"Oh, well, thank you! It's quite the workout but also incredibly enjoyable. Experimenting with new drink creations and perfecting their presentation can truly make or break an evening. So, my dear, is there a particular drink that tickles your fancy?" As she engaged in casual conversation, she effortlessly tended to her duties of cleaning glasses, wiping the counter, and attending to the beverages of the passengers. Her efficiency and flawless service left my head spinning in admiration.

"I'll have a whiskey sour, please. Crown Royal, if you don't mind," I requested, casting a glance toward the ladies occupying the prime round booth in the corner. "And they would like a generous pitcher of margaritas. Salt-rimmed glasses, please."

Curiosity laced the bartender's voice as she poured two fingers of Crown into the tumbler. "Whiskey sour, huh? Is everything alright, love? Anything on your mind?"

Chuckling lightly, I responded, "Ah, just another part of the job, isn't it? Playing the role of an onboard therapist? You *are* intuitive, but I don't tend to spill my own troubles to strangers." I held my hand out, claiming the tumbler of whiskey sour.

With a warm smile, the bartender introduced herself. "Well, my name is Zoe. I hail from Melbourne, Australia. And if it matters to you, my horoscope sign is Cancer. It's truly a pleasure to meet you." As she handed me a neatly folded napkin, she filled the pitcher with margaritas and passed it to a waiter destined for our waiting table.

I grinned, taking a sip of my drink before responding. "Touché, Zoe. Pleasure to meet you as well. Lisa-May here, but you can call me Lisa. And since we're friends now, I think I'll go for something stronger to drown out the frustrations caused by a hateful man who bumped into me, left me with a sore shoulder, and probably knocked the name tag off my luggage. And wouldn't you know it, my suitcase has gone missing. So here I am, stuck in the same clothes I started the day in, unable to wash away the weariness of travel."

I needed to steer clear of delving into the unfortunate circumstances surrounding my job loss, where I was pushed aside for a younger, more cost-effective replacement. Some things were best left unsaid, even with a newfound acquaintance like Zoe.

"Oh, it's been quite the rough start, indeed," I replied, a mix of frustration and exhaustion evident in my voice. Zoe's offer of advice caught my attention as she continued to wipe down the counter.

As I observed Zoe more closely, it became apparent that despite her youthful appearance, her gaze betrayed an old soul. Worry lines etched around her mouth and a tightness in her eyes revealed a depth of experience beyond her years. The weight of her own struggles was evident, aging her prematurely compared to the smile lines most people bear.

"You know, I'd be eager to hear your perspective," I said, taking another satisfying sip of my whiskey sour, savoring the slight burn traveling down my throat.

Zoe glanced around, checking for any pressing customer needs, but the lull in activity allowed her a momentary respite.

"There are men out there who thrive on gaslighting," Zoe began, her scrubbing growing more vigorous with each word. "They manipulate, making you question your worth and emotions, isolating you from loved ones. They are bullies, cruel in their ways. It's crucial to reclaim your power and show them you refuse to be a victim." It was clear she had personal encounters with the kind of men she spoke of.

Sensing the rawness behind her words I remarked with caution, "It seems like you speak from personal experience."

Zoe met my gaze, a mix of shock and sadness reflecting in her eyes. She realized the depth of her disclosure, acknowledging the unexpected intimacy that had unfolded between us. Sometimes, sharing with a stranger was easier than confiding in a therapist or family member.

"Let's just say my journey to the other side of the world wasn't solely fueled by wanderlust," Zoe replied, her grip tightening on the rag as her hand trembled. "I need to attend to a couple over there. If you need anything else, just let me know."

As Zoe walked away, I noticed a slight limp in her step, a subtle hint at hidden battles. Yet she greeted the couple with a radiant smile, effortlessly switching gears. It was a disorienting contrast, witnessing her ability to exude warmth despite the underlying anger. There was clearly something terrible she endured, yet she held her own. The question was: Could she learn to harness and channel that anger?

I yearned to delve deeper into Zoe's story, but time would grant us further conversations during our remaining days on the boat. The whiskey sour was exceptional, prompting me to leave a generous tip as I made my way toward the girls at the corner booth.

My encounter with Zoe ignited curiosity within me, fueling a desire to learn more about the complex individuals onboard this voyage.

Chapter Eight

Our spirits were soaring as we finished off the pitcher of margaritas, knowing we had ample time to freshen up before the mandatory safety meeting and the upcoming dinner. The discomfort of my missing luggage had taken its toll on me, and I yearned for a reprieve. There was only so long I could endure wearing the same clothes and going without my toiletries before feeling on the verge of madness. I teetered on my limit, longing for a quick rinse, some dry shampoo, and a fresh set of garments that didn't reek of travel.

After a revitalizing shower, Wilma kindly offered me some of her more elegant clothes for dinner. Our similar sizes worked in my favor, and any minor differences in weight were compensated by my height. Adorned in a sleek pair of dark black capris and a flirtatious strappy black tank top that showcased my well-toned arms, I couldn't help but notice the hint of playfulness in Wilma's fashion choices. Her packed attire, whether short, sheer, strappy, or form-fitting, exuded a flirty charm. I couldn't help but wonder what transpired in her life. Ever since losing her husband, she remained unattached. Could she finally be opening herself up to new possibilities?

Wilma, radiant in a vibrant flowery skater dress boasting a plunging V-neckline, exuded an air of romance. The spaghetti straps and delicate lace-back design added an alluring touch. With a high-waisted seam drawing attention to her toned figure, the tiered short skater skirt flirtatiously flared just above her knees. Her long silver hair was elegantly swept into a French braid, and she sported dangling bamboo earrings, completing her charming ensemble.

Grabbing her clutch, Wilma turned to me and asked, "Ready to head over?"

"Yes, ma'am! Lead the way!" I replied, a mixture of excitement and nervous anticipation coursing through me. Finally, I was surrounded by my closest friends, embarking on a week-long adventure together. Completing the safety briefing would mark the official start of our memorable journey.

We walked to the room next to ours and knocked on the other girls' door, which Charlotte graciously opened for us. I couldn't contain my laughter at the striking contrast between Wilma's and my attire compared to Charlotte and Beverly's. Granted, I wasn't wearing my own clothes, but even so, I would have likely opted for a similar style. Charlotte, on the other hand, donned a pair of khaki slacks, a black V-neck shirt, and a delightful cardigan adorned with an embroidered sea turtle above the left breast. She embodied the typical librarian and author in every way.

Squinting her eyes at me with feigned suspicion, Charlotte stepped aside, allowing Wilma and me to enter. I couldn't help but smirk as we stepped into their room.

"What, Lisa? Not a fan of my outfit?" Charlotte playfully quipped, twirling around before settling down on the sleeper sofa to put on her trusty Mary Janes.

"Your cardigan is perfectly on theme, Charlotte! I absolutely adore it!" Beverly chimed in as she emerged from the bathroom, having changed into her evening ensemble.

Beverly sported a more relaxed yet still beautiful wrap-around sundress, accentuating her curves, and gladiator strappy sandals complemented the outfit while providing comfort.

"Ladies! Look at us! We're a fierce bunch!" I hollered, grabbing everyone in for a group hug.

"Let's take a picture!" Charlotte suggested, producing a peculiar contraption from one of her bags. She attached her phone to the end, extending her arm out.

"Oh, my goodness! The things these youngsters come up with!" Beverly exclaimed. "What do they call this one?"

"It's called a selfie stick. It helps you capture great angles while taking group photos," Charlotte explained.

"Now, Charlotte, angle the stick up! We want to eliminate those second and third chins, not accentuate them," Wilma chimed in as she gathered everyone for a selfie.

As the pictures were snapped, a voice boomed over the ship's intercom system, catching our attention.

"Why, hello, ladies and gentlemen! It's Gaaaarrrrrry, your cruise director! It's time to start embarking and preparing for a week of unforgettable fun. We'll soon be out of cell service range. Please make your way to your designated dining room for a quick safety presentation, followed by a delightful evening of dinner, drinks, and desserts!"

We quickly sent texts to our loved ones, letting them know we'd be out of reach for the next week, eagerly anticipating the adventure ahead.

Chapter Nine

We made our way to deck ten, where the mouthwatering scent of food beckoned us to the dining hall. The ship's culinary scene was an absolute delight, offering a smorgasbord of options to satisfy any craving.

As we explored the ship, we discovered a variety of eateries to suit every taste. Poolside burger joints were enticing with their juicy patties and mouthwatering toppings, perfect for a quick and satisfying bite under the sun. Nearby, the aroma of freshly baked pizzas wafted from charming parlors, promising cheesy goodness with every slice.

For the little ones, the children's area transformed this part of the boat into a playful haven , serving up kid-friendly treats and bringing joy to their young hearts.

And then there was the buffet, a treasure trove of flavors available for breakfast, lunch, and dinner. It was a laid-back affair, where we could help ourselves to an array of scrumptious dishes without the need for fancy attire. It offered a casual dining experience, allowing guests to enjoy our meals at our own pace, with a wide variety of tasty options on display.

But the true charm awaited us in the dining hall. Stepping inside, we were greeted by an air of sophistication. Tables adorned with crisp white tablecloths, folded napkins, and sparkling crystal water goblets exuded a sense of refinement. The attentive waitstaff in their dashing uniforms were ready to cater to our every whim.

In this haven of culinary delights, we would savor each bite, indulging in delectable dishes crafted with skill and passion. The dining hall was sure to be a place of relaxed enjoyment, where we could relish great food and engage in delightful conversations with our fellow passengers.

As we entered the dining room, we were greeted by Rachelle, our server from the buffet. "Hello, lovely ladies! Don't you all look stunning tonight!" She greeted us as though we were old friends.

"Follow me to your table. We have everything set up, and there is a set menu for tonight's services.." Rachelle motioned for us to follow her through a maze of tables with perfect place settings, bowls of bread and butter, and comfy-looking leather chairs.

"I believe we should eat here every night on the ship!" I exclaimed, taking in the luxurious surroundings.

"I don't want to have to dress up EVERY night, Lisa, but I do have to admit this is really nice!" Beverly said as she scanned the room. Her gaze made its way up to the stunning chandeliers hanging from the ceiling.

Rachelle graciously led us to a table perfectly positioned to offer a picturesque view of the dining area. As we settled into our seats, we couldn't help but be captivated by the sight before us. The room buzzed with an undercurrent of first-night excitement as elegant individuals glided to their tables, their attire meticulously chosen to display their wealthy status. The effort they put into their appearance granted them an extra dose of confidence, charisma, and attention, as if dressing up elevated their very essence.

Around us, conversations flowed like a symphony of animated chatter. Strangers embraced each other with warmth as if reuniting with long-lost friends while others introduced themselves to their tablemates with enthusiasm, their voices filled with exuberance. It was a spectacle of human connection, where the joy of meeting new people was celebrated.

Noting we filled four of the five chairs at our table, I commented, "I'm so glad we have this table to ourselves! Can you imagine being forced to have drab conversations with a complete stranger?"

We had a front-row seat to observe the ebb and flow of fellow passengers. The ship was a paradise for my penchant for people-watching, a delightful pastime I shared with my companions. We reveled in the opportunity to invent elaborate tales about these individuals, imagining grandiose life dramas rivaling the most gripping soap operas. Each passerby became a character in our collective imagination, and we couldn't help but weave intricate narratives around them, fueled by our own playful interpretations.

"Hey, look at those four over there," I said, nodding toward a table across the aisle. "Something's definitely going on."

The others turned to look; indeed, four people seemed like they were in an intense conversation.

"I bet they're plotting something," said Wilma with a sly grin.

"Oh, I know," said Beverly, leaning forward conspiratorially. "They're probably secret agents on a mission to save the world."

The four of us burst out laughing, imagining the four people at the other table as slick spies with gadgets and guns.

"But what if they're actually aliens in disguise?" suggested Charlotte, taking a sip of her wine.

"Aliens? Really?" I said, rolling my eyes. "That's so cliché."

"Okay, fine," said Charlotte, grinning. "How about they're time travelers from the future, trying to prevent some kind of catastrophic event?"

Wilma snorted. "You know what? I bet they're just a group of friends who accidentally got on the wrong cruise ship and are now stuck here with us."

The four of us dissolved into laughter, imagining the four people at the other table as hapless tourists who stumbled into a ridiculous situation.

As we continued to joke and laugh, the other diners around us couldn't help but glance over and wonder what was so funny. But we didn't care—we were having too much fun making up stories, teasing, and enjoying each other's company.

As we all sat back in our seats and grabbed our beverages, a handsome older gentleman walked up to the table's only empty seat beside me.

"Good evening, lovely ladies. I've been instructed that this is my dining table for the remainder of our voyage. Is this seat taken?"

Charlotte, Wilma, and Beverly sent subtle looks of acceptance to each other. They scooted their chairs a little over to give him more room while I sent him a not-so-welcoming look. I was not in the mood for a wanna-be Prince Charming. I'd rather sit next to a trash panda.

"Of course! You're more than welcome to sit at our table, Mr.?" Wilma rested her head on her hand and looked up, batting her eyelashes, awaiting his response.

"Taylor, Richard Taylor." He spoke with a low baritone British accent. I hated to admit it was as smooth and warming as a hot toddy on a sore throat.

I took in the appearance of this "Taylor, Richard Taylor" before me. He was my usual type…at least six feet tall, with piercing blue eyes, a healthy build, and not too muscular where cuddling would be like hugging a rock.

He must have sensed my gaze roaming his body because he sent a cunning smile aimed directly at me. I could feel the heat travel up my neck onto my face. I had a flutter in my stomach like I was a teenager again. This was ridiculous. I've been married four times. Each one was the wrong man. I'm just not meant to have a soul mate. Now was not the time to dive into another relationship.

"And my dear…" He reached for my hand and my body betrayed me by giving him my right hand to kiss. "Who might you be?" he asked as he sat down in his seat between Wilma and me.

Charlotte, Wilma, and Beverly shared humorous glances and laughed under their hands like schoolgirls.

"My first name is Lisa. My last name is none of your business. Are you sure you aren't meant to sit somewhere else?" My voice held no emotion, and I did not return his smile.

"Nope, here is my ticket they gave me at the front. Looks like I get the pleasure of dining with you four lovely ladies for the remainder of the trip," Richard responded with a lilt of humor in his voice. Beverly, Wilma, and Charlotte introduced themselves to allow some melting time on the freeze I just put over the table.

"Where are you from, Mr. Taylor?" Beverly asked.

"Please, call me Richard. I am originally from London, England. But I have lived all over due to my job in banking. From England to America and even Africa for a while," he responded.

I lifted my eyes from my menu. "Africa? Where did you spend time in Africa?"

I remember my time in Africa very fondly. It was the first time I set out as lead anthropologist at my own dig site. Maybe he wasn't as bad as I first believed, but if he started in on how he went for safari and didn't spend any actual time with the locals and learning the culture it would set the tone for the remainder of the cruise. It would also help me decide if I ate at the buffet for the remainder of the trip.

Richard was about to dive into captivating African tales, but the safety briefing abruptly interrupted the flow of conversation. With a collective sigh, we turned our attention to the mandatory instructions, our minds temporarily diverted from the delights awaiting us.

After the briefing, Rachelle graced our table with her presence armed with menus reading like a culinary adventure. As we nibbled on warm bread and indulged in the creamy embrace of butter, our taste buds were primed for the feast soon to arrive.

The appetizer selection presented a delightful dilemma. Each offering seemed more tempting than the last, from succulent shrimp cocktails to vibrant and refreshing summer salads. The velvety allure of the lobster bisque whispered promises of maritime decadence. We all exchanged glances, our eyes sparkling with anticipation, and quickly made our choices, eager to embark on this gastronomic journey together.

Then came the moment we had all been waiting

for—the main course selections. The menu unveiled a treasure trove of options, each more mouthwatering than the last. The butter-braised steak, the tantalizing vegetarian creations, and the array of seafood delights that graced the page, catering to every discerning palate.

While Rachelle jotted down our selections, the air crackled with a mix of hunger and excitement. We leaned back, exchanging knowing glances, and took a moment to savor the anticipation before our taste buds were tantalized.

"How has your trip been so far, ladies? Where are you from?" Richard asked as he pushed his plate away and picked up the bottle of wine from the middle of the table, offering it out to each of us before pouring his own.

Engrossed in the lively conversation, we shared the details of our eventful journey—the mishaps during our drive, the baggage fiasco, and the unfortunate encounter with an insufferable neighbor for the week. I participated in the discussion, relishing the opportunity to bond with my fellow ladies. After all, this trip was envisioned as a cherished getaway for us girls and the unexpected presence of a strange man at our table dampened the atmosphere I envisioned. However, I reminded myself rudeness was not in my nature, and it was unlikely he had deliberately been seated with us to provoke me.

As we continued recounting our stories, the object of our earlier frustration made a conspicuous entrance into the dining room, accompanied by his stunning girlfriend. My attention shifted to Rachelle as she guided the couple to a cozy, intimate table positioned diagonally from ours. It was the perfect vantage point to witness the unfolding drama, a spectacle requiring no embellishment on my part. From the moment they sat down, it was evident this encounter would be a trainwreck of epic proportions, captivating in its raw and unscripted chaos.

Chapter Ten

As the young woman made her way to the table, the man, initially appearing charming and suave, abruptly grabbed her arm with an unexpected force. His demeanor shifted, revealing a darker side beneath his handsome exterior. Anger etched across his face, he barked at Rachelle, "Excuse me! We need a bigger table than this!"

Maintaining her composure, Rachelle responded calmly. "I'm sorry, sir. We have assigned seating in the dining room. You are welcome to explore other dining areas on the ship and choose a table suiting your preference."

Annoyed by Rachelle's polite explanation, the man's aggression escalated. He raised his voice and demanded, "Do you have any idea who I am? I want to speak to your manager."

Attempting to diffuse the situation, the young lady with him stepped in and addressed him gently. "Seth, honey, please calm down. This table is lovely and intimate. We don't need a bigger one."

Disregarding her attempt to pacify him, Seth's hostility intensified. He dismissed her with a growl. "No one asked you, Robyn. Just sit down and be quiet."

He shoved Robyn away in an act of physical aggression, causing a chair to topple over. The situation was on the verge of spiraling out of control. Just as I was about to intervene, Richard, showing admirable courage, rose from his seat and positioned himself between Rachelle, Robyn, and the volatile Seth.

"Young man, this is not a way to conduct yourself. You are not meant to be in the presence of others if you cannot handle your emotions and act like a civil human being." I noted Richard had straightened to his full height. The dining room instantly quieted in response to the disruption.

"Who are you, old man? No one needs a wannabe Sean Connery up in their face. Go back to retirement, geezer." Seth ended his slew of insults by shoving Richard.

Richard grabbed Seth's shirt front and pulled him up on his toes. "Young man, you need to remove yourself from this situation, or I will be the one to remove you from it."

The atmosphere in the dining hall grew palpably tense, with all eyes fixated on the unfolding confrontation. As the seconds ticked by, the room held its breath in anticipation. I could feel the collective tension in the air, and my teeth clenched involuntarily. Leaning forward on the edge of my seat, I braced myself for what might come next, unsure of how the situation would escalate or resolve.

In a sudden burst of aggression, Seth pushed Richard away, his body language indicating a readiness to escalate the conflict further. Feeling the tension mounting, I moved to step in, but before I could make a move, a security guard made a timely entrance, drawing everyone's attention. The guard, with fiery red hair and visible arm tattoos, exuded an air of authority and determination, instantly commanding the situation. It was evident he was there to swiftly diffuse the escalating tension and put an end to the brewing fight.

As he approached, the uniformed man began, "Excuse me. I am Martin Wick, the head of security on this ship. What seems to be the issue here?"

With a calm yet firm tone, Richard addressed the situation. "This young man put his hands on this young woman, Robyn, and was being aggressive with our waitress, Rachelle. He pulled a full-on temper tantrum. I stepped in to stop it."

Unyielding in his anger, Seth responded defiantly. "Listen, old man. This is none of your business. How I handle my woman or act toward 'the help' is none of your concern. You have no idea who you're messing with. Now go take your dentures out, eat some JELL-O, and go to bed for a night of eternal sleep."

The surrounding diners shifted their attention, some avoiding eye contact with Seth, no longer willing to support or indulge his deplorable behavior. It became apparent his actions caused him to lose any sympathy he may have initially had. Whispers and murmurs circulated, turning this incident into a hot topic of conversation throughout the room.

Martin maintained his composure and calmly placed his hand on Seth's arm. In a low whisper, almost drowned out by the buzz of the dining hall, he stated, "Sir, you must come with me now." Only our table, closest to the unfolding scene, caught their exchange.

Enraged, Seth refused to accept his fate and struggled against Martin's grip. With a sudden motion, he swung his free arm, forming a tight fist, and landed a forceful punch squarely in Martin's eye. The head of security staggered, visibly dazed by the blow. After a deep breath, he regained control, grasping Seth by the arm and marching him toward the dining hall doors.

As Seth was forcibly removed from the dining hall, he couldn't resist throwing a parting insult back at Richard. His voice was laced with contemptuous amusement. "You better watch out, old man! The elderly tend to fall, and there isn't a Life Alert system here," he taunted, his smirk leaving a bitter taste in the air.

"Well, that was all very exciting," Wilma commented when Richard returned to the table and took a big swig of his bourbon. I observed his hands trembling. He was shaken by the confrontation.

"Quite. I haven't felt so much blood pumping through my veins since I was a much younger man. What are your plans after this?" Richard asked us as our table was being cleared by the waitstaff. Rachelle was noticeably absent and must have left the floor to calm down after the incident.

"Well, there is a Singles Mixer right now!" Wilma squealed. "Who's coming with me?" She looked around the table, and I could feel her gaze boring into me.

"I am way too tired after the day of driving and this drama tonight. Plus, I have a nice stack of books calling my name." Charlotte sighed in contentment as she was probably daydreaming of the new worlds awaiting her from the stack of books she packed as she stood up and pushed in her chair.

"I agree. I can't believe the drive took as much of my energy as it did. Char, how about we try out the Tranquility Deck? You can read, and I can lay down and watch the stars while listening to my audiobook." Beverly pushed in her chair after folding her napkin and stacking the remaining dishes on the table for ease for the waitstaff.

"Sounds perfect!" Charlotte clapped as she and Beverly interlocked their arms and turned to look at me.

I was not in the mood to be single and mingle, but the look on Wilma's face made me give in. Something was going on with her, and I also wanted to get some one-on-one time with everyone before the end of the week.

"Come on, Lisa. You know you want to come. At least to keep me from getting in trouble! We haven't had a night out together in decades! Plus, you're single now, right? You ready to find husband number five?" Wilma winked at me and gave a pointed glance to Richard, who was generously tipping our waitstaff with Ben Franklin bills.

Richard turned back to us right as Wilma mentioned husband number five. I could feel myself blush again; this couldn't be good for my heart rate or blood pressure.

"Husband number five, eh? What happened to the other four? You kill them off with your icy looks?" Richard asked with a twinkle in his eyes and a hint of humor in his voice.

"Yes. And they are scattered all over the world. United States. Africa. Yucatan. Iraq. You'll never be able to find the bodies. Who knows, I could get hitched here and get to add Cozumel to the list. There are plenty of caves and beaches to hide a body in." I responded with a witch's cackle for extra emphasis.

"Annnnnd with that lovely bit of information, we will go to our rooms, grab our things, and head to the Tranquility Deck. See you later, girls. Be safe!" Charlotte said while tugging Beverly along with her.

Wilma turned to Richard. "You are more than welcome to join us. Unless there is a Mrs. Taylor, we don't know about?"

"No, ma'am. There has never been a Mrs. Taylor. I never found the one to settle down with. It is just me, myself, and I. I've always been the lonely bachelor."

I maintained my composure as Richard's gaze attempted to meet mine. Refusing to show any hint of curiosity or interest in his personal life, I met his eyes with a smile. "It would seem to me there are plenty of fish in the sea, so to speak, here on the ship. There is a good deal of women I see even now vying for your attention in this very room."

And indeed, there were. I couldn't help but notice the presence of numerous single ladies, their anticipation evident as they eagerly awaited Richard's conclusion of our conversation. Some stood in awkward limbo while others exuded poise and confidence in various poses, all hoping for a chance to capture his attention. His standing up for young Robyn and Rachelle enhanced his allure in their eyes, elevating his attractiveness even further.

"Come on, Wilma. I need my clothes if I'm going to this mixer with you. I refuse to settle for more stretchy attire, leaving everything hanging loose. I need my trusty Spanx and an excellent push-up bra. Let's leave Mr. Taylor to his admirers and head to the service desk to find my missing bags," I declared, tugging Wilma's hand to urge her toward the entrance. Turning back to Richard, I bid him farewell with a nod and a knowing smile, fully aware of the swarm of women circling him like hungry piranhas.

"If you ever get bored, Richard, you know where to find us!" Wilma called out mischievously, her playful flirtation aimed solely at having some harmless fun. After all, Wilma never allowed herself to open her heart to another person since her painful experience with her high school sweetheart, Daniel. And from what I could see, it wasn't about to change anytime soon.

Chapter Eleven

Wilma and I made our way toward the service desk, the hub of activity and resolution for lost items on the ship. As we drew closer, the sound of raised voices reached our ears, indicating some sort of dispute taking place. The circular desk itself was encircled by an assortment of misplaced suitcases, creating a visual reminder of the unfortunate mishaps that could occur during travel.

I couldn't help but feel a sense of anticipation mixed with a touch of anxiety as I hoped my bags would be among those waiting to be claimed. I simultaneously found myself silently wishing for the swift recovery of everyone else's missing belongings as well, understanding the frustration and inconvenience it must cause.

Around the desk, strategically placed brochures showcased a plethora of exciting excursions with thrilling experiences such as whale watching, cave exploration, underwater adventures, and local historical tours. The glossy images and enticing descriptions painted vivid pictures of unforgettable escapades, whispering promises of extraordinary memories waiting to be made.

The door to the security office was left open a few inches, an accident I assumed due to the nature of the conversation spilling out. I could just make out the side

profile of Seth leaning against the wall with a smug
expression while Martin's familiar Irish voice yelled. I
couldn't make out what he said, but whatever he ended
the conversation with replaced the smug look on Seth's
face with anger.

"You wouldn't. You owe me too much, and there is
little bird to think about, eh?" Seth's voice dripped with
acidity.

Whatever the Australian man said caused Seth's
smugness to return. Smirking as he triumphantly walked
out of the room, his gaze turned to fixate on Wilma and
me. An air of arrogance hung around him like a cloud,
his self-assured smile serving as a silent declaration of
his perceived superiority as he strode by us. It was clear
he took pleasure in leaving with the last word, relishing
the opportunity to display his supposed dominance.

"People like him could get away with murder while
others like him should be murdered," I mumbled under
my breath, and Wilma snickered behind her hand.

Martin walked out of his office right as I finished
my statement with a grim look on his face. He cocked his
eyebrow at me and replied with a thick Irish lilt, "You
know, lass, you should watch what you say aloud. You
never know who might be listening. Now, what can I do
for you?"

"I am here to pick up my missing luggage," I said,
ignoring his warning as I looked around for my luggage,
relieved to spot it in the corner. "Ah! It is right over
there!" As I made my way over to my bags, Wilma
started talking with Martin.

"How is he not in a cell right now? He assaulted you,
his girlfriend, and was aggressive with the staff. Even on
a ship, basic law applies, right? Did you not press

charges?" Wilma asked nosily.

"No, ma'am, I did not, and neither did either of the young ladies. The issue is resolved, and other things are more important right now. No need to add paperwork to my already full schedule." Martin changed the subject by asking about our plans for off-ship days, but Lisa and I were on a mission like a dog with a bone. We weren't going to let it drop.

"He isn't very kind, and I think he is cruel to Robyn. You might want to keep an eye on him," I responded. Of course, my opinion was probably not warranted or needed. Still, I had a gut feeling this could get a lot worse before it would get better.

"As I said, I'll keep an eye on it. Everything is as handled as it could be." Martin's Irish accent grew noticeably stronger, carrying a tinge of emotion or agitation. His words became laced with a more pronounced inflection as if his accent manifested itself more prominently when he was upset. I was reminded of my gramma's Oklahoma accent, which tended to thicken and truncate vowels and consonants in moments of distress.

"Now, unless I can help you with anything else, I have other duties that need attending to." Martin nodded curtly at us, turned back toward his office, and closed the door. I swore I heard him talking again to someone but couldn't tell if there was someone in his office or if he was talking on the phone or walkie-talkie. And it wasn't my business, as he had so rudely pointed out.

As we left the service desk, Wilma proposed a question aloud. "I thought the person talking to Seth was Australian. Could my hearing be that off? Could I have confused an Irish accent with an Australian?"

"No, I don't think so. If it is, then my hearing is going as well. But I am pretty sure we both made out the same thing. Quite interesting. I wonder who else was in the room." As we got in the elevator, I had a nagging feeling in the back of my mind; I heard his voice before. I just couldn't put my finger on where.

Wilma and I exited the elevator and headed to our room to prepare for the Single's Mixer on the fifth floor. As we were about to enter our room, we ran into Beverly and Charlotte. They were both dressed in comfy clothes and looked ready to relax on the Tranquility Deck. Honestly, I would much rather join them, but I promised Wilma to flirt and make some new friends.

"Hey, ladies!! On your way to falling into a fictional world? You know the real world is pretty cool, too!" Wilma teased.

"Alas, Wilma, I tend to find more comfort in my fictional friends. They have also done very well for me and my lifestyle," Charlotte retorted.

"Too true!" I chimed in. I still wanted to find out what happened with Charlotte. Maybe we could have some coffee soon to chat. I was still feeling guilty for throwing her under the bus at Beverly's house. I needed to apologize.

"Actually, we have something we need to talk to you about. Let's go to your room for a second while you both get ready, and we can explain," Beverly whispered conspiratorially as she looked around the hall, expecting someone to be listening in or coming around the corner.

We entered the room and saw the state we had left it in when we went for dinner. It looked like Wilma's whole wardrobe had exploded all over the room. There were at least three pairs of shoes on the counter, the bed was covered with all the clothes we threw on it as we tried on outfits, and the pillows from the bed and sleeper sofa were on the floor haphazardly. A person walking in wouldn't know if this room belonged to retirees or teenagers. Some things never change.

Wilma started picking things up as Beverley sat on the little sofa, which was a pull-out couch, and almost sat on some very lacy unmentionables. I opened the armoire and started unpacking my things, searching for what I might want to wear tonight. Charlotte leaned against the wall by the sofa. The cruise ship rooms were notoriously compact, leaving little space to maneuver. With four full-sized humans sharing a cabin, it felt even more cramped. Every square inch was occupied by beds, furniture, and storage compartments. Trying to navigate around one another without bumping into walls or stepping on toes was a constant juggling act. Even simple tasks like changing clothes required a careful dance to avoid accidental collisions. The limited room made it evident that personal space was a luxury on this voyage.

"Beverly left her headphones in our room, so we headed back here. As we were approaching our room, we heard arguing in the room next to yours where that horrible young man, Seth, and his sweet girlfriend Robyn are staying." Beverly waited a couple of beats before continuing to make sure she had a captured audience.

Impatient to get ready and to start having a smashing time at the mixer, Wilma huffed. "Yes? And? What did you hear?" She glanced up from hanging and folding her items into the armoire beside where I was unpacking my bags.

Charlotte took over as Beverly found a shoe poking her backside. "Apparently, Seth got out with barely a slap on his wrist. Just like he said he would. I wonder who he knows who could get him off from causing such a scene and punching the head of security."

Beverly continued the story, not wanting to be left out of the juicy gossip they stumbled upon. "We couldn't make out everything through the door, but it was bad. We could hear shoving and glass breaking. We barely made it to our room before Seth slammed open the door and stomped out to the elevator to God knows where."

"We went back out to the hall to see if we could hear anything else, and we could hear Robyn crying." A somber atmosphere settled over the room as Charlotte finished recounting the story. The weight of the situation hung heavily in the air, and the emotions stirred within us.

We could sense the pain and injustice Robyn must have felt at that moment, hearing her tears echoing through the hallway. It was a stark reminder of the pervasive issue of men belittling and demeaning women, a reality far too many of us experienced or witnessed firsthand.

"He is such a horrible person. I can't believe he is getting away with assaulting Martin." I proceeded to tell Beverly and Charlotte what Wilma and I witnessed at the service desk.

"Sounds like he knows someone pretty high up on the ship to get off that easy," Charlotte pondered out loud.

"Wilma and I were thinking the same thing. I'm still wracking my brain to pinpoint why the Australian man's voice sounded so familiar."

"I'm not sure, but what I am sure about is you two need to go read so Lisa and I can get ready for some hot gents downstairs!" Wilma responded while twirling one of her lacy tidbits in the air.

"Alright, alright. We know when we are overstaying our welcome. Please have fun but be safe," Beverly said in a motherly tone. She has been and will always be the mom of the group. I don't think any of us would have it any other way.

As we were getting ready for the mixer, I started reminiscing about the past and what we had gone through to get to where we are now.

This might be the only time to approach this topic, so I cleared my throat. "Hey Wilma, if this is overstepping or makes you uncomfortable, we can change the subject. But why didn't you try to find someone after Daniel? You were so young. You had more than enough life and love to give."

Wilma settled herself on the stool, removing the hot rollers from her hair as he said, "You know Daniel passed when we were just twenty years old. I wanted to try and figure out who I was without him," Wilma began, her voice tinged with a mix of sorrow and reflection. "He was my everything, my laughter. He'd been there for all our shenanigans throughout our whole childhood. I didn't know who I was as a person."

I listened attentively, realizing the weight of her words and the depths of her emotional journey. Tears welled up in her eyes; an outpouring of emotions had been suppressed for far too long. I hesitated for a moment, unsure if I should change the subject or allow her to continue. But something in her gaze urged me to hold space for her, to be present in this moment of vulnerability.

Wilma continued, her voice trembling with the

weight of her experiences. "I came back from the Peace Corps when Momma was getting really sick. I felt like I was needed there, and it would have been so much harder to date while taking care of her. Plus, I was going to night school to become a nurse. There was only so much time in the day, and I didn't want to start something I couldn't give myself one hundred percent to. When Momma finally passed two years later, I thought, 'This is the time for me!' I was twenty-eight, almost done with college and a career, and was ready to start looking for someone new and start a family…until…"

Wilma's voice trailed off, her tears flowing freely, as she struggled to find the words to convey the profound impact of another tragic event. I moved closer, taking a seat beside her on the stool, my heart aching for her pain. "Until your sister got into an accident with Evan in the car." I finished her sentence softly, realizing the immense weight of that event in her life.

A mixture of gratitude and sadness washed over her face as she looked into the mirror, her hands twisting the napkin she used to help remove the rollers from her hair. "It's okay, Wilma. You don't have to talk about it anymore," I reassured her, feeling a pang of guilt for bringing up such a painful memory.

But Wilma surprised me, her voice laced with resolve as she gently pushed through her tears. "No, Lisa, it's okay. It is a valid question. And I know we haven't been able to talk much about this since you've been out of the country and taking care of Veronica. After my sister didn't make it and her deadbeat boyfriend was out of the picture, I received sole custody of her son. At that point, I was given an instant family. A small family of two in an instant. It didn't feel right to introduce someone else into our lives after all the trauma we'd both gone through. I finally finished school but felt I needed to be there for him more than I needed to find someone else."

Wilma's words hung in the air, the weight of her sacrifices and devotion to her nephew palpable. I searched for the right response, but no words seemed sufficient to convey the empathy and admiration I felt. So, instead, I embraced her in a tight squeeze, offering solace and understanding. Through our unspoken connection, we both acknowledged the need for a change of subject, silently agreeing to redirect our focus and prepare ourselves for the single's mixer.

Chapter Twelve

Stepping into the fifth-floor ballroom felt like being thrown into a whirlwind of sights, sounds, and sensations. A sensory overload in the best possible way. The place was packed with seniors of all ages, shapes, and sizes, each one exuding a youthful energy defying their actual age.

As I looked around, I couldn't help but notice some of the endearing quirks that come with getting older. There were men rocking their trusty comb-overs, battling the hair loss with slick precision. A sight making me grin, appreciating their tenacity and sense of self-expression.

The ballroom was alive with chatter, laughter, and gentle melodies playing in the background. The air was infused with a medley of scents, as perfumes and colognes mingled together, creating a unique aroma adding to the ambiance.

The room was filled with a contagious sense of liberation. People mingled unapologetically embracing the joy of the moment. Age melted away as they danced, laughed, and reveled in the sheer pleasure of being alive.

I caught glimpses of familiar faces of fellow shipmates who embarked on this adventure with us. They were lost in animated conversations, sharing stories and laughter with newfound friends.

As Wilma and I navigated through the crowd, a

sense of anticipation swelled within me. Who were these individuals, adorned with the beautiful lines of life etched upon their faces? What tales of love, loss, and triumph lay hidden beneath their twinkling eyes? The ballroom was a treasure trove of experiences waiting to be unraveled.

I felt a deep appreciation for the tapestry of life, where age was merely a number, and the spirit of adventure knew no bounds. A celebration of the human spirit, reminding me no matter our age, we all carry stories worth sharing.

As I stood at the bar, waiting for the bartender's attention, I found myself next to Richard, the charming English businessman. His presence was undeniably alluring, and his greeting made me raise an eyebrow.

"Well, hello there, duckie," he greeted with a hint of mischief in his voice. "Long time no see." His transformation from dinner attire to a more casual ensemble made him even more irritatingly handsome. He oozed charm from every pore without any effort.

I couldn't deny Richard had a way of getting under my skin, but I was determined not to let my hormones cloud my judgment once again. After all, they had let me down on four separate occasions already. I wasn't about to give them the satisfaction of leading me astray for the fifth time.

Suppressing a smirk, I replied, "Oh, you know, just enjoying the festivities. Trying to keep up with the dance floor and all." I bobbed my head to the rhythm of the music, playing it cool despite the subtle flutter in my stomach.

As the bartender finally approached, I ordered two glasses of white wine, keeping all my attention on the task at hand. Richard might have been standing beside me, but I wasn't about to let his magnetic presence derail my focus. The night was young, and I had a plan with Wilma to stick to—let the "boys" come to us; no need to beg for attention.

I collected our drinks and nodded politely to Richard, subtly asserting my independence. "Enjoy the evening, Richard," I said with a knowing smile before making my way to the table where Wilma waited.

It was a battle of wills, a game of flirtatious banter and self-control. And this time, I was determined to keep the upper hand, even if Richard's annoyingly handsome charm continued to test my resolve.

"Hey hey hey! I saw that interaction at the bar! Hubba hubba!" Wilma said a little louder than usual to get over the music as she grabbed the white wine in my hand.

As we took a few sips of our wine, I looked around at the action going on in the room. With my new positive outlook, I was happy to see many people having fun. I could feel the stress released from everyone as they danced, drank, and chatted. There was so much going on in our lives that we rarely stopped and smelled the flowers. In my generation, it was seen as lazy to take vacations. Rest and relaxation were only acceptable for a specific class of people. I was happy glancing around and seeing more people our age with apparent disregard for social norms.

Gone were the walls people built up around themselves. The classist decorum was apparent when we were in the dining hall. Here, everyone was having drinks, dancing with each other, and having the time of their lives. This is why I came this week. To have these moments.

My attention was momentarily diverted as I spotted the cruise director making his grand entrance. He appeared disheveled, perspiration glistening on his forehead. I couldn't help but wonder if he indulged in one too many drinks before joining the mixer. I silently hoped he wouldn't lose his composure in front of the crowd.

With an unsteady gait, he made his way toward the raised stage at the center of the dance floor. It was a marvel he managed to climb up without stumbling over his own feet. I couldn't help but feel a mix of concern and amusement as I watched him struggle.

Finally reaching the stage, he raised his arm to wipe away the perspiration collecting above his eyes. Then, with a microphone in hand, he cleared his throat dramatically, capturing everyone's attention.

"Hellooo, ladies and gentlemen!" he boomed through the microphone, his voice amplified to the entire ballroom. "I must apologize for my tardiness to this fabulous party, but it seems like you're all having an absolute blast, as the youngsters would say. Let's keep the energy high and continue the festivities into the early hours of the morning, shall we?" His attempt at rousing the crowd with a loud cheer only resulted in a few startled glances and a step back from the stage, as his unsteady twirl gave off an air of awkwardness rather than slickness.

I couldn't help but stifle a chuckle as I observed the cruise director's earnest yet slightly comical performance. Despite his less-than-graceful entrance, I admired his determination to create an entertaining atmosphere for the guests. It was clear he embraced the spirit of the evening, even if his coordination had deserted him temporarily.

As he continued to address the crowd with enthusiasm, I smiled, ready to immerse myself in the lively ambiance of the party. The night was young, and with the cruise director's offbeat charm setting the tone, it promised to be a memorable and eventful evening aboard the ship.

A hushed stillness settled over the room after Gary's enthusiastic proclamation, his words hanging in the air with an uncomfortable weight. The DJ, eager to break the silence, swiftly resumed playing the music, hoping to restore the energetic atmosphere.

Meanwhile, Gary, clearly unsteady on his feet, descended from the stage only to collide with Martin, the head of security. Their chance encounter ignited a tense exchange between the two. I couldn't help but notice the bruise on Martin's right eye, its discoloration catching the light just as the shimmering disco ball descended from the ceiling to the delighted applause of the crowd.

Curiosity flickered in my mind once again as if a puzzle piece had fallen into place. There was an undeniable connection between the altercation earlier involving Seth, the head of security, and now this interaction between Gary and Martin. Something deeper was at play, and the events of the evening were becoming increasingly entangled.

With my senses heightened and an unrelenting curiosity gnawing at me, I made a mental note to keep a keen eye on the evolving dynamics and unravel the mysteries lurking beneath the surface of this idyllic voyage. There was more to this story than met the eye, and I was determined to uncover the truth, even if it meant venturing into uncharted territory.

"Wilma, did Cruise Director Gary's voice sound familiar to you?" I quickly glanced at Gary and Martin before turning to Wilma to give her my full attention.

"Hmmm?" Wilma responded, tapping her foot to the beat, clearly wanting to be dancing on the floor but not wanting to abandon me.

"Gary, did his voice sound familiar?" I repeated, knowing this was not the line of conversation Wilma wanted to be having right now. Still, I was unable to stop myself from continuing.

"I'm not sure. There are a lot of Australian men and women on the boat, but maybe." Wilma drained her wine and started to sway with the music. I lost her to the smooth and relaxing voice of Fleetwood Mac's "Second Hand News". I needed to reset for the night and head back to the room.

"Wil? I'm getting pretty tired, but I think you should stay. Go out on the dance floor and have fun. I promise I'll be fine." I drained the rest of my wine and set it back on the table before standing up and pushing my chair in.

Wilma, startled out of her thoughts, turned her gaze to mine. "Are you sure? I don't want to leave you alone. You've had a lot of changes going on in your life recently, and I want to be supportive." But I could see her attention travel back toward the dance floor and her body starting to sway to the music.

Wilma would return to the room if I asked her to, but I needed time to think about everything that happened. Wilma was also trying to get out for the first time in a long time, and I didn't want to hinder her.

"Wilma, I am okay. I am just drained. We are going to be together for a whole week. Please, go have fun." I leaned in and gave her a big hug and kiss on her cheek. "Don't do anything I wouldn't do." I teased. The problem was there were many things I would do, and some were not legal.

Chapter Thirteen

I felt much more centered, calm, and relaxed the following day. I had spent the rest of the evening watching mindless reality TV about a group of kids stuck together, competing to stay in a big house. I would have a blast doing an introspective study of people who agreed to be in a house full of strangers for the slim chance of winning a hundred-thousand-dollar grand prize and mild celebrity fame while showing embarrassing aspects of themselves on national TV.

I had tossed and turned for a while, checking often to see if Wilma had made it back yet. I finally gave in to exhaustion and dropped into a sleep. My first thought when I woke up was to check for Wilma's presence again. I hadn't heard the door open last night, but I had slept pretty hard, so a stampede of elephants might not have woken me up. Wilma was indeed in her bed, sporting her eye mask, her hair in curlers, and sleeping like a baby with a little bit of drool puddling on her pillow. I smiled, released my legs from the burrito of blankets, and tiptoed to the tiny bathroom and shower stall.

The shower, a mere afterthought in the corner of the tiny bathroom, boasted a flimsy plastic sheet posing as a shower curtain. I chuckled, realizing I could reach out and touch all four walls with outstretched arms. But I had experienced far worse bathing situations on my travels, so I wasn't fazed. All I needed was hot water, soap, and a trusty washcloth to feel clean, refreshed, and invigorated. The satisfying act of rinsing away the grime of travel and banishing the remnants of dry shampoo from my hair was nothing short of heavenly.

Emerging from the bathroom, I felt like a transformed woman; donned in my ultimate comfort ensemble: a pair of sleek black leggings, a wireless sports bra providing the perfect support, and a soft sage green t-shirt. Overall, I felt like I projected tranquility in this outfit. Completing the look was a delightfully worn-in jean jacket. I felt comfortable, confident, and ready to take on whatever the day had in store.

Heading towards the small "living" room, if it could be called that, I spotted Wilma diligently folding the sleeper sofa, creating much-needed space in our cozy abode. She then embarked on her morning yoga routine of stretching and contorting her body with a dedication that impressed and intimidated me. I couldn't help but admire her commitment to health and wellness. Now that we would spend more time together since I was back home for good, Wilma could become my accountability buddy in pursuing a healthier lifestyle. But alas, it would have to wait for another day. This morning, my body craved the life-giving elixir of caffeine, preferably delivered through an intravenous drip.

"Good morning. Did you have fun last night?" I asked as I walked around her to slide my socks on.

"It was enjoyable. I spent most of the evening dancing with a certain English gentleman." Wilma winked at me as she moved seamlessly from standing to downward-facing dog.

I turned from where I was on my bed, tying my black

and white striped pair of Adidas trainers. When I met Wilma's gaze, I could see a twinkle of humor in it, and I knew she was messing with me.

Wilma jumped up and pointed at me dramatically. "Ha! I knew you had something for him!"

"What?! No. Not at all. Wilma, I've had enough romance for four lifetimes. I'm happy you spent the evening dancing with him." I felt the acid rise in my mouth as I fibbed. I finished tying my shoes and flopped onto my back on the bed like a petulant teenager.

I knew the feelings of jealousy Wilma's teasing evoked in me were momentary and ridiculous. Wilma and I both deserved to have our own adventures and fully enjoy this cruise. After all, being in our golden years didn't mean we were dead or devoid of desires. It was only fair we each took advantage of the opportunity to meet someone and have a fling if we so desired.

With a renewed sense of understanding, I made a promise to myself. The next time I crossed paths with Richard, I would be more open and welcoming. I would set aside any lingering reservations and embrace the possibility of a genuine connection. Life was too short to let jealousy or insecurities get in the way of potential friendships or relationships.

"Oh really? Good to know. He is meeting us for drinks before tonight. Put on your best dress and smile. We will have fun and we don't need a Grumpy Gus joining the party," Wilma stated while finishing her yoga set.

Wanting to give Wilma space to finish her yoga and meditation session, I left to knock on Charlotte and Beverly's door. The door opened just a crack, revealing a dimly lit room and Charlotte, her face illuminated by a small book light attached to the paperback she was holding.

"Good morning, Lisa! What brings you here so early?" Charlotte greeted me with a warm smile, glancing at her beloved gold wristwatch, a timeless accessory she never left behind. While Wilma embraced the latest technology with her Apple Watch, Charlotte preferred the simplicity of a classic timepiece. One of the ways she detached herself from the digital world, especially after the events surrounding her Inkwell Investigations series.

I furrowed my brow with concern and asked, "Is Beverly still asleep?" It was unusual for her to be the last one awake. She was usually the one rousing everyone for breakfast. Beverly had always been an advocate of making the most of the day and avoiding the temptation of wasting precious hours in bed.

Charlotte glanced back into the cabin, then turned to face me, her expression filled with worry. Evidently, she didn't want to risk Beverly overhearing our conversation. I understood her silent communication and nodded in response.

"Shall we go down to the cafe together and grab some coffee for all of us?" I suggested, hoping to lift the spirits and kickstart the day on a positive note.

Charlotte's eyes lit up, and she eagerly nodded in agreement. "Absolutely! Let me just grab my trusty fanny pack." She disappeared for only a moment, popping out of the room dressed in her vibrant yellow cardigan embellished with embroidered owls and books. She had her fanny pack in hand, carefully stuffing her current paperback inside. Charlotte had a lifelong love affair with books, a constant comfort in her ever-evolving life. No matter how much we changed, some things remained steadfast and reliable.

We set off through the ship's corridors on our mission to find our morning jumpstart beverage. The soft hum of activity echoed around us as we strolled toward the aroma of freshly brewed coffee wafting through the air. The anticipation of a warm cup in hand brimming with caffeine-induced energy brought a spark of excitement to our step.

The friendly barista greeted us with a bright smile as we approached the cafe counter. "Good morning! What can I get for you today?"

"I'll have three medium coffees and an herbal tea, please," I requested, reaching for my wallet for my room card. Charlotte rummaged in her fanny pack, retrieving hers first. Insisting on treating the group this time, she handed her card to the barista.

"And please hold off on making the herbal tea and one of the coffees for thirty minutes or so." I paused to look at Charlotte hoping she would agree that we needed some one-on-one time, she nodded.

With coffee in hand, we found a cozy table near a window with a breathtaking and peaceful view of the endless expanse of the ocean. The early morning light cascaded through the glass, casting a gentle glow on our faces.

Charlotte took a sip from her cup, savoring the rich flavor. "Ah, the simple pleasure of a hearty cup of coffee. It never fails to bring a sense of calmness to the morning."

I nodded, cradling the warmth of my mug. "You're absolutely right, Charlotte. Amidst all the changes and uncertainties, some things remain constant and dependable."

As we sipped our coffees while taking in the oceanic view, the tranquility of the moment enveloped us like a warm hug. The day's worries and concerns faded, replaced by a sense of closeness and a shared appreciation for the small joys in life. I couldn't help but feel grateful for the enduring friendships which had weathered the storms of time.

"We all need comfort and familiarity in life," Charlotte absently repeated the phrase she used earlier when talking about coffee.

As Charlotte spoke, her gaze fixed on the vast sea expanse, she wasn't still talking about coffee. I sensed something significant was on her mind. I felt the weight of her words resonating within me, urging me to confront the situation brewing within me since the prickly exchange between us at Beverly's house. The time had come for me to address it, apologize, and set things right.

Summoning my courage, I cleared my throat and prepared to express my remorse, but Charlotte continued speaking before I could say anything. Her voice had a contemplative tone, and her words held a deeper meaning.

"Some things remain constant and dependable," Charlotte mused, her gaze still fixed on the horizon. "But other aspects of life require change and growth as we, the human race, change and grow ourselves."

Her pause lingered in the air, and I turned to look at her. Her face had become as familiar to me over the years as my own reflection. Time had left its mark, evident in the gentle lines tracing her features. However, there was an added depth to those lines, etched with traces of concern I hadn't noticed before. It became clear to me this conversation was significant beyond a simple apology.

A mix of gratitude and guilt washed over me as I realized Charlotte trusted me enough to share her thoughts and concerns. I was acutely aware I had thrown her under the bus during our encounter with Beverly. I vowed to make amends through words and genuine actions reflecting my remorse and respect for our friendship.

Taking a deep breath I gently placed my hand on Charlotte's, hoping to convey my support and willingness to listen. We sat there for a moment in comfortable silence, allowing the weight of her words to settle between us. In that brief respite, I prepared to offer the long overdue apology.

"Charlotte," I began, my voice filled with sincerity. "I want to apologize for what happened at Beverly's. I should never have put you in that situation, and I am truly sorry for any embarrassment or hurt it may have caused you. You deserve better, and I hope you can find it in your heart to forgive me."

As I spoke, Charlotte turned her gaze from the sea to meet mine. Her gaze had a flicker of appreciation and understanding and a glimmer of something more profound. She gently squeezed my hand, her touch a reassurance confirming we were in this together.

"Lisa," she responded, soft yet resolute. "Friendship is about growth and forgiveness. We have been through so much together, and I understand mistakes happen. It takes strength to acknowledge them and seek reconciliation. Your apology means a great deal to me, and I forgive you wholeheartedly."

A wave of relief washed over me mingled with

gratitude for Charlotte's understanding and forgiveness. Our bond, forged over countless shared experiences and a deep sense of camaraderie, had weathered many storms, and this was just another testament to its resilience.

As we sat there, hand in hand, we knew our friendship would continue to evolve and grow, just as we had as individuals. We would navigate the challenges ahead, supporting and uplifting each other every step of the way. The storm within me had found its resolution, replaced by a renewed sense of peace and a determination to cherish the constants while embracing the necessary changes ahead.

As I cautiously broached the subject of her series, Charlotte took a sip of her coffee, using the momentary respite to gather her thoughts. Her response was measured, and I could sense the weight of her words as she embarked on sharing her journey.

"I needed to start something new," Charlotte began, her voice carrying a mix of resolve and vulnerability. "I've been writing the Inkwell Investigations for over fifteen years, and it was time for Inspector Tidwell's story to end. We had created a whole world around him with a television show, comics, and merchandise. But both he and I grew weary of the endless cycle. I know you may find it silly that I feel connected to my fictional characters, but from my perspective, they are my companions when I feel alone. Before I had you girls, my love for the written word was often misunderstood, and my dreams of becoming a librarian were met with skepticism."

She paused, taking in a deep breath of the refreshing ocean air as if drawing strength from the vastness of the sea before continuing.

"So, I did something drastic. I pulled a Sir Arthur Conan Doyle move and killed off Inspector Tidwell," Charlotte admitted, her gaze fixed on the horizon. "But my fan base wasn't exactly receptive to this turn of events. They couldn't accept the end of the series and the demise of their beloved character. To make matters worse, the publishing company that had profited from my work for years abruptly dropped me as a client. They refused even to consider the pitch for my new series. Their lack of loyalty and trust in my craft really hurt. Now my agent is scrambling to reach indie publishing houses and it's been an uphill battle."

A profound sadness lingered in her voice, mingling with a hint of frustration. The weight of public opinion and the media's relentless scrutiny had taken its toll on Charlotte. This trip, our shared adventure on the cruise, offered a much-needed respite from the outside world's disappointments and demands.

"I needed to escape from the public eye, from the constant news articles and the relentless presence of social media," Charlotte admitted, her gaze momentarily shifting to meet mine. "This journey came at the perfect time for me, a chance to recharge and find solace in the company of dear friends like you. It's a chance to rediscover my passion for storytelling, explore new horizons, and create something fresh. I hope the right opportunity will eventually present itself, and my voice as a writer will be heard again."

As she spoke, her words carried a mix of resilience and determination, a reminder that even in the face of setbacks, Charlotte's creativity and spirit remained unyielding. I reached out and placed my hand on hers, offering support and understanding.

"Charlotte," I murmured, "I agree with you and am happy to hear you're approaching this with such a healthy perspective. Your talent as a writer is undeniable. Your impact on readers and fans is immeasurable. I believe in you, and I have no doubt your storytelling prowess will find a new avenue to flourish. This journey is not just a break from the noise; it's a chance for you to rediscover your voice and embrace the possibilities ahead. And you're not alone in this. We're here for you every step of the way."

I felt renewed hope in the quiet morning at the cafe, surrounded by the gentle rhythm of conversations and the distant sound of waves. We were embarking on a cruise filled with possibilities and adventure. It was up to us to embrace the day and create new memories, fortified by the unwavering bonds that had carried us through the years. I didn't know just how much our bonds would be tried on this new journey.

Chapter Fourteen

The day continued in tranquil camaraderie as we strolled along the Lido Deck, relishing the gentle ocean breeze sweeping through our hair. We indulged in the various offerings of the ship, from savoring delectable meals to luxuriating in the steam room's comforting embrace. Laughter and stories filled the air as we basked in the joy of each other's company, creating new memories that would linger long after the voyage's end.

As the sun descended, casting a golden glow upon the horizon, we collectively decided to retreat to our respective rooms, eager to freshen up and prepare for the anticipated gala in the Cruise and Groove Ballroom. With renewed energy, we headed for our rooms, sharing lighthearted banter and inside jokes along the corridors.

Upon reaching Charlotte and Beverly's room, Arba appeared at the door carrying a stack of fluffy towels. His warm smile illuminated the room as he greeted us, his presence a comforting reminder of the ship's unwavering hospitality.

"Hello, ladies! I hope you have enjoyed our lovely ship and are taking in all the vitamin D the sun can provide." He was looking over his shoulder as he started folding a towel in a very intricate way.

"Yes, Arba, we did," I responded. "What have you got there?" I was more interested in what he was doing with the towel than in retelling what we did today on the

Tranquility Deck.

Arba turned around with a bunny made of a body towel and a few hand towels. He rested it on the counter in the room. "Oh, this little guy? I love making towel animals. I have been the ship's towel champion for two years running! Wait until you see what I have for tomorrow's towel animal! You'll just love it!"

"This is really clever, Arba!" Charlotte exclaimed as she picked up the bunny and turned it around. "I DO love it!" She took her cell phone out. Without service, Charlotte was using the camera on her phone to document the trip. She took a selfie with the bunny-shaped towel.

Arba's eyes crinkled with a smile as he nodded. "It's my pleasure. Ensuring your comfort and satisfaction is my top priority. If there's anything else you need, please don't hesitate to let me know." His voice exuded genuine warmth until the door next to ours opened.

Seth poked his head into the hallway and scoffed. "Making towel animals, Arba? What are you—six years old?" Seth shook his head and laughed at his own joke as he closed the door hard and headed toward the elevators.

"Ignore him, Arba. He is just a horrible man with nothing but mean bones in his body." Wilma patted Arba on his shoulder in comfort.

"Oh, I know," Arba grumbled under his breath, dripping in sarcasm and what felt like a tinge of hatred.

"Have a great evening, ladies." Arba hung his head, and with a final nod and courteous farewell, he went on to his next duty leaving a sense of anxiety and sadness behind.

Something bothered me about how Arba responded

to Seth's bullying, but I couldn't quite put my finger on it. There was no time to think about that right then. We all had to get dolled up and didn't have much time to make it to pre-dinner drinks, which was quickly becoming a tradition I enjoyed.

As we freshened up and prepared for the evening's festivities, the air buzzed with anticipation. The gala held the promise of elegance and glamour, an opportunity for us to showcase our individual styles and revel in the magic of the occasion. We donned our finest attire, carefully selecting each piece to reflect our personalities, adding excitement to our already vibrant spirits.

The Cruise and Groove Ballroom was awash with a sea of exquisite ball gowns, shimmering with sequins and intricate embroidery, and dapper tuxedos, exuding a timeless charm. Every guest embraced the spirit of the occasion, displaying their finest attire with a touch of personal flair.

The crowd parted naturally to allow our group of four to move toward the bar before we split off. Beverly and Charlotte spotted a corner booth and headed off to secure it while Wilma and I headed to the bar to get our drinks.

The graceful Australian, Zoe, swiftly maneuvered behind the bar, getting all the drink orders shouted across the bar to her, pouring them out into different-sized glassware without spilling a drop. I knew I wouldn't be able to keep up in Zoe's place. I'd spill every bit of the beer and liquor while trying not to trip over my feet.

The crowd at the bar lessened as people took their drink orders to tall tables and booths, allowing the perfect amount of room for us to squeeze up to the bar. Of course, as we inched closer, it felt like I was in an old-time movie. The crowd split, and there Richard was, leaning up against the counter, martini in hand, scanning the crowd with a devilish smile.

"Awe! Ladies! Looking radiant as always!" He leaned down to Wilma to give her a kiss on the cheek.

"How are you feeling from last night? Are your puppies aching?" Richard smiled as he met my gaze and nodded an acknowledgment of hello toward me.

"Not too bad. You forget I do yoga. I'm not young chronologically, but I am young in heart and body." Wilma flirted and smiled as she turned away to ask Zoe for a pitcher of margaritas and a whiskey sour for me.

Richard's voice broke through my swirling emotions; his words carried a hint of playfulness that caught me off guard. "Missed you last night, Lisa. Would have loved to take you around the ballroom floor a time or two." His gaze locked with mine, and a rush of heat flushed my cheeks, my palms growing clammy.

Attempting to maintain a light-hearted tone, though my unease lingered beneath the surface, I said, "Oh? I think you had your hands full with our Wil here. Plus, my dance card has been filled for years. I've run out of spots for signups." I theatrically fanned myself with an imaginary dance card.

Needing a distraction from Richard's flirtatious advances, I turned my attention to the bustling crowd to engage in some people-watching. I was uncomfortable with the flirty conversation and how my traitorous body was responding to it, especially with Wilma standing right there beside us. The last thing I wanted was to create tension within our close-knit group.

Just then, Seth and Robyn made their grand entrance into the bar, drawing my focus away from the conversation with Richard. Seth's assertive hand cleared a path through the crowd, pushing and jostling people aside, while his grip on Robyn's wrist appeared tight and possessive.

Inwardly, I rolled my eyes. *Does he EVER just hold her hand??*

As they came closer, it was clear Robyn had applied an excessive amount of makeup, obviously trying to hide discoloration on her otherwise lovely face.

Zoe was busy preparing our drinks, but I knew she was aware of Seth's presence. Predictably, a few seconds of Zoe's inattention was all it took for Seth's impatience to get the best of him. He slammed a ten-dollar bill onto the bar and demanded a Budweiser and…nothing for Robyn.

Zoe's professional demeanor transformed into firm disapproval, saying, "There are other people ahead of you. This isn't how you place orders in my bar. You can wait." She shot us a reassuring smile as we finalized our drink orders.

In a fit of aggression, Seth knocked over two of our drinks, causing them to spill onto the floor before we could pick them up from the counter. Anger boiled within me, but my attention was redirected to the disturbing revelation unfolding as the interaction between Seth and Zoe continued.

Leaning closer to Zoe, Seth sneered, "Listen, witch, this isn't your bar. You don't know who I am, but I can make your life harder." He turned to Robyn, whose face was growing red with embarrassment. "Can't I, babe? Your brother would have something to say about this, seeing as the customer is always right."

I looked closely at Robyn's face and, as the layers

of makeup failed to conceal the truth, a pang of concern welled inside me. Dark bruises took shape beneath her cosmetic mask under her left eye, resembling the outline of a giant fist. Glancing down, I noticed Seth's hand still tightly gripped her wrist, the physical evidence of his abuse becoming unmistakable.

Also obvious was how differently Robyn and Seth presented themselves in their appearances. Robyn stood before us in a stunning little black dress that accentuated her delicate figure. The elegance of her outfit was complemented by the grace with which she carried herself, her confidence shining through despite the shadows looming beneath her eyes. Her black heels added a touch of sophistication to the ensemble.

On the other hand, Seth's appearance starkly contrasted with Robyn's refined style. He exuded an air of immaturity, dressed in a tuxedo t-shirt, which was out of place amidst the formal atmosphere. His ripped jeans and Converse sneakers completed the image of a middle-aged man clinging to his youth.

As my gaze lingered on Robyn, my concern for her well-being evident, Seth caught my intense scrutiny and his eyes narrowed. I was loudly telegraphing the weight of my judgment against him and his deplorable behavior. Though his gaze met mine, he seemed more defensive than remorseful, defiance etched onto his face.

I was silently condemning him. My holding him accountable for his actions didn't go unnoticed by him and a few people around us as well. Seth's behavior further reinforced my determination to stand up for Robyn and confront the abusive dynamics that had become all too apparent.

Though frightened and subdued, Robyn muttered

under her breath to suggest she and Seth proceed to dinner.

Ignoring her while directly challenging me, Seth sneered, "What are you looking at, hag?"

"I'm not sure. I hope you know there is a dress code for tonight." I looked him up and down with the meanest look of distaste and derision I could summon. "And *that* is not going to make the cut." I motioned my hand up and down, indicating his outfit.

We grabbed fresh drinks from Zoe and returned to the table where Charlotte and Beverly were waiting. Our table offered a perfect vantage point to observe the bar and dance floor. Beverly pointed to the escalating confrontation between Seth and Zoe, and I shifted my attention back toward the bar. The intensity of their argument was palpable, their voices rising above the crowd's buzz. Seth's gestures became more animated, his face contorted with anger, while Zoe's frustration grew evident as she struggled to maintain her composure.

Richard leaned in and offered to intervene, if necessary, but I hesitated. Something told me this confrontation needed to play out. Zoe had a well of deep strength and independence within her; from our earlier conversation, I didn't think she would appreciate anyone intervening at this point. She would call on her inner core to face this battle. I couldn't tear my eyes away from the unfolding scene, my heart pounding in anticipation.

The tension peaked when Seth, in a moment of aggression, seized Zoe's left arm tightly. I remembered her earlier remark about self-defense skills. Zoe reacted immediately, her voice pierced through the chaos, filled with determination and defiance. "No! Do not touch me!" she exclaimed, her words carrying the weight of her resistance.

In a swift and decisive motion, Zoe pushed Seth away with such force he stumbled backward, losing his balance and landing hard on his ass. Robyn squeaked a sound of surprise and ran toward him. She tried to help him, but he just glared and shoved his way up from the floor. He turned to Zoe and hissed something I couldn't hear, grabbed Robyn, and limped away, nursing his newly injured ankle. The crowd surrounding the bar erupted in cheers and applause, a resounding show of support for Zoe's act of self-empowerment. It was evident Seth's behavior had worn thin on everyone there.

The rest of pre-dinner drink time was filled with laughter and camaraderie, the weight of the confrontation eventually lifting from our shoulders. We relished in each other's company until the attendants kindly reminded us it was time to move into the Cruise and Groove for the gala.

Dinner was enjoyable with no drama, only fine food and conversation. We entered our room later that night to find a delightful surprise—a meticulously crafted towel sculpture in the form of an eight-legged octopus, courtesy of Arba. Little did he know his creation would be etched in our memories to symbolize the horror we would share in the morning.

Chapter Fifteen

"Rise and shine, Lisa-May!" The sound of the curtains sliding and the rush of the morning breeze against my bedsheets stirred me from the depths of a warm and cozy dream. Reluctantly, I resurfaced from the realm of slumber, feeling the tangled sheets around my legs and the perfectly molded pillows cradling my head. Every fiber of my being resisted opening my eyes.

"Hmm? What do you want?" I muttered, attempting to bury myself deeper into the pillows and slip back into the inviting realm of sleep.

Wilma's voice carried a sense of determination, breaking through my half-conscious state. "We need to keep ourselves in shape. We can't turn into blobs on this trip. Get your butt up. I'm going to wake up the other girls. We'll take a stroll around the Lido and then treat ourselves to a healthy breakfast," she declared, punctuating her words with a playful slap on my backside. The message was clear—I needed to rise and prepare for the day. I dared to crack open one eye, only to confirm that the sun was indeed still beneath the horizon.

On the Lido Deck, Charlotte, and Beverly looked just as tired as I felt. I wanted an excellent French press breakfast blend of coffee and strawberry jelly toast. A dash of Kahlua may be acceptable; I am on vacation.

Wilma looked like she had already had her coffee

with a double espresso. She bounced from one foot to the other to keep her blood pumping. It was an unseasonably cold morning. The Lido Deck was open to the elements, and the ocean could be frigid without the sun bouncing off it.

"Alright, ladies. This is what we are going to do. First, a couple of laps around the Lido, and then the dining hall will be open for breakfast by the time we're done." Wilma looked at each of us and smiled as she picked up her speed to a fast walk, not even looking back to see if we were keeping up.

We began our circuit at the stern of the ship, making our way clockwise toward the middle. Ahead in our path were two inviting pools—one designated for adults to relax and swim and the other a playful splash pad designed for children's enjoyment. A delightful sight stopped us in our tracks as we neared the poolside lounging areas.

A multitude of meticulously crafted animal towels occupied every available lounge chair, each one distinct and unique. The scene was a whimsical display of creativity and thoughtfulness. Smiles spread across our faces as we took it all in, appreciating the care and effort put into this charming surprise. Elephants, monkeys, cats, and dogs—beach towels transformed into cuddly creatures—waited patiently for the awakening of the ship's passengers as if anticipating the joy and laughter that would ensue.

It was a heartwarming sight, evoking a sense of childlike wonder and reminding us of the simple pleasures that can be found in unexpected moments. We couldn't help but feel a renewed appreciation for the small, delightful details making this journey even more special.

"This is something the kids are going to really enjoy!" Beverly said through deep breaths. She wasn't used to speed walking and was the shortest of us at five foot two inches tall.

"This is a lot of fun!" Wilma agreed. "All right, ladies, let's keep moving to get our muscles warmed and our heart rate elevated. Break time is over."

As we started to resume our walk, a peculiar sight caught my attention and caused me to halt abruptly. There, on one of the lounge chairs, lay a figure who appeared to have fallen asleep in a very uncomfortable position. It struck me as odd since it was against the ship's safety regulations for guests to sleep on the deck chairs. Everyone was encouraged to return to their quarters by two in the morning to ensure a peaceful night's rest.

Concerned about their well-being and mindful of the discomfort sleeping on those chairs could bring, I gestured to the ladies that we needed to investigate further. As we approached, this person was clearly not sleeping off a night of revelry; something deeper was at play. Worse yet, I recognized him.

"Hey, Wil?" I looked back to see if we both had come to the same conclusion about the situation. Her reaction told me we were on the same page. Yoga and running enthusiast Wilma was no longer there; ER Nurse Wilma had come to the forefront.

"I see him, Lisa. Will you please step back? I need to check his vitals." She leaned forward, but I felt she already knew the answer. She turned back to us with a grim expression and a sadness only people who have seen death before could feel. "Charlotte? Beverly? Will you find Martin in his office at the service desk? One of the passengers has passed away."

Charlotte and Beverly stood in shock, unresponsive. I walked and rested my hands on both of their arms.

"Bev? Charlotte? Are you both okay? Did you hear Wilma?" I knew Charlotte wrote about death and murder but seeing it up close and personal was probably not what she expected to happen during her vacation. I worried more about Beverly, though. Her face had lost all the color it had gained during our short workout.

Pale as a sheet, Beverly whispered, "Um…" She shook her head to get her bearings and said, "Yes, I heard her." She turned to Charlotte, who was returning from the shock. "Come on, Char. We need to get going." Charlotte nodded her head, and they both jogged to the elevators to get to the service desk.

"He wasn't a very nice person. But no one deserves to die like this." Wilma said as she stood up from her crouch on the ground.

Seth lay twisted, his body contorted on the lounge chair. However, it wasn't his contorted posture that struck me the most. It was the shocking evidence of foul play becoming immediately apparent. An octopus towel animal encircled his neck, the skin exposed under the towel was discolored, and there were signs of petechial hemorrhaging showing in his open eyes. It was a chilling realization that this man had been choked to death.

As I surveyed his lifeless form, a wave of dread washed over me. The severity of the injuries became evident as I noticed his swollen face, his nose grotesquely misshapen, likely broken during the struggle. It was a disturbing sight, one that confirmed without a doubt Seth's demise was no accident—it was a deliberate act of violence. The implications were profound, and the reality sank in that this was a homicide with a long list of potential suspects, all of whom were still on board this ship.

Suddenly, a realization struck me with jarring force—*I could be considered one of those suspects*. The unsettling thought sent a shiver down my spine as the weight of the situation settled upon my shoulders.

Soon after, Beverly and Charlotte arrived, accompanied by Martin. Also approaching the scene were the ship's doctor and nurse. I quickly moved away from Seth's lifeless body, joining Beverly and Charlotte off to the side. I strongly wanted to put as much distance as possible between Seth and me.

Glancing back at the approaching medical professionals, Martin nervously raked his hand through his striking red hair, causing it to stand on end. "You haven't touched anything, have you?" he asked us, concern etched on his face.

I shook my head and replied, "No, I haven't touched anything. Wilma checked his pulse and breathing, though. She's a retired ER nurse, so she knows the necessary precautions." Wilma stepped away, creating space for additional security staff who swiftly erected caution tape and set up cones to secure the area.

"What time did you find him?" Martin asked.

"It couldn't have been more than fifteen minutes ago. We sent for you the moment we understood the situation," I responded, clutching my hands to keep them from shaking.

I observed Martin as he diligently scribbled notes in his notebook, his tired eyes overshadowed by dark, deep bags. The fading bruise on his face, courtesy of Seth's assault, showcased an uncomfortable array of black, blue, yellow, and purple shades.

Interrupting his notetaking, Martin looked up at us with a furrowed brow. "Was anyone else present when you ladies arrived?" he questioned, his tone tinged with suspicion. "And why were you out of your rooms so early?"

Beverly, finally recovering from the shock of discovering a lifeless body amidst innocent animal towels, retorted, "Excuse me, but I don't appreciate your tone, young man."

"Ma'am, you don't have to appreciate my tone, but these questions are necessary. We can do this here or in my office, but you must provide answers," Martin asserted, the weariness evident in the corners of his eyes and the tautness of his mouth.

Offering support to Beverly, I placed my hand on her back and rubbed it gently, providing comfort and warmth to ease her chills induced by shock. I turned to Martin, explaining, "Wilma is a health and exercise enthusiast. She roused all of us at the crack of dawn for a power walk before the ship became crowded."

Martin turned to the other ladies, observing their sneakers and workout attire, and nodded in understanding. "Listen, ladies, this was clearly a homicide. It was no accident. Do you know someone who might have held a grudge against Seth?"

Suppressing a snort and hastily covering my face with my hand to mask my response of untimely humor, I realized it was an inappropriate reaction given the circumstances.

Wilma, however, blurted out, "Other than you?" before quickly covering her mouth in shock. Martin's lip twitched, displaying either amusement or annoyance—I couldn't discern which.

"Yes, ma'am. Other than me. You know, dealing with disgruntled individuals comes with the territory of my job. I have a much thicker skin than to let a boy's punch affect me," Martin replied, glancing around as his team erected caution tape and blocked the entrances to the deck. The doctor prepared to remove the body.

"Um, yes." Charlotte finally answered. "There's his poor girlfriend, Robyn. Though I'd be surprised if she did it."

"Why is that?" Martin asked as he looked up from his notebook.

"Well, it's just that she's timid and scared as a mouse when around him from what we've seen. She was constantly flinching and moved away if she could when Seth made any sudden movement. That is not someone likely to kill anyone. She's also quite small; I wouldn't think she'd be strong enough to…do *that*…with the octopus, I mean."

"Hmm. I have seen abused women snap once they have reached their limit. You can't immediately take her off a suspect list because she is a small woman," Beverly whispered.

"And how would you know?" Martin asked.

"I worked as my husband's secretary in his medical practice for over forty years. I've seen countless women and men walk through those doors with unexplained bruises, fractures, and concussions," Beverly revealed, her face etched with weariness and her gaze distant, lost in memories of a different time and place. "Some of them ended up making headlines because they had finally reached their breaking point. They either became victims or the perpetrators themselves."

Her words hung heavy in the air, carrying the weight of her experience and the countless stories of pain and struggle she had witnessed. Beverly's journey had exposed her to the dark realities lurking behind closed doors, leaving an indelible mark on her spirit.

"I see. There is also the man he fought with on the first night. I have seen you dining and with him in various places around the ship."

"Excuse me? What is that supposed to mean? He was assigned to our table, so we've gotten to know him a little. You can't possibly think he had anything to do with this just because he stuck up for those two girls." A flush was moving from Wilma's neck up to her face. She was a fiercely loyal person to people she considered her friends. I wouldn't want to get on her wrong side.

I needed to get in between her and Martin before she clocked him and gave him a matching shiner. "His name is Richard Taylor, a gentleman from England. I don't think he killed this young man."

I hesitated to accuse anyone without concrete evidence, but I knew there were several other possible suspects to explore. The expression on my face must have revealed my thoughts as Martin arched an eyebrow and asked, "Are you considering someone else?"

I took a deep breath, determined to make it clear that my intention was not to divert attention away from Richard. "There are two other individuals who come to mind. Last night many witnessed Seth and Zoe engaged in a heated argument at the bar. He was impatient and rude, grabbed her arm at one point, and fell hard on his butt when she pushed him away. I had the impression he then verbally threatened her right before he left."

Martin nodded, jotting down notes. Without looking up, he asked, "And the other person?"

"This may be a stretch, but I have a gut feeling about our steward, Arba. There seemed to be a connection between him and the victim," I explained. I recounted the interactions we had observed, Seth's constant barrage of derogatory remarks towards Arba, and how Seth seemed to flaunt his relationship with Robyn as if they shared a history. I also mentioned Arba's exceptional skill with animal towels, notably his signature octopus design.

Martin's gaze intensified as he closed his notebook and surveyed the area. The body had been taken away, and his team diligently documented the remnants of the scene.

He turned back to us and said, "I recommend you stay cautious but go back to your rooms for now. I will come to find you if I need to have you answer any more questions." He turned away in dismissal.

"I guess he doesn't need to tell us not to leave town," I muttered to the ladies as we went to the elevator to lighten the mood. Everyone smiled slightly, and I knew they would all be okay. This wasn't the first body *I* had come across.

Chapter Sixteen

We went to our rooms and stopped at Seth and Robyn's door. We needed to talk to Robyn before Martin did. Something in my gut told me Martin wouldn't be as sensitive as we seasoned women would be to what this young woman was going through. Wilma and Beverly agreed they needed to wash up before they could do anything else.

Charlotte and I exchanged a knowing glance, resorting to our usual method of deciding who would take on an unpleasant task: a game of Rock, Paper, Scissors. Unfortunately, luck was not on my side, and I found myself with the duty of knocking on Robyn's door.

In response to my knock, a cacophony of stumbling, expletives, and a shattering sound reached our ears, accompanied by the sound of feet shuffling toward the entrance. Robyn opened the door slightly, appearing disheveled and clearly just awakened.

Robyn, clearly not fully grasping the situation, responded, "Arba? I don't need anything right now. Seth isn't here. Can you come back later?" Her voice sounded hoarse, hinting at her need for a glass of water, and she started to close the door.

I placed my hand against the closing door and interjected, "Um, dear? We're not Arba. We have something vital to discuss with you. Is there any way we could come in just for a second?" I attempted to channel my inner Grandma Beverly, hoping to convey both urgency and a comforting presence.

I gently pushed my way into her room without waiting for a response. Robyn appeared startled by the sudden intrusion of two elderly ladies but didn't appear inclined to argue. Unlike Seth, she was raised with respect for her elders.

Taking in the chaotic state of the small cabin, it looked like a violent whirlwind had blown through with clothes scattered about, the bed unmade, and items haphazardly lying everywhere. My gaze landed on a towel, soaked in blood, lying amidst the disarray.

Robyn's appearance was a big clue to the reason for the bloody towel. Her face bore the signs of recent violence—a split eye, dried blood clinging to the wound, and the dark spots peeking through her makeup the night before now stark against her pale, makeup-less complexion. She seemed lost and bewildered.

Charlotte, ever the leader, guided Robyn to sit down. She exchanged a knowing look with me, silently conveying that I should continue exploring while she talked to Robyn.

"My dear, what happened to your beautiful face?" Charlotte's voice dripped with an Oklahoma accent she skillfully exaggerated. We knew the power of elderly Southern charm—some people underestimate us, thinking we're less astute than we actually are. Our age only adds to that inaccurate perception. We have often used the misconception to our advantage.

Robyn avoided making eye contact, offering a quick and smooth lie. "I tripped on the clothes and hit my head on the entertainment center." It was a well-practiced fabrication, and I wondered how often she had to deceive others during her time with Seth. Perhaps she had honed her skill of lying throughout her life.

"Now, now, darling. We know there's more to the story. You can trust us," Charlotte coaxed, her hand rubbing gently on Robyn's back as she began to sob silently.

Robyn put her face into her hands and started to shake uncontrollably. "This isn't what was supposed to happen. We were supposed to get married and move to Mexico. He isn't normally this way. It is the stress. He can't handle the stress. And you know what they say. You lash out at those you love because you are safest with them. This was supposed to be the perfect week. We were going to get everything. Everything we deserved."

Robyn had surely been given horrible advice on what love was supposed to be. I could tell she really believed what she saying.

"Honey, anyone worth their salt would not abuse someone like this. If they truly loved you, they would never raise a hand or voice against you." Charlotte spoke calmly, her hand continuing to provide comfort on Robyn's back.

I paused my search of the room, leaning against the dresser-entertainment combo, and asked Robyn, "What did you mean by this being the perfect week? Is this your pre-honeymoon?" I observed her closely because I wanted to see how she would react.

"Seth and Gray, my brother, were supposed to be closing a deal with the cruise line. I'm unsure about the specifics, but they were both excited. Gray was going to get a promotion, and Seth said we would be set for life and never have to work again," Robyn explained, wiping her nose on her bare arm, a gesture that made me cringe and avert my gaze to the ceiling.

Charlotte took over the conversation, probing further. "What do you mean by 'would never have to work again?' What does your brother do for the cruise line? Did you also work with him?"

Robyn's eyes widened, betraying the sense she had revealed too much. The extent of what she had divulged was still unclear. I had no knowledge of who her brother was or why he held a significant position.

Attempting to cover her tracks, Robyn stumbled over her words. "I'm a licensed cosmetologist, and I sometimes do makeup gigs for the ship's entertainment. I've worked on and off ships since Gray and I were old enough to work. It's actually where Gray and I met Seth about ten years ago." Her voice trailed off as she seemed lost in her thoughts of the past.

Realizing time was short, I signaled to Charlotte to expedite our conversation. She nodded her understanding and said, "I have some news we need to share with you. Would you like a glass of water or ice for your eye?"

"No, I'm fine. What's wrong? Have you seen Seth? He's been gone since last night. We had a big fight," Robyn replied, gesturing to her battered face and the chaos in the room.

"We have seen Seth, but he won't be coming back to the room," I interjected, meeting Robyn's gaze.

"Has he gotten himself locked up in the Brig? Did Gray let that happen?" Robyn's face revealed confusion, and I wondered who Gray was. Could it be Martin? Was he the only one with the authority to detain someone? Did she know him before this trip?

Before I could inquire further, Charlotte dropped the bombshell. "No, honey. Seth is not coming back. We found him this morning on the Lido Deck. He's gone."

I maintained my gaze on Robyn, observing her reaction to this shocking news. She appeared relieved. First, her shoulders sagged, and then a weight seemed to lift off her. Suddenly, as if remembering she wasn't alone in her cabin, she started crying uncontrollably.

An interesting response, I noted to myself.

As Charlotte was comforting a now inconsolable Robyn, I tidied up the room, hoping to find something to tell us more of the story. Before I could say anything else, a knock sounded at the door, startling everyone in the room. I looked at Charlotte, hoping Wilma and Beverly were coming to help with this soft interrogation. Robyn got up to answer it and Martin walked in with his security team. I assumed he was here to tell her the news about Seth.

Martin took in the messy room, Charlotte sitting on the couch, me standing with a towel in my hand, and suspicion grew in his narrowed eyes. "Robyn, I need you to come with me to Guest Services. We have a lot of things to talk about," he said firmly.

Robyn nodded, grabbing a shawl from the floor to wrap around her arms. As she stepped into the hallway, Martin turned his attention back to us. "Ladies, this is an investigation. I don't need a bunch of Miss Marples or Jessica Fletchers to help me solve it. Please make your way back to your quarters as I recommended before. I will be coming back to ask more questions."

With that, Martin held the door open and gestured for us to pass through and return to our rooms. He may have been able to confine us to our quarters, but he couldn't prevent us from discussing the case or attempting to solve it ourselves. We had some details to share and debate amongst ourselves.

We all gathered in Wilma's and my room to discuss the events that had unfolded.

"I understand that young man might think we're just little old ladies who don't know how to mind our own business," I began, voicing my frustration.

"And he's probably right. We are here to enjoy ourselves, not to get into trouble or cause any," Beverly chimed in with her grandmotherly voice. Her tone was smooth, slow, and calming, with a touch of authority. It reminded me of how adults would reason with a child, gently guiding them toward the right decision. But in this case, Beverly didn't realize I was determined to get to the bottom of this, no matter what.

"I don't know about you, Charlotte and Wilma, but I feel the same way as Lisa," Beverly continued. "We must uncover the truth. We can't let Lisa or Richard be falsely accused of this murder. Is 'pinned' the right term, Charlotte?" Beverly asked, turning to Charlotte for confirmation.

Charlotte nodded; her eyes gleaming with excitement. As a seasoned mystery writer, she knew how to approach such situations. "You two are right. Martin may not have the expertise of a homicide detective, so it's up to us to gather the important information. We can't afford to let any crucial details slip through the cracks. However, we must be careful not to overstep our boundaries and jeopardize the investigation."

"Agreed, we need to take this one step at a time," Wilma said.

I took a deep breath, acknowledging the gravity of

the situation. "That's true. We need to consider all possibilities, even if they may seem unlikely. Our goal is to find the truth, no matter where it leads us. But let's not jump to conclusions about Martin. We should approach this with an open mind and rely on the evidence we uncover."

Beverly, always the voice of reason, chimed in, "Girls, we'll work together and share what we discover. We can support Martin's investigation while ensuring we aren't dismissed or overlooked. We'll use our collective wisdom and intuition to navigate this mystery."

I felt a renewed sense of purpose and determination. This was an opportunity to prove that I still had what it took to unravel a complex puzzle. It wasn't about seeking validation from others but about reaffirming my worth and capabilities. With that thought, I eagerly joined my fellow sleuths in our quest for the truth.

"All right, girls. Let's order room service and start getting a timeline together. We have a lot to figure out before we hit port in Cozumel in three days. Should be plenty of time, right?" I cleared off the small coffee table in our room. I took out some notebooks and pens I always had with me. We had a murder to solve and a killer to catch.

Chapter Seventeen

With our thoughts fueled by room service, we settled into spots around the small cabin room. I sat on the couch next to Charlotte, and Beverly took a comfortable cross-legged position on the bed. Wilma, always restless, claimed the chair in front of the vanity but then quickly thought better of it and began rolling out her yoga mat in the small entryway.

Feeling the need to organize our thoughts, I grabbed a notebook and pen, ready to delve into the details. "The first person who's been bothering me is our room steward, Arba," I stated, writing down his name on the notebook and circling it. "I think creating a bubble chart will help us analyze his potential involvement and gain a better understanding of the situation."

"You are so right, Lisa!" Wilma agreed from her stretching position on the floor.

Beverly held up the spoon for attention while swallowing her last bite of cake. "You saw that an animal was around Seth's neck, didn't you? It was an octopus, just like the one we had in our room. Didn't he say it was his specialty and had won awards for his towel animals?" She placed her empty plate on the side table by the bed.

"You're correct!" I made a new circle webbing from Arba's name. I wrote *Octopus Towel*. Adding another point to our growing chart, I said, "Arba's behavior around Robyn was peculiar, like he had some kind of connection to her, perhaps even a crush. Robyn's gentle demeanor and captivating doe eyes could have easily caught his interest."

"And Seth made fun of him about the animal towels and hinted at something more sinister going on with Arba. I saw anger flash in Arba's eyes whenever Seth talked," Charlotte chimed in. "But what about Martin? Seth punched him in the dining room and later you saw him arguing with Seth in his office when you went to pick up your luggage. Then Seth seemed to have gotten off scot-free for giving Martin a black eye. That *must* put Martin higher on the list of suspects than poor Arba."

I turned to another page in the notebook and started a web outline for Martin. Two circles webbed off of his name: *Altercation & Black Eye (Dining Room)* and *Argument (Office)*.

"Tell us more about the argument in the office, girls," Beverly asked as she moved more pillows behind her back to get more comfortable on the bed.

I took a moment to recall the details of the argument in Martin's office. "When we approached Martin's office to pick up my luggage, the door was open a few inches. We could see Seth's face through the crack, and he was clearly agitated. His tone suggested he was trying to assert authority over Martin as if he was Martin's superior."

Wilma added, "Yes, Seth was confrontational, like he was intentionally trying to provoke Martin. I couldn't make out the exact words, but there was tension in the air. Still, Martin appeared to be composed, though I could tell he was irritated."

Beverly listened, her eyes narrowing in deep concentration. "So, Seth was trying to assert dominance over Martin. There might be a power struggle between the two of them. There has to be more going on behind the scenes we don't know about yet."

Still holding her yoga pose, Wilma added, "Maybe Seth said something while they were arguing that finally pushed Martin to his limit."

"True! But there's another factor!" I exclaimed. "Another voice was coming from that office! I swear it wasn't Seth talking to Martin. The voice sounded Australian, not Irish. What's weird is that voice also sounded super familiar, like I've heard it somewhere recently." I added another smaller circle in the corner of Martin's page, *Unknown Australian Male Voice*. "I don't know who the voice belongs to yet, but I feel it's important to find out who he is. Seth was bullying *that* man, not Martin, and Martin was forced to let Seth go."

We exchanged glances, realizing the conflict in Martin's office could be a crucial piece of the puzzle— hinting at a complex dynamic between Seth and Martin that might have escalated and led to tragic consequences. We made a note on our chart to explore this further, determined to uncover the full extent of the conflict and potential implications of Seth's murder.

"Oh! Charlotte! We didn't tell Wilma and Lisa about Martin's reaction when we told him Seth was hurt." Beverly bounced up and down as she spoke like a child remembering something she couldn't wait to tell.

Anticipation filled the room as Charlotte leaned forward, her expression pensive. "When we informed Martin about Seth's condition, he didn't react in the way we expected. There was no visible shock or concern on his face. Like he already anticipated, *maybe knew,* about Seth's fate."

Beverly, sitting cross-legged and leaning elbows on her knees, interjected, "I saw a flicker of something in Martin's eyes. A flash of emotions I couldn't quite decipher. There was a hint of surprise, but then something else showed before he quickly masked it, finally settling into security guard mode. Whatever it was, it didn't align with the typical reaction one would have upon hearing about a death, especially by murder."

Charlotte nodded vigorously, her eyes wide with recollection. "Yes, yes! And his body language was guarded, like he was hiding something. Something felt off, considering the circumstances. I couldn't shake the feeling there is more to Martin's involvement than meets the eye."

I furrowed my brow, pondering the implications of Martin's peculiar reaction. "We need to dig deeper into Martin's background and relationship with Seth. It could be a crucial piece of the puzzle if he did have prior knowledge of Seth's death or some level of involvement."

"I think it would be best to get more 'deets' on Martin. That's how the cool kids say details, right?" Wilma said from a happy baby pose on the floor. She was on her back, feet in the air, and her hands held her feet as she rocked back and forth.

"Do you have to do that? It is making me nauseous just watching you," Beverly asked, suddenly turning green.

"You sure it isn't that we are on a ship or maybe because you decided to eat half of a chocolate cake after eating a bowl of spaghetti and garlic bread?" Wilma asked as she finished her yoga routine.

Beverly shook her head and got up from the bed, not

looking like her happy and cheery self. "I'm not feeling very well. I think I need to go lie down for a little while. Can we reconvene in a few hours? At dinner, maybe? Y'all, could you do some reconnaissance about Martin and maybe this mystery man with the accent? I'm sure we will run into Arba again, and we can probe him for more information. Sorry to miss the fun, but I've got to rest for a bit. Good sleuthing!" Beverly headed for the door on unsteady feet.

Charlotte rose from the couch, her gaze sparkling with enthusiasm. "I'd love to join you, ladies, if you're up for it. Sitting around and eating isn't exactly my idea of a thrilling vacation. How about we take a stroll around the deck and see if we can gather any information from the staff and other guests? People share gossip more freely with little old ladies like us."

"Lisa, why don't you and Charlotte go get more information? I have a massage appointment I don't want to miss. Treat yo'self as Evan says." Evan was Wilma's nephew, and he was such a fun young man.

"Let's go! I know just the person to start with for the best gossip!" I exclaimed, excitement bubbling within me. I swiftly grabbed my trusty tote bag and tucked the notebook and pen inside, ready for our investigative adventure.

"Oh, who could you possibly know so well already?" Charlotte asked, curiosity twinkling in her gaze as we made our way toward the elevator.

A mischievous smile spread across my face as I revealed my secret. "Why, the ship's therapist, of course!"

Charlotte's eyebrows shot up in surprise. "You've seen the ship's therapist?"

I chuckled. "Well, she's not exactly the conventional counselor. I prefer therapists who serve whiskey sours and possess a healthy dose of sass."

Understanding dawned on Charlotte's face. "Ah, so we'll be paying a visit to Zoe the bartender slash therapist. It could be important to find out more about her argument with Seth last night."

I was stopped short by Charlotte's comment. *Should we also consider Zoe as a potential suspect?* She did display a wicked anger issue, and her forceful shove that sent Seth sprawling to the ground was far from gentle. Perhaps our encounter with Zoe would yield more information and add another name to the ever-growing list of suspects. This investigation was shaping up to be more complex than I had initially anticipated.

As we stepped into the elevator and the doors closed, our journey to uncover the truth began—as all adventures do—with one step at a time. Little did we know what twists, turns, and unexpected revelations lie ahead. We were determined to face them head-on, armed with wit, charm, and a burning desire to solve the mystery that had interrupted our peaceful cruise.

Chapter Eighteen

Charlotte and I walked into the pub and saw we beat the lunch crowd. Zoe was wiping the bar down and getting glassware put up for a busy day. There weren't many downtimes in any of the bars on a cruise ship full of people who couldn't go anywhere. After all, there were only so many times a person could go to the spa, swim, eat, and gamble. Drinking would probably be the ship's most lucrative endeavor.

As we approached Zoe, I noticed a bruise had bloomed on her right arm. It stood out against her skin, and she was favoring it, using her left hand more often than her right. The injury appeared recent, raising questions in my mind. Was it from Seth grabbing her arm as we saw last night or was it from a later encounter with Seth...or maybe someone else?

Zoe looked up from her task and greeted us with a warm smile. "Hiya, ladies! You all are looking amazing today. What can I get you? Let me guess, a whiskey sour," she said, nodding in my direction. Her kind and open demeanor and bright smile made it hard to believe she could be involved in a murder. *But appearances could be deceiving*, I reminded myself. I had no prior experience in identifying murderers.

With a slight hesitation, I decided to deviate from my usual choice. "Actually, since it is brunch-*ish* time, is there any way we could have mimosas?" I asked, hoping to break the routine and gather a new perspective on the situation.

Zoe's smile widened, revealing a glimmer of excitement. "Mimosas it is, ladies! Coming right up." She prepared our drinks with a touch of elegance in each pour. Her movements were smooth and practiced, giving no indication of the turmoil that might have transpired the previous night or that she was bothered by anything today.

As Zoe placed the refreshing mimosas before us, the bubbles dancing in the flutes, I couldn't shake the nagging feeling there was more than met the eye when it came to her. We sipped our drinks, relishing the tangy sweetness. At the same time, our minds worked tirelessly to connect the dots to uncover truths lurking beneath the surface.

Zoe was distracted by a group of people who had just sat down to order, so I turned to Charlotte and quietly said, "Do you think she would have the strength to kill Seth?"

"In my research for *Inkwell Investigations: The Deadline for Death*, I found out women can be just as dangerous as men when it comes to killing, and even have the same amount of strength if their adrenaline is pumping fast enough. So, I'm not sure. You said she also told you she knows how to handle herself. She managed to put Seth on his butt last night, all by her lonesome. She might have taken classes for self-defense."

Overhearing the end of Char's comment, Zoe walked up to join the conversation. "Are you ladies looking for self-defense classes? It's never too late to start learning how to defend yourself. And you can do many other things to make sure you are protected."

This was the perfect opportunity to dive into what happened between her and Seth. "I saw you fend off that man, Seth, last night when he grabbed you." I motioned to her arm, where the bruise seemed darker every time I looked at it.

Zoe's face flushed as she lowered the sleeve on her arm. "I can't believe he had the audacity to grab me. All because I cut him off and his 'charm'," saying charm in air quotes, "wasn't getting him what he wanted. I could have killed him for grabbing me. *No one* touches me without my consent."

"Have you heard about what's happened to Seth?" I asked, whispering so as not to get anyone else's attention around us.

"No, what? Did he accost someone else and land on his butt again?" she joked, then grew serious when our faces remained somber. "Is it something bad?" her eyebrows tented in worry.

"I'm afraid so, dear. He was found strangled on the Lido Deck. He is dead." I made sure to keep my eyes on Zoe's face to gauge her reaction.

Zoe's expression turned into a mask of shock and disbelief. Her grip on the glass she held loosened, causing the glass to slip from her fingers and crash on the floor, glass shards flying in all directions. The sound sliced through the air, a sharp echo of the shattered peace that had befallen the ship.

The color drained from Zoe's cheeks, leaving her pale, and visibly shaken. "Wait, how? When did this happen?" she stammered, her voice trembling with a mix of fear and confusion.

"We don't know many details yet," Charlotte reassured her, offering a comforting smile and gently touching Zoe's trembling fingers. "We found him during our walk this morning before sunrise. It appears he was strangled sometime last night."

Concern filled her eyes, and Charlotte and I exchanged glances, acknowledging our shared opinion that Zoe's reaction was genuine…but it didn't rule out the possibility of her involvement. We couldn't afford to overlook any potential leads or suspects. We needed to get more information from her to remove her from our list.

"Did you know him well, dear?" I asked, my voice tinged with curiosity. "He acted like he had the run of the ship, seemed to think everyone knew 'who he was.' And he was so confident he wouldn't face consequences for any trouble he caused."

"I'd never seen him before this cruise," Zoe said. She became distant, her mind visibly retreating to somewhere far away from the present. As she fell silent, I moved behind the bar to grab the broom and dustpan from the wall. I carefully gathered the larger pieces of broken glass, mindful of their sharp edges, before sweeping up the shattered debris. "You'll want to be sure someone runs a vacuum cleaner over this, dear, to make sure all the glass has been picked up."

Zoe suddenly came back to our conversation with, "But you said you felt he had a run of the ship. What are you talking about?"

I didn't know if we were being hoodwinked, but my gut said she was being honest and didn't know Seth. *Or she was an excellent actress and my character judgment had dulled with age*. We told her a little bit about our experiences with Seth. Recounting how cruel he was to the staff and his many rude remarks to us. For the cherry on top, how mean he was (verbally and physically) to Robyn.

Zoe immediately spoke up about Robyn. "That sweet girl. She is a battered woman. I saw her flinch every time he talked, meekly obeying, being agreeable as some women do while they are bullied. But before the end of my shift, she looked like she was getting to the end of her acceptance of his abuse. I've seen that look before. I've seen it in the mirror. She was done being his mouse."

"Why do you say that?" I probed.

"Well, she slugged him for starters, broke his nose, it looked like," Zoe said with a satisfied smile as if she took pride in Robyn standing up to Seth. My gasp was stifled by my hand flying to my mouth. This revelation erased my perception of Robyn as a timid, submissive person. *Robyn was capable of hitting back…hard.*

Zoe nodded; her eyes gleaming with intrigue as she continued her tale. "It happened after everyone had left for the gala. I was tidying up tables and cleaning up leftover drinks to be ready for the next rush. Big groups often make big messes, so I was still cleaning when I heard them arguing."

Charlotte and I leaned closer with anticipation, hanging onto Zoe's every word. "She was yelling, telling him she was done being abused, and he had crossed a line. What 'line,' I don't know," Zoe paused for effect. "He grabbed her shoulders and shook her, saying something like, 'If you and your no-good brother don't know what's good for you, then it will be your fault if we all rot in prison.'"

A surge of emotions stirred within me as I imagined the distress and fear Robyn must have felt at that moment.

"She must really have had enough, though. She shook off his grasp and landed a solid punch on his nose with a fine right hook," Zoe continued, relishing the details. "He cried like a baby and ran off, muttering threats I couldn't quite make out. But what I did hear was Robyn hollering back, 'If you touch me again, I'll kill you!' "

We fell silent as the weight of those words settled upon us. Puzzle pieces were coming together, painting a picture of a troubled relationship and the tensions boiling between Seth and Robyn. We might have stumbled upon a dark secret. It was becoming clearer that there was more to Robyn than met the eye. She may have played a part in Seth's demise.

"Well, that adds her to the suspect list!" Charlotte blurted as she tapped the bar with her fingers, motioning to my bag with the notebook inside.

"Suspect list?" Zoe's brows creased in confusion. "Are you ladies snooping into this? You should really leave that to Martin. He knows what he is doing, and you could get hurt."

"What do you mean Martin knows what he is doing?" I asked as I pulled out my notebook to write some items down. Now that Zoe knew we were investigating Seth's murder, I didn't feel the need to hide it.

"Well..." Zoe whispered. "Have you done any digging into Martin's past yet?"

Charlotte and I both shook our heads. Zoe gave us a one-minute sign with her left hand while she went to take care of a customer and their bill, my pen poised to get all the details as she returned.

Zoe lowered her voice to avoid eavesdroppers. "Have you noticed how tattooed and big Martin is?" She waited for both Charlotte and me to nod our heads.

"He has a *police record*! I've been told by people I trust that he did time at Mountjoy Prison in Ireland. And not as a security guard. Those tattoos? It's not something he got in a regular tattoo parlor. He is known to have a temper and doesn't take being disrespected lightly. I accidentally walked by his office a couple of weeks ago. He was yelling at someone on the phone about being extorted." Zoe shrugged her shoulders and finished making our drinks.

Interesting that someone on this ship had hired an ex-con as the head of security, adding *Ex-Con* to our suspect web notes. I knew we needed more information on Martin, but this was a great start.

"What about Arba? Do you know anything about him?" Charlotte asked as I finished adding my notes to Martin's page.

"I don't know much about Arba. He is semi-new to this ship and doesn't hang out with my group of people. I heard he has been mending a broken heart. But I don't know. He doesn't talk to a lot of people. You should ask another room steward." Zoe paused, picking up some broken glass I missed.

Suddenly, Zoe's demeanor changed. "Wait a minute, you were talking about self-defense when I walked over, then you asked about my fight with Seth. Do you have a page in there with *my* name on it?" Zoe's voice dripped with anger, her hot gaze locked on us with accusation and distrust. I could feel the tension building in the room as she confronted us.

I understood her frustration and resentment toward

our probing questions. We were strangers, digging for information about her and her colleagues, potentially suspecting they were involved in something sinister.

I took a deep breath, carefully choosing my words. "I'm not going to lie to you, Zoe. Your fight with Seth last night looked personal. The intensity of anger you displayed, and your knowledge of self-defense made it appear there might be a deeper connection between you. Our logical conclusion, given the circumstances, was to add you to our suspect list until we could clear you." I looked down at my drink. Suddenly, I was nervous Zoe might kick us out of the bar for prying into her personal affairs. The atmosphere was thick with anticipation as we awaited her response.

Zoe gripped the towel she had used to clean some of the broken glass with and hissed in pain, blood blooming from a cut on her hand. "You don't have a right to assume you know me or my trauma. You need to leave me and my name out of this," Zoe said between clenched teeth.

Charlotte grabbed the napkin under her drink, handed it to Zoe, and said gently "We apologize, Zoe. We didn't mean to pry into your affairs." Charlotte had a knack for calming people down by projecting the persona of a favorite aunt or grandmother. "We are just trying to get to the bottom of this and figure out who killed Seth. Lisa remembered you talking about abusive men and knowing how to take care of them. That made us curious about you, especially after everything that happened last night."

Zoe pressed the napkin on her hand and took a deep, self-soothing breath. I had seen Wilma take those types of breaths every time she was about to lose her temper.

"I can see where you might get that. But I am not the killer. I have what Americans would call 'daddy issues,' and I'm working on them."

"Do you want to talk about it, dear?" Charlotte offered. I was trying to become invisible in my chair, remaining quiet to observe the conversation.

Zoe's words hung in the air, heavy with a mix of resignation and fear. Her voice quivered with the weight of her confession, adding an extra layer of suspense to the atmosphere. It was as if the room itself held its breath, awaiting another revelation.

"My dad is a very well-known businessman in Sydney," Zoe began, her voice conveying a haunted past. "He controlled every aspect of our lives, from what we wore to who we talked to. I think my mother knew something dark and dangerous about his business dealings. She paid the price for it, dying unexpectedly and under suspicious circumstances. I know he killed her."

A chill ran down my spine as I listened to her story. The room grew colder, the shadows deepening around us. Zoe continued, her words flowing with a mix of determination and vulnerability. "She left me an auto-send email, a hidden testament of his crimes. I turned the email in to the authorities and became a witness in his upcoming trial. He found out and sent people to find me."

We all gasped at the realization that Zoe herself was currently in grave danger. She took a deep breath, glancing around cautiously. "I was forced to learn to defend myself, to protect what little of my life was left. My lawyer advised me to go into hiding until the trial was over. That's why I'm here on this ship, hiding in plain sight, tending bar."

The room fell silent for a moment, the weight of Zoe's situation sinking in. I felt a surge of empathy and a newfound understanding of the intensity she displayed during the altercation with Seth. Her words painted a picture of a desperate struggle for survival where trust was a luxury she couldn't afford.

Zoe's voice broke the silence, interrupting the suspense-laden atmosphere. "Now, if you don't mind, I must go to the med bay to get this looked at."

Zoe stormed out of the bar and headed toward the medical office for help with the cut on her hand. I felt terrible about even suggesting she killed Seth. But like she said, we didn't know her, and we couldn't just assume she wasn't a part of killing Seth just because she was a female.

"It looks like we have a few more people to investigate. Martin can't be taken off the list. If anything, he has been pushed to the top," I said.

Chapter Nineteen

"I know you don't want to think about it, Lisa, but we must confirm we can officially rule out Richard," Charlotte said, casting a glance in my direction as we made our way back to our rooms. The tension in her voice hinted at the seriousness of the situation.

The sea salt air conspired against me, blowing my hair into my eyes, and tangling it around my mouth as we walked. I let out a frustrated sigh, brushing stray strands from my face. "I don't understand why you're looking at me. Richard is smitten with Wilma, so she'd be the one most likely to be upset," I replied, my words muffled by the gusts of wind.

Charlotte's expression shifted to one of disbelief, her gaze narrowing as she studied me. "Lisa, you have to be blind not to see he's into you. It's been obvious from the way he looks at you and the way he tries to engage you in conversation. It's not Wilma he's interested in."

My heart skipped a beat at Charlotte's words, and I quickened my pace, hoping to outrun the conversation. If it had been Beverly beside me, I might have been able to slip away, but Charlotte was no slouch. She may not be a yogi like Wilma, but she took care of herself, and her legs were a smidge longer than mine.

As we reached the corridor leading to our rooms, I couldn't help but feel a mix of confusion and unease. *Could it be true? Have I been misreading Richard's attention all this time, too preoccupied to see the truth?*

"You are blind, my dear," Charlotte went on. " Wilma has been what your Veronica would call a 'wingman', or 'wingwoman', in this case." My daughter Veronica was the quintessential millennial and would probably know what a wing-whatever was.

But Veronica wasn't here, so I had to ask, "What the hell is a wingman or wingwoman?" I was huffing at that point, feeling the strain in my breath as I tried to keep up with Charlotte's brisk pace. I slowed down to continue our conversation and breathe at the same time.

With a self-satisfied smile, Charlotte replied, "A wingman or wingwoman is someone who takes on the role of supporting a friend, like *Wilma*," she emphasized her name, "when they need help approaching a potential romantic partner." Her confident tone suggested she was rather pleased with herself for imparting this knowledge.

I let out a chuckle, finding her enthusiasm amusing. "I'll take your word for it! But I don't need a wingwoman. I'm not in search of another significant other. Four marriages are more than enough, don't you think?" I had married and divorced four different men across the globe over the past three decades. The image of venturing into another relationship wasn't appealing to me.

Charlotte's retort was swift and direct. "That's because, even including your marriages, you've never let anyone get close enough to become a permanent special someone in your life. You haven't been open to finding 'your person.' "

Her words struck a chord within me, stirring a mix of emotions. Perhaps there was truth to what she said. I built walls around my heart, shielding it from potential pain or disappointment. But as we walked along the ship's corridor, with the mysteries and secrets swirling around us, I wondered if it was time to reconsider my stance. The ship's journey was far from ordinary, and unexpected connections challenged my preconceptions.

I glanced at Charlotte, her expression holding a hint of concern and understanding. Maybe it was time to let my guard down, to open myself up to the possibility of finding companionship amidst the intrigue unfolding around us. With that in mind, I matched Charlotte's pace, ready to embrace whatever the journey had in store for us.

As we walked along in silence, I thought about the path of love I had taken. Husband number one was in the United States. I fell in love while an undergrad at Oklahoma University. But we weren't right for each other. Rather than support my career choices, it turned out he preferred a wife who wanted to take care of 2.5 kids, a dog, and a house with a picket fence.

While I didn't judge others like Beverly who wanted and craved that life, it wasn't the life for me. I couldn't be that wife. I was young and needed something more, to find myself and who I was really meant to be. Our divorce was quick and painless. We are cordial when we occasionally meet in the grocery store in town. He is now married to a lovely woman with four children and two grandchildren.

Fast forward to 1978, when destiny took me to Africa, an extraordinary twist of fate granted me the remarkable opportunity to embark on a thrilling excavation expedition. This arduous journey would forever shape my life's trajectory, transforming my passion for digging into an unyielding flame of discovery.

I found myself collaborating with the illustrious Professor Mary Douglas Leakey, a trailblazing British archaeologist whose name echoed with reverence across the scientific community. Her groundbreaking discoveries at Laetoli, where she unearthed a collection of footprints etched in volcanic ash by early human ancestors over 3.5 million years ago, held the promise of unraveling the mysteries of our ancient past.

The opportunity to work with Professor Leakey was more than a mere stroke of luck—it was a watershed moment for me as well as all women forging a path in the field of archaeology. Thrilled to be a part of breaking through the barriers of a historically male-dominated realm, I was driven by a profound determination to leave an indelible mark in the annals of scientific exploration.

Amidst the stirring landscapes and captivating scientific endeavors, another unforeseen, yet undeniable, force shaped the contours of my experience—husband number two. I was totally caught by surprise when this man, with his striking features, towering stature, and an alluring charm that could bewitch even the most guarded heart, crossed my path. As my Nonnie would say, he was a tall drink of water. He possessed a rare blend of kindness, compassion, and a refreshing embrace of gender equality that impacted every facet of our connection, including the intimate confines of the bedroom. Just thinking of him now made the flames of passion reignite, my pulse quickening with the memory of his tender touch.

Reality interjected swiftly as Charlotte's gentle touch on my wrist pulled me back to the present. Being lost in the past wasn't unusual for me, but it wasn't what we needed now. We needed to figure out the present mystery.

"Lisa? I didn't mean to snap or hurt your feelings." Charlotte's brows creased with worry as we approached our cabin doors.

"Oh, Charlotte! No, I am fine. I just started thinking about one of the Golden Boys." I laughed at the nickname the group had given to my troupe of ex-husbands. Beverly came up with this after we all fell in love with the Golden Girls show in the 80s. She bestowed the name to them soon after my divorce from my last husband.

Charlotte's eyes crinkled with humor as she knocked on her and Beverly's door, checking to see if everyone was decent. We walked in when there wasn't an answer. A note from Wilma and Beverly was on the table in the middle of the room. *Richard stopped by looking for Lisa and offered to take us to the Tranquility Deck for rest and relaxation! Come on up! XOXO Wil & Bev.*

"Well, you'll want to change into something a little more…" Charlotte paused as she took in my workout outfit, wind-swept hair, and lack of makeup. "…cute?" Charlotte would be the first to admit she wasn't into current fashion trends. She lived in her cardigans, fanny packs, and comfortable shoes. The fashion she preferred, to be honest, looked a lot more comfortable than a lot of the clothing Wilma and I wore.

Charlotte knew I wouldn't dress like this to attract a potential suitor. I'd have to talk with Wilma later to ensure whether she was trying to be a wingwoman for me or if *she* was smitten with him. If it turned out that she was trying to help me land him, so to speak, I didn't yet know if I even liked him or if he even wanted me. Signs my body was giving me indicated that, although I haven't had companionship with anyone for over a decade, my libido was good to go.

I didn't want to give Charlotte the satisfaction of knowing she was right about my outfit, so I said calmly, "I'll go change, but this doesn't mean anything. This will give us the perfect opportunity to pull Richard's ear and ensure he doesn't need to stay on our list of suspects."

Chapter Twenty

I changed into a cute red tennis skirt, a tight black supported tank top, and black and red tennis shoes. I arranged my long silver hair into a high ponytail, swiped my eyelashes with mascara, dabbed my cheeks with blush, and finished my look with Burt's Bees Chapstick. I nodded at my reflection in the mirror, satisfied and ready to meet Charlotte at the elevator to head to the Tranquility Deck.

Rounding the corner, I ran into Arba leaving a supply room. He looked a lot happier than the last time I saw him. In fact, he had a bounce in his step as he turned the opposite way with his cart. I wondered for a second if he was happy about Seth's demise, but then I chided myself for having such a dark thought about a seemingly sweet kid like Arba. Maybe he just received an excellent tip or woke up on the right side of the bed this morning. I shook my head to clear it as Charlotte and I boarded the elevator.

"What are you shaking your head about?" she inquired as she pushed the button to the Tranquility Deck.

"Nothing. I'm just trying to clear my head and get my thoughts put together. Richard the Suave will be more difficult than Zoe to get information from. He is closer to our age and isn't likely to underestimate us."

"That's why you need to use your charisma and

persuasive skills to get his attention focused beyond just his immediate thoughts," Charlotte said. I paused before getting out of the elevator, my jaw dropped from shock. Charlotte grinned and motioned for me to follow her out.

"*You* have been hanging around Wilma a little too much, Charlotte. She has turned you into a little harlot." I giggled as we approached the table and lounge chairs Richard, Wilma, and Beverly procured in a nice little corner of the deck.

"Harlot? Who is a harlot? You're not talking about yourself, are you, my dear?" Wilma asked with a twinkle in her eye. "Here, come sit down." She stood up and patted the seat she had just vacated. "I've kept your seat warm." She moved to another empty chair to the right, giving me the perfect spot on the couch with Richard. If I didn't know any better, this was exactly what Charlotte talked about when she said Wilma was a wingwoman. I could feel the blush rise up my chest and onto my face.

"No, I wasn't talking about me. I was talking about you corrupting our dear Charlotte."

Wilma laughed a deep belly laugh, and Beverly snickered in her hand as she put her book down on her ample bosom to give us her full attention. The scene before her was obviously more interesting than the book she was reading.

"You look lovely, Lisa," Richard whispered as I sat down next to him and crossed my legs the opposite way to avoid touching him accidentally.

"Um, thank you." Suddenly shy, I didn't know what to do with my hands but finally decided to rest them on top of my crossed legs.

"Now, ladies! What have you discovered?" Beverly asked.

I raised my eyebrows at Wilma, Charlotte, and Beverly, signaling we probably shouldn't discuss this in front of Richard. Wilma rolled her eyes, grunted in annoyance, and turned to Richard. "Richard, dear? Did you kill Seth?" she asked without beating around the bush.

He took a nice, slow drink of his martini and then chuckled a deep, soothing laugh. The kind of laugh that put you instantly at ease and made you want to cuddle deeper with your ear to their chest to hear its full glory. "Um, no. I did not kill that young man. He needed to be taught a lesson about treating women and others, which I would have done in a discussion. I am not one to use violence to make a point."

Wilma smiled at me as though saying, *See! He isn't a killer. Get over it.* I rolled my eyes, and Charlotte and I filled them in on everything we learned over the past couple of hours.

"So, it looks to me Zoe should no longer be on our list, but Martin has been lifted higher in our suspect pool," Beverly said as she flipped through my notes, taking in everything. She would have the whole thing memorized by the end of our conversation. I was amazed by the human brain.

"And don't forget, Robyn finally hit back." Wilma took a drink of her fruity cocktail and made a toasting gesture. "Good for her. However, that does put her on the list, doesn't it?"

"That is my thought exactly. We need to learn more about the suspects before we can start taking people off the list," I said. I took my notebook from Beverly to make a new page with Robyn's name on it when everyone got suspiciously quiet.

I looked at the group and noticed they were all looking behind me. I turned around to find Martin standing over my shoulder, looking at what I had written. "Suspects? You wouldn't be meddling in my investigation, would you?" I could see the fire in his eyes because we were talking about his crime scene and acting as, what I could only presume he would call us, amateur sleuths.

Unfazed by the sudden tension, I squared my shoulders to meet his piercing gaze with an unwavering resolve. "Well, Martin, we discovered the body. We are Seth's next-door neighbors and all. And we've been accidental witnesses to several unpleasant scenes and interactions involving him and others around the boat," I retorted, my voice laced with a subtle edge of indignation. Though we may not have been seasoned detectives by any means, I refused to allow him to dismiss our presence and insights so readily. After all, the passing of time had bestowed upon us a wealth of wisdom and experience that demanded respect. As a young woman, I often despised the phrase "respect your elders," but it carried a certain satisfaction at this moment, and I now embrace the reminder of the value of knowledge attained through decades of living through life's trials.

"Oh? Do you think you can do my job better than me? Who do you have on your list? Want to compare?" He moved around the couch Richard and I were on to sit on the arm next to me, peering at the open notebook on my lap. Robyn's name was circled, and a few webs connected her name with blank bubbles I had been about to start filling in.

"Robyn? The young, battered, and abused girl of

Seth's. Really? You think she had the strength to strangle a man of his size?" He scoffed with indignation.

"She would have if he was inebriated and unaware of his faculties," Wilma interrupted the interrogation.

Martin looked up and met Wilma's gaze with interest as though this was the first thing anyone in the group said with merit. I added, "We have also talked about the fact that women can be seen as weak, but with proper training, they can be as deadly as a man."

Martin looked at Richard. "Are you really giving into this theory? Or are you happy they aren't pointing fingers at you?"

"I trust these women know exactly what they are talking about. But I'd love to clear my name right now. Do you have the time of death for the young man?" Richard inquired.

"Actually, we do. He was killed between 1 a.m. and 3 a.m. That is the closest we can get to the time of death. Do you have an alibi?" He turned a smug look at Richard.

"Actually, I do," Richard interjected, his voice calm and composed amidst the growing tension. He leaned in slightly, a hint of assurance in his gaze. "I take it you have security cameras in the vicinity where the computers are located? You see, I was engaged in a last-minute business meeting with my bank. A matter of utmost importance involving a Japanese counterpart. I had to diligently prepare and exchange email correspondence with them, including signing and submitting an e-contract. If you'd like, I'd be more than happy to provide you with their contact information so you can verify my alibi's authenticity."

Richard's request for pen and paper was met with a

momentary pause. I turned my gaze toward Martin, who was visibly irked by the possibility that Richard possessed a valid alibi. With a touch of skepticism, Martin extended his hand to receive the slip of paper, silently acknowledging Richard's offer to corroborate his whereabouts during the time of the incident.

"You can bet I will. Did any of you see Seth that night?" Martin questioned, looking at each of us with a piercing gaze.

Wilma and I glanced at each other before answering. I turned my notebook to the page marked with Zoe's name. "We did see him get into a confrontation with Zoe, the bartender of the Below Deck Pub. He grabbed her arm pretty hard. We talked to her a little bit today during brunch, and she didn't seem too happy. But who would after being harassed? Did she report it to you?"

"As a matter of fact, she didn't." He looked annoyed that we knew something he didn't. "Anything else?"

Charlotte and I exchanged a meaningful glance, our silent agreement reinforcing the importance of sharing what we had learned. With a determined nod from me, Charlotte turned her attention toward Martin, her voice steady and resolute. "In addition to what Zoe shared with us earlier, she mentioned Robyn retaliated against Seth last night. She socked him in the nose after he forcibly grabbed her, and she even went so far as to threaten him with death if he ever laid hands on her again." Martin's disbelief was evident, but he diligently jotted down our accounts, his attention fixed on us as he awaited further revelations.

Richard cleared his throat, breaking the silence, ready to contribute his observation. "Actually, as I was making my way back to my room from the computer area around one-thirty in the morning, I happened to spot Seth engaged in a heated exchange with a rather portly, older gentleman. Their voices carried an air of aggression as if it was a recurring argument they had been embroiled in before." Richard's statements hung in the air, casting a new shadow of suspicion over the unfolding investigation.

"Oh? Any reason why you'd think that? And did you know the man? Any distinguishing features?"

"I heard the shorter man say, 'Seth, I've told you. I've got nothing left to give. You need to get off at the next port without her and leave for good.' I couldn't tell you what he looked like, but his accent was from down under. Australian. I am positive about that." Richard leaned forward to grab his drink and took a sip.

Richard paused for a moment before realization crossed his face again. "Seth had responded to the man with a scathing comment that also made me wonder if they knew each other before this trip. He said something along the lines of, 'You know they really call you Gray because your personality matches the color. You are about as exciting as watching paint dry. She will never choose you over me.' "

This was news to me. Something tingled in my mind about Seth arguing with an Australian man when we went to grab my bags from the service desk. But Wilma swears she didn't think anyone else was in the room with him except for Martin. I pulled out of my thought processes when I realized Martin was talking to me.

"And, ma'am, I'm going to need your notebook," he said, indicating my composition notebook in my hands. I tightened my grip around it and felt my heart pattering. We were so close to figuring everything out.

Martin continued over the sound of blood pumping in my ears. "It is evidence of a current homicide, and I need you to stop looking into it. You're on vacation. You should go to the spa, mingle with others, and play bingo. Let the authorities handle this." He got up to leave; grabbing for my notebook, it slipped through his hands and fell to the ground.

As Martin stooped down to pick up the fallen notebook, his gaze fell upon the page bearing his name. I watched as his eyes scanned the contents of the graphic organizer, absorbing my notes and probing questions about his past. A visible tension gripped his features, his jaw clenching in a display of mounting frustration. Our gazes locked for a brief, charged moment, but no words were exchanged. He snapped the notebook shut with a resolute motion. He briskly walked away, leaving behind an unnerving silence in his wake.

A shiver traveled up my spine, an instinctive reaction to the intensity of Martin's stare. The revelation of his evident displeasure only solidified his position at the forefront of my list of suspects. There was an unsettling air about him, a simmering anger threatening to boil over at any moment. The potential danger lurking beneath his calm exterior was a stark reminder of the thin line between civility and explosive violence. I shook off the chill settling within me, refocusing my attention on the ongoing group conversation, my mind fully attuned to the urgent task.

"Don't worry, Lisa. I can recreate everything you had in your notebook." Beverly smartly tapped her head and winked at me. It was handy to have talented friends. And sometimes it was really lovely being old and unsuspecting.

Chapter Twenty-One

The setting sun cast a warm golden glow across the ship as Richard, the girls, and I gathered around a table in the Below Deck Pub, huddled together conspiratorially. We knew we needed to speak with Robyn directly to figure out her status as a suspect. While we caught whispers in the air and gathered information about the other suspects, Robyn remained an elusive piece of the puzzle we were determined to solve.

We devised our plan over pre-dinner drinks amidst the hum of conversation and clinking of cocktail glasses. If Robyn were to walk in here or maybe at dinner, we would invite her to join us at our table. As luck would have it, just as we ordered our drinks, Robyn entered the bar. I heard Wilma's intake of breath and noticed Robyn's presence was commanding the attention of several other bar patrons.

Gone was the timid and unassuming woman we encountered before. In her place stood a transformed Robyn, exuding confidence and style. She wore a chic tea-length red dress tailored to perfection, elegantly accentuating her curves. Her choice of black flats provided a hint of sophisticated practicality, a subtle reminder that beneath her newfound allure, she remained grounded. Her makeup was flawlessly applied, enhancing her natural features and showcasing her already captivating presence.

Robyn looked around the bar, her gaze scanning the room as if looking for someone. I raised my hand to wave her over, beckoning her to join. Catching my wave, she gracefully made her way to our table.

"Good evening," she greeted us with a voice carrying a hint of vibrancy and resilience. Every syllable was laced with poise and, one could assume, added strength that came from recently breaking free from the clutches of her oppressor.

It's remarkable, I thought, *how much Robyn has transformed since Seth's death.*

I gestured to an empty seat at our table. "Would you please join us, Robyn? It's so good to see you."

Robyn looked around the table at all our open, smiling faces and nodded. Richard jumped to his feet to pull the chair between me and Wilma out for her, saying, "You look lovely this evening, especially after all you've been through in recent days."

"Yes, dear," I said. "We are all so sorry for your loss. No one should be alone during a time like this."

Robyn, again, glancing around the room, said, "My brother was supposed to meet me here, but maybe he got tied up."

"Your brother?" Wilma injected as she salted her buttered bread. Sometimes, she really does confuse me with her suggestions of living a healthy life. But what did I have to say about that? She works it off daily with walking and yoga. Adding salt to her food was her call, and I wasn't about to give her any ideas about policing *my* often unhealthy choices.

"Your brother is onboard?" Wilma asked before taking that double-salted bite.

"Um, yes," she replied, her voice tinged with a

mixture of hesitation and avoidance. "He works on the ship. We aren't close. He is probably busy," Robyn said rapidly, reaching for her water. The huge gulp of water she took provided symbolic punctuation, signaling her desire to shift the conversation away from her brother. She clearly preferred to keep certain aspects of her personal life guarded.

Respecting her boundaries, I changed the subject to one that might yield more fruitful insights—her deceased boyfriend, Seth. It may have been considered tactless to probe into such sensitive matters under normal circumstances, but time was ticking, and the urgency to solve the murder before reaching Cozumel was increasing with each hour that passed. We needed answers.

We girls had earlier discussed what approaches to take with Robyn, deciding it would be best to begin the conversation with a tone of gentle prodding, an exploration into the depths of Robyn's past.

"How long had you and Seth been together? How did you two meet?" I inquired, inwardly relishing in the freedom to indulge my nosiness in the name of justice.

A flicker of vulnerability danced across Robyn's eyes, complex emotions swirling within her. She hesitantly began sharing their history. "Seth and I were together for a long time. Five years. Since I was twenty-three," she revealed, her voice laced with a hint of nostalgia. She went on to explain the connection they shared spanned a significant portion of her young adulthood, fostering a deep bond in her young heart.

Her tale took an unexpected turn as she flashed back to the circumstances of their initial encounter. "We met through my brother, Gray, actually," Robyn continued, her voice tinged with a blend of fondness and melancholy. "They were working together, and my brother asked me to come onto the cruise liner he was about to join; they needed help with makeup for a modeling gig that was going on in port. I am a cosmetologist by trade. I specialize in theater makeup and hair."

As she delved into her memories, the tears welling up in Robyn's eyes appeared genuine. Recalling the past and likely cherished moments with her brother and Seth was exposing a vulnerability she had been guarding until now.

"That's an exciting career. You must be very good; your makeup is flawless tonight." Wilma indicated where she knew a bruise was underneath Robyn's mask of makeup.

Robyn laughed sardonically. "Yes, concealer can hide many flaws."

Before we could ask more questions, Zoe came by to check on us, bringing with her a fresh glass for Robyn. We decided to extend our time with Robyn by ordering more appetizers; the garlic bread was disappearing fast. Zoe poured wine for Robyn from the table bottle while we decided which appetizers to order. Out of the corner of my eye, I noticed Robyn taking a couple of big gulps of wine before Zoe was off with our order and we could resume our conversation.

"I am so sorry your relationship was so volatile," Beverly said over her plate as she grabbed another piece of bread. "I've seen many women not make it back or even try to fight back when it happens. Good for you."

"Pardon me?" Robyn's voice wobbled, uncertainty threading through her words. The sudden mention of a confrontation with Seth caught her off guard, her eyes widening as if grappling with conflicting emotions.

With compassionate resolve, Charlotte chimed in, contributing to the conversation with a touch of empathy. "We heard you had a confrontation with Seth last night. He put his hands on you, but you finally fought back. You broke his nose!" Her words carried a mixture of admiration and understanding, acknowledging the immense courage it takes to stand up against an abuser. The gravity of the situation was not lost on her, as she added, "It takes a lot to stand up to your abuser. I wouldn't have blamed you if you killed him."

As the conversation unfolded, I stared at Robyn's face, searching for any telltale signs of guilt or remorse. I understood the deep reservoirs of anger that could accumulate over years of enduring gaslighting and abuse. It was evident Robyn shouldered the weight of Seth's mistreatment, a burden with wounds that would take significant time and effort to heal.

I was tired of putting this poor girl through memories of abuse she had been taking for years. It was time to move on to current events.

"Out of curiosity," I asked. "Where were you last night between 1 and 3 a.m.?"

"Oh, um, I was in my room, asleep." She fumbled through her words, obviously telling a blatant lie to everyone at the table.

Richard patted her hand. "Come, come, my dear. You can tell us. We are not judging. I feel like there won't be many people to mourn the death of this young man. We might be able to help if we know the truth of where you were."

Robyn cleared her throat, a flicker of nervousness

betraying her as she glanced around the room, gauging the level of attention on their conversation. "I was actually visiting with another steward, James, in his room. I wanted to avoid Seth after our fight. I've known James for a long time so I went to see him; we stayed up most of the night talking and drinking wine," she revealed, her voice tinged with a hint of wistfulness as she recalled the evening's events. Her words hung in the air, hinting at a connection with James that went beyond mere friendship.

While Robyn was talking, I sensed an opportunity to uncover more. "I'm glad you could find comfort in a friend on the boat. It's fortunate you know so many people on the ship," I commented, hoping to find out more about how well she knew Arba.

Robyn smiled with a glimmer of recognition as she picked up on the implication. "Actually, I know a lot of people. My brother has been in the cruise line business for a long time. You know our room steward, Arba?" she asked.

We all nodded, and I could feel my pulse quickening with anticipation. "He and I used to date before I met Seth. I don't know if you could tell, but Seth hasn't been very kind to him in the past few days. He liked to rub it in Arba's face that we were together. I have tried over the years to stop Seth but, as you could see, he wouldn't listen to reason. He and Arba had a hate-hate relationship. The last time the three of us were together, they threatened to kill each other." At that, Robyn suddenly rose, wished us a good evening, excused herself, and left the bar.

We all sat there in shock, mouths slightly agape, taking a moment to process that bombshell and its implications. The puzzle pieces were starting to come together, and the emerging picture wasn't quite what we expected. Arba, the towel-obsessed maestro, suddenly had a shady connection to Seth while newly freed Robyn seemed more like a victim than a suspect.

"Well, well, well," I said, leaning back in my chair, a mischievous grin spreading across my face. "Looks like our friendly neighborhood towel artist might have some explaining to do. And here I thought he was just passionate about fluffy bath accessories."

Charlotte raised an eyebrow, her eyes gleaming with curiosity. "You think Arba saw an opportunity to get rid of Seth and have Robyn all to himself?"

"It's a possibility!" I nodded, excited by the unfolding drama. "This is like a twisted soap opera. Before we jump to conclusions, we should have a little chat with our towel-wielding mastermind, don't you think?"

The group nodded in agreement, renewed energy buzzing around the table. The game was afoot, and we were ready to dive deeper into this whodunit.

Unfortunately, the rest of the evening was uneventful. We decided to skip dancing in favor of being bright-eyed and bushy-tailed for tomorrow when we would go full steam ahead to answer the million-dollar question—who among us was a killer?

Chapter Twenty-Two

The next morning, I jolted awake, my eyes blinking rapidly as I tried to shake off the remnants of sleep. My ears were greeted by an obnoxiously cheery voice echoing through the ship's intercom. It was Gary, the enthusiastic cruise director, delivering a wake-up call that was anything but soothing.

"Goooooooood morning, ladies and gentlemen!" Gary's voice boomed, penetrating the silence of my cabin. "We have one more delightful day and one last fun-filled evening at sea before our grand arrival in Cozumel tomorrow at 8 a.m. sharp. However, fate seems to have thrown a little wrinkle into our plans. Due to an unforeseen incident, we might experience some delays disembarking. But fear not, my dear passengers, for we shall make it up to you with an extended stay in port! Yes, you heard it right: two extra GLORIOUS hours of adventure await you onboard the great ship *Oceanic Odyssey*!"

I rubbed my eyes, still trying to process the information. An incident? What had possibly happened? My mind raced with wild scenarios, ranging from pirate attacks to alien invasions. I pushed those ridiculous thoughts aside when I woke up enough to remember ship security was still in the middle of the investigation of Seth's death. I focused on the next part of Gary's announcement.

"As a token of our sincere apologies for any inconveniences caused," Gary continued, "we have graciously added one free drink voucher to each and every one of your accounts. Yes, my friends, a little libation to soothe the soul and wash away any worries or frustrations. So go forth, explore the ship, indulge in the amenities, and have the time of your liiiiiives!"

I groaned, wondering to myself if I would ever be able to sleep in on this vacation. I turned over toward the pull-out couch. "Wilma? Are you awake?" But the bed was empty. I heard the shower turn off and Wilma rumbling in the tiny bathroom. I missed my clawfoot tub and rain shower head from home.

As Wilma hogged the bathroom, taking her sweet time getting ready, I couldn't help but get lost in my thoughts about the Golden Boys. Did I let true love slip through my fingers without even realizing it? Was I too stubborn to see the sparks flying right in front of me?

Back in the early 80s, when dinosaurs roamed the Earth and big hair was all the rage, I embarked on a crazy adventure with a bunch of thrill-seeking archaeologists. That's where I crossed paths with husband number three, a genius archaeologist with a face that could launch a thousand paparazzi cameras. His infectious Latino zest for life and love for his people and their ancient treasures made my heart do all kinds of crazy salsa moves.

Together, we journeyed across the mystical lands of Yucatan, exploring ancient ruins, unearthing hidden artifacts, and stumbling upon the occasional snake like a real-life Indiana Jones movie (minus the fedora and whip). He and I had something special, or so I thought.

But then, life threw us a curveball in the form of little Veronica. She arrived fashionably early, putting my age-old womb through some serious acrobatics. Bed rest (per doctor's orders) and stir-craziness were my daily activities. And as my belly grew, so did his protective instincts. Suddenly, he had this fear of losing us and it transformed into overbearing suffocation.

Fast forward a bit, after a year of juggling motherhood and trying to figure out how to be a working mother, loving wife, and keep my career afloat, I was over being overprotected. I pulled the plug on our love boat. Divorce papers were filed, and I hightailed it back to my home turf, seeking solace in the loving arms of friends and family. Husband number three, bless his heart, stayed down in Yucatan, occasionally popping up to visit Veronica, but he and I never rekindled our relationship.

Now fully awake on the *Oceanic Odyssey* cruise ship with my besties all these years later I was still digging for answers. Only this time, I was searching for a killer.

Wilma emerged from the bathroom, her yoga pants hugging her curves, and her determined look told me she had a plan brewing in her head.

"We need to get Zoe's alibi for the night Seth was killed," Wilma announced, her eyes glinting with mischievous excitement. "So, put on your detective pants, my friend. We're hitting the road!"

I chuckled and nodded, ready for whatever crazy scheme Wilma had cooked up. Because when it comes to unraveling mysteries, we've got just the right amount of quirk and sass to make things interesting.

Chapter Twenty-Three

As we sailed into the Below Deck Pub, the clock struck brunch o'clock, and my stomach began its own little symphony of hunger growls. All that introspection about my past drained me, and I desperately needed a pick-me-up. Coffee, food, and maybe a mimosa were the top items on my agenda. The mimosa from yesterday was a real winner, and I was already fantasizing about the blissful combination of bubbly champagne and fresh orange juice.

With anticipation, I glanced over to the bar, fully expecting to see Zoe expertly mixing drinks and ready to cater to my brunch desires. But to my surprise, there was a new face behind the counter, a bartender I hadn't laid eyes on before.

"Do you see Zoe?" I asked Wilma as I went on my tiptoes to look around the bar's tables, which were all full of people laughing, eating, and enjoying their vacation.

Wilma and I scanned the room, searching for Zoe among the sea of brunch-goers. Finally, Wilma pointed to a secluded corner, far away from the bustling crowd. There she was, sitting alone at a table, surrounded by the evidence of her liquid breakfast—a nearly empty pitcher of mimosas. Well, this interrogation was shaping up to be either a cakewalk or a bumpy ride.

We made our way over to Zoe's table. As we approached, she lifted her gaze and greeted us with a sly smirk accompanied by a hint of mischief in her demeanor. "Well, well, well, if it isn't Nancy Drew and Miss Marple," she quipped, waving for us to take a seat.

Wilma couldn't resist a playful retort as we settled in. "So, Zoe, who's Nancy, and who's Miss Marple in this dynamic duo?"

Zoe, clearly tipsy, squinted her eyes in an attempt to focus. "What?" she slurred, struggling to grasp Wilma's words.

Wilma repeated her question with a mischievous grin. "I said, which of us gets to be Nancy, the young, pretty, and crafty sleuth? And which one is the brilliant, feisty Miss Marple?"

Zoe pondered for a moment, using her drink as a pointer. "You, my dear, are definitely Nancy," she declared, nodding at Wilma. Then, gesturing toward me, she continued, "And you, with your wit and wisdom, make a perfect Miss Marple."

Wilma couldn't help but playfully react. "Well, I don't know if I should be offended or flattered. At least she thinks I'm young and pretty!"

Wilma and I clinked our drinks together while Zoe, in her inebriated state, attempted to join in but chose to settle for a sip from her own glass instead.

"What can I help you, ladies, with? You already took my job from me."

"Excuse me? How did we manage that?" I asked, aghast.

"That little notebook of yours? Martin showed it to me. He said I was seen accosting a customer. That is against the ship guidelines, so *I* will be let go at the next port." Zoe's words slurred more, and she took another drink.

"Oh, dear. I am so very sorry. That certainly was not my intention. Martin took my notebook when he realized we were doing our own investigation. I didn't mean for you to lose your job." I was sorry to have caused her so much trouble when she had been kind to me.

"Wait a minute, he is letting you go?" Did that mean she had an alibi? He hadn't arrested her and was, in fact, going to let her go when the ship docked at Cozumel?

"Yes, I assaulted a guest, but I didn't kill him. He wasn't worth my time to kill," Zoe said, indicating that maybe there was someone who might be worth her time to kill, maybe her father.

"But if you didn't kill him, where were you that night after your altercation?" Wilma asked while finishing her glass and reaching for the pitcher to pour another drink, only to realize Zoe had drained it minutes before.

"I was with the ship's therapist. I have mandatory anger management sessions, and that requirement follows me onto the ship. Since I shoved Seth down that night, I needed to make amends and talk to the therapist. I was going to apologize for my behavior the next morning, but you all know what happened."

"Is there any way we can help to save your job? I am sure we could all write letters to account for what happened. You shouldn't lose your job for protecting yourself." I finished my drink. I didn't want her world to turn upside down because of something that wasn't her fault.

Zoe looked up from her empty glass with hope in her eyes. "You would do that? You would talk to Martin and Gary about not firing me?"

"Of course! We would love to do that for you.

Especially now that we know you aren't a killer." Wilma winked and patted her hand in a grandmotherly way. Zoe grinned and winked back as she took another "drink" from her empty glass.

We stood to head back toward our rooms for reconnaissance with the rest of the ladies when Zoe's voice stopped us.

"Um, ladies? Do you remember when I told you Robyn broke Seth's nose that night?" We both nodded.

Sighing, Zoe continued. "Well, someone followed them when they left. A short Asian man with a ship's steward uniform on. I think it was Arba. I saw him around the ship following Robyn a few times, but he followed Seth out of the bar that night after Robyn hit him. I don't know if that is helpful. Thank you for offering to help me keep my job." We both nodded and promised we would send positive notes to Martin and Gary.

Wilma and I figured it was time to regroup with Beverly and Charlotte. As we made our way to the Lido Deck, I couldn't shake the uneasy feeling lingering around Arba and Martin. Something about them just didn't sit right with me. They were hiding something.

Speaking of hidden things, we needed Beverly's mind magic to work its wonders once again. I hoped she could recreate everything she had seen in our suspect notebook before Martin confiscated it.

Beverly and Charlotte were eagerly waiting for us at our table in the buffet. "You're just in time! We're thinking of detective names for our group."

Wilma held her hand up to stop Beverly. "Too late. Zoe has already named me Nancy Drew and this," she gestured to me, "is Miss Marple. Maybe you two can be

142

Cagney and Lacey or Risoli and Isles."

"Maybe you could be Ms. Magic Mind. Would you try to recreate the notebook Meanie Martin stole from me?" I asked while handing Bev the new notebook I'd picked up at the gift store.

Beverly nodded in agreement, her eyes already glimmering with anticipation. "Don't you worry, dear. I'll use my mind magic to unlock the secrets hidden in your notebook. We'll get to the bottom of this, one memory at a time."

I couldn't help but feel a surge of hope as Beverly agreed to dive into her unique talent. With her remarkable abilities and the combined efforts of our team, it was possible we could unravel the truth behind this perplexing mystery.

Wilma and I filled Beverly and Charlotte in on what we had learned from Zoe, including her comments about the Asian man, probably Arba, whom she had seen following Seth and Robyn.

Charlotte leaned forward, murmuring, "That's interesting! Another bubble on Arba's web."

"And Arba used to date Robyn?! That confirms the odd feelings we picked up from Arba's demeanor around Robyn," Beverly added.

"I'm concerned about Arba and Martin as well," I went on. "Something about those two gives me the heebie-jeebies, girls. They're acting mighty suspicious. We need to keep a close eye on both of them."

Wilma yawned and spoke up. "Let's go back to the rooms for a bit to give Bev a chance to fill in that notebook. We can continue talking in comfort…and I need a stretch."

As we entered the corridor to our rooms, who was

outside of Beverly and Charlotte's room? None other than our animal towel-making steward, Arba.

"Arba! It is so good to see you!" Wilma hollered as we walked closer to the rooms, and she grabbed him for a hug and pinched his cheeks.

"Please come in! We have questions for you." I winked as I saw his shoulders creeping up to his ears in anxiety. He nodded and entered the room with us, and Charlotte closed the door.

"What's the matter, ladies? Are your rooms not to your satisfaction? Let me know if you need anything to make your stay more comfortable," Arba said, inching towards the door like he wanted to escape from us nosy old ladies. And honestly, I couldn't blame him.

"Arba, have a seat. We won't keep you too long," I said, gesturing to the chair at the vanity. Charlotte and I plopped down on the couch while Beverly and Wilma took spots on the bed. It was a tight squeeze, but we made it work.

"Sorry, I really have to go. I have other rooms I must attend to," Arba said, trying to excuse himself.

"Before you go, Arba. Did you know Robyn and Seth before they joined this cruise?" I already knew the answer from my conversation with Robyn the other night, but I wanted to see if Arba would come clean.

He shifted uncomfortably, realizing he was under interrogation. Finally, he sighed and spilled the beans. "Yeah, I knew both of them. Robyn and I used to date, but she left me for Seth. And he loved rubbing it in my face."

"Sounds like your relationship with Seth was a fiery one, huh?" I grabbed another tiny notebook from my bag and started jotting down notes.

"It was far from rainbows and sunshine, as you Americans like to say. I tried talking to Gray about how toxic Seth was and how badly he treated Robyn, but they worked together and Gray didn't believe a word I said. We've all been working on different cruise liners for a long time," Arba explained.

I needed to know if he had an alibi for the time of the murder. This line of questioning wasn't getting us there.

"Hey, how did you three all meet?" Charlotte popped the question.

"We were in the same training class for the cruise line. Gray and Robyn were siblings trying to turn over a new leaf. I had just landed in the States and believed this job would be the perfect way to see the world and pick up English. Plus, I needed the cash to send back home to my family. Seth, on the other hand, was just here for the heck of it. Honestly, I couldn't believe he even passed the employment tests to get on board," Arba said sullenly, leaning against the door to our room.

"And you and Robyn fell head over heels during training?" Beverly gushed, clasping her hands to her chest.

"We did. Both of us had tough childhoods, you know? Robyn had been bounced around the system, and I got deported with my family when I was a little kid. I only recently managed to get back into the U.S. We connected instantly. We stuck together during training until Seth decided he wanted her." Arba's face darkened with anger.

"I can imagine that caused some serious tension within the group," Wilma added, nodding sagely. "How did Gray handle it all? I mean, Robyn is his sister, after all."

"Gray always had this overprotective streak when it came to Robyn. But once she made up her mind about something, he usually went along with it. Plus, he and Seth were tight, you know? That is, until things turned sour. After what happened, we all drifted apart. And now, here Gray is, climbing up the ranks." Arba paused abruptly, realizing he might have said too much.

I wondered what he meant by "after what happened," but sensed he would bolt if I asked him about that right now. Better to continue along the lines of information we learned today and hear his alibi for the time of Seth's death.

"Word on the ship is you've been tailing Robyn and had a few confrontations with Seth. So, tell us, do you have an alibi for the night of the murder?" I asked, raising an eyebrow.

Arba blushed in embarrassment. "Unfortunately, I do. I wish I'd been the one to kill Seth. He was pure poison. That night, I followed Robyn out of the bar, begging her to leave Seth and come back to me. I promised I'd take care of her, but she laughed in my face and said she'd never tie herself to me. Then she hopped into the elevator. Didn't seem upset at all that she had just broken my heart again."

Tears welled up in Arba's eyes as he remembered Robyn's harsh rejection. He continued, "When I turned around, I spotted Seth heading towards the service desk area. I trailed him, and what do you know? He met up with Gray, just like always, and they started arguing. I couldn't stand being around them anymore, so I grabbed a bottle from an outside bar and drowned my sorrows. I wanted all the pain to go away. The next thing I knew, I was on the floor outside Robyn's room. I had passed out cold until a maintenance guy woke me up and took me to the drunk tank to sleep it off. The orderly there can vouch for my time in and time out. You can check with them." Arba made a move to leave the room.

"Thanks for telling us, Arba. Just one more thing, though," I called out, stopping him in his tracks.

He sighed, turning around to face us. "Yeah?"

"Did you have any idea that Robyn and Seth would be on this ship?" I asked, hoping for a lead.

Arba shook his head vigorously. "No clue. I was shocked and thought it was cruel of Gray to bring them on board. And putting them on my floor? That was even worse. I planned to give Gray a piece of my mind before Seth was killed." Arba shook his head and reached for the doorknob. "I didn't like the guy, but I didn't do it."

As Arba exited the room, I turned to the rest of the gang, a puzzled look on my face. "If he didn't do it, then who the heck did?"

We needed to uncover more about Gray and figure out how he had the power to put Seth and Robyn on Arba's floor. We should try to track him down and see if he had any beef with Seth. Martin was another possibility. Time to put our snooping skills to work!

Chapter Twenty-Four

"Well, ladies, where do we go from here?" I looked at all of them, and they all had pensive looks.

"I'm not sure. I feel like we can't get too much more information about anyone else on the boat. If only we could get some assistance from the mainland." Wilma's face lit up with an idea I was sure I wouldn't like.

"Mainland?" Beverly asked. "Do you mean someone from home? Can we even get in touch with anyone? I know our phones have no service."

An idea popped into my head, probably the same one Wilma had. "You guys remembered our conversation with Richard yesterday? How did he prove to Martin he didn't kill Seth?"

Wilma smiled knowingly as Charlotte and Beverly nodded. "He said he was on an important call or email during that time in the computer lab! We could email Veronica and see what she can dig up! She is a wiz on the computer and has been able to find me some of my long-lost friends from over the years. I am sure she could find out a little more through some internet sleuthing!"

Everyone was in agreement. Wilma, Charlotte, and Beverly would go to the dining hall to order our lunch, and I would reach out to Veronica to see if she could do some research for us. She knew a thing or two about digging, literally and digitally. She followed me to many dig sites and even followed my footsteps into the anthropology world. I couldn't be more proud of the young woman she was becoming.

I made my way up to the Lido Deck, where the computer lab was located, and turned on one of the computers. The system required me to swipe my room key to charge an obscene amount to use the computer. Fifteen dollars every twenty minutes was a bit extreme, but desperate times called for desperate measures.

I logged into my email and was surprised Veronica had already emailed me. She recently graduated from the University of Oklahoma in the same field as I did. And she was now on the job hunt. I told her before I left that if she heard any news, she should email me and let me know. I promised to get on the internet when we hit our first port. I got on sooner than intended but couldn't wait to open the email. My heart rate increased as my mouse hovered over the email to open it.

I must confess my initial reaction to Veronica pursuing a new and exciting job was selfishness. I couldn't help but feel a tinge of sadness at the thought of her being so far away from me. It is quite ironic, considering I've spent the majority of my adult life living far from home. However, as the years have gone by, I've come to recognize the immense value of family and dear friends in leading a fulfilling life. I've missed out on significant moments while being away, such as the passing of my mother, the birth of babies, and the joyous milestones of those closest to me.

Nevertheless, I wouldn't change every aspect of my life's journey. Through the culmination of countless events and the experiences of my various marriages, I have become the person I am today. Now, as I was poised to open the email, a familiar voice caught my attention, interrupting my train of thought.

"Why isn't this a nice surprise? I didn't think I'd ever get to spend time with you alone." Richard's warm and inviting voice made me shiver as he stood behind me.

"Well, you're not actually spending time alone with me. I am answering and sending some emails. And there are a ton of other people in the lab," I said, motioning to the two other young kids glued to the computers.

Richard laughed. "I didn't mean to intrude. You looked like you were upset about something when I walked in. I wanted to make sure you were okay. You haven't gotten any bad news, have you?" His face showed worry.

As we grow older, it's not uncommon to see friendships fade away with the passing years. That's why I wanted to make this vacation happen with my girls. I didn't want to look back and regret not spending enough time together. We might be getting older, but we're far from being dead! We still have dreams, goals, and a lot of life left in us. And we're here to support each other in reaching those aspirations. Rest can wait for later—I want to make the most of every moment with my amazing friends.

"I'm actually not sure. I have an email from my daughter. She just graduated and is trying to get a start in her life. I don't know if it is good news or bad. Or if it is good news for her but bad or sad news for me. I am trying to get up the courage to open the email." I stopped suddenly, realizing I was babbling. I couldn't believe I just told a complete stranger this.

"Ah. You are afraid she isn't going to be within a car drive away, or maybe she will move so far it will be

hard to even talk to her due to the time difference." He
nodded. "I can stand next to you if you need me to. I
won't read the email, but I will be here if you need to
talk."

I finally raised my gaze to meet his. His piercing
blue eyes were not as cold as I originally believed they
were when we first met. I smiled at how warm they
looked, like an onsen waiting for me to wade in, and I
nodded.

"You can stand next to me. Thank you. I appreciate
the support." I turned to the computer. I had taken long
enough to press the open button.

When I opened the email, there was a gif at the top.
Lorelai Gilmore, a young woman I recognized from
Gilmore Girls, was telling her daughter Rory that she got
into Chilton. Below the gif, the email read:

*Hey Mom! I hope you and the aunts are having an
amazing time, and they aren't allowing you to pout and
sulk too much. You need to relax and have fun! This is a
trip of a lifetime with your friends.*

*Alright, now that I've mom'd you. I have some news
to tell you! A student at Wichita State University made a
discovery going back to the 1600s! It is a nail of Spanish
origin. They are calling all willing and local
anthropologists to come and help excavate. I know it
isn't Iraq or Africa, but it is a start! They are letting me
lead my own team on part of the dig site.*

*I am going to be moving to Kansas for the next six
months. I know, I know, it isn't too far from home, and I
promise to call you every week with updates! I'm going
to need your advice! Please don't worry about me. I love
you and can't wait to hear about your trip!*

Love, Veronica

I sigh in relief. Kansas. She was moving to Kansas. I could handle Kansas. It's flat. Not much is going on. That was safe. This wouldn't be the only place she would be traveling to in the years ahead, but I felt better knowing she would be close to home for now. It was not too close that she would feel suffocated by me, but close enough it wouldn't be hard for us to hop in the car if we needed each other.

"I take it that it is good news. The breath you just released makes it seem like it isn't bad news." He arched his eyebrow in intrigue.

"Yes, she has gotten a job offer in Kansas. It is less than half a day's drive from where we live now. I feel a lot better. My first job took me to Africa. I was very young and naive. I didn't have anyone but me to count on." Tension was releasing from my muscles.

"That is wonderful news, Lisa! I am so relieved for you." Richard grabbed my hand and squeezed it in support. An electric shock ran from my hand through my body as my face became flushed. Was it getting hot in here, or was it just me? The heat had to have been all of the computer towers in the room. They were making it extremely warm.

"Very much so! She was the one I wanted to talk to in the first place. Now I can give her congratulations and ask her for a favor."

"What kind of favor? If you don't mind me asking. Is it about the investigation you ladies are doing about Seth's death?"

"Actually, it is. We have come to a roadblock when it comes to the suspects, and I feel like a good ol' Google search, as my daughter would say, is in need." I clicked the reply button and gave my daughter their names:

Martin Wick, Robyn Leed, Gray Leed, Seth Shannon, and Arba Chen.

Beverly and Charlotte were able to snoop and find out the full names of our suspects through their magnificent sleuthing powers and the ship's crew log they found left at a concierge's desk in the dining hall. They kept track of the ship's guests and workers' eating logs and habits. It was weird to think about it, but I guess it helped them keep up with what was liked and not liked by the voyagers on the ship.

I told her I wasn't sure if Gray was Robyn's brother's real name. Still, anything she could find on anyone would be greatly appreciated. She was very quick to read and answer her emails, but this snooping would take her at least a few hours before she could give us anything.

"So, Richard, shall we meet up with the ladies in the dining hall for lunch and see what other bit of trouble we can find ourselves in?"

"Are you asking me out on a date?" I couldn't help but notice how his eyes crinkled in an extremely attractive way. It was just unfair how well most men aged. They became more debonair and sexy with every silver strand and wrinkle. There's something about a man who laughs more than he frowns, who's comfortable in his own skin, and embraces his age without resorting to hair dye or other tricks to appear younger. A quality that only adds to their charm.

"I wouldn't call it a date, Richard. Just friends having lunch with each other. Don't push your luck."

"You are correct, madam. I will woo you one day, but first, let's meet up with your Cruising Crew, shall we?" He motioned for me to go first through the

153

computer lab's doors.

"Cruising Crew?" I looked up in confusion.

"Why yes. I have been talking with the ladies about how you all met, and they talked about the cruises and vacations you have all gone on throughout the years. The road trips and how your goal is to cruise through the rest of your lives by each other's sides. I think it's fantastic. In my head, I started calling you ladies "The Cruising Crew." Do you like it?"

I couldn't help but smile to myself, overwhelmed with gratitude for the incredible blessing of having my best friends. It's rare and precious to have even one best friend, and here I was, fortunate enough to have three. We may come from different walks of life with unique perspectives and journeys, but that's what strengthens our bond. We complement and support each other, making each of us better versions of ourselves. There's truth in the saying lifelong friends are like cheese and wine—they only get better with age.

"Actually, Richard, I love it. Absolutely love it." As we headed toward the dining hall, I put my arm through his crook. Who knew? Maybe this old dog could learn new tricks and be open to trying new relationships. I shook my head to clear the thought. The first thing I needed to do was find this killer. Hopefully, Veronica will be able to find something useful.

Chapter Twenty-Five

We ended our afternoon in the Below Deck pub, reminding me we needed to talk to Martin, and Gary the cruise director, about Zoe's predicament and ensure she could keep her job. It wasn't fair for her to lose her job over something she couldn't control.

Speaking of the devils, Martin and our cruise director strolled into the bar, engrossed in a serious conversation. Oblivious to our presence in the cozy corner, I observed their every move. Body language is remarkable; it can unveil a person's true emotions, actions, and even reveal when someone is concealing something. I discreetly informed the ladies and Richard that Martin and Gary had just made their grand entrance into the bar.

"I am going to talk to them about Zoe. I really feel guilty that she might lose her job. Especially if it is because of what we wrote in our notebook." I excused myself from the table and walked to their two-person table around the corner.

As I was approaching, I overheard their conversation. "Martin, mate. You need to keep this to yourself. This isn't something that needs to be taken to the authorities when we dock at the port." Gary was saying in his thick Australian accent.

"I feel like I need to be forthcoming. Rumors are going around that I might have killed him. We both know it wasn't me. They need to look into her and have the whole story of everyone involved." I peered around the corner, seeing Gary's face tighten in frustration.

"Everyone deserves to be able to start over from their past. Including you, aren't I right? Leave Birdie out of this. She doesn't have anything to do with this. If I were you, I'd keep this to myself. You have your daughter to think about. Any negative attention could get in the way of your processing." Gary's voice turned cold and unfeeling.

It was like seeing a totally different person. I could see the perspiration on his face as he took a drink of his water and grimaced with a smile as people waved to him around the room.

"Don't you dare bring her into this. My past is my past, and it has nothing to do with what is happening on this ship. You need to worry about your past. You brought this onto yourself when you agreed to the demands. I know about your past, Gary." Martin's voice dropped a couple of octaves, so I had to lean forward more into the half-wall of fishnets and fishing equipment.

Gary scoffed as though he didn't care, but his gaze darted back and forth, traveling through the crowd to ensure no one was paying too close attention. "What do you want, Martin? Money? I can get you the money once we land in Cozumel. It could be enough for you to take your daughter and disappear. But you'd have to give me anything you have on him, Birdie, and myself."

Martin tensed like he wasn't expecting Gary to try and bribe him. He leaned forward like he was going to respond. I leaned forward more to get all the details, but as I leaned forward on the fishnets, my hand knocked one of the anchors, and it fell to the ground in a big crash. Gary and Martin turned quickly to see me squatting on the floor behind the half wall.

Gary's cruise director mask fell back on as he smiled and helped me. "There you go, chicky. You need to be careful as you walk around here. There are a ton of things you could get hurt by." He helped me up from the ground as though I had tripped. I wasn't going to correct him.

His hands turned chilly on my arms as he turned to Martin. "We will finish this discussion later. Please see that this young lady gets her refreshments paid for on us and ensure the staff here clean up and the walkways are cleared." With that, Gary nodded to me and left the bar.

"The pathway was clear when we got here," Martin responded. "How much of that were you eavesdropping on, eh?" His eyes narrowed in suspicion as he bent over to pick up the anchor.

While he diligently tidied up, I shifted my attention back to the table where my dear friends were seated. Richard, with his kind nature, seemed poised to approach us. I shook my head, signaling I was fine, and gestured for them to remain where they were, keeping their distance.

"I heard enough. You have a daughter?" I asked.

"Yes, I do. What is it to you?" he asked as he started to put the anchor back into the fishnet webbing.

"It's tough to be away from mine as well. Even when we were in the same country, I worked so much that she was normally asleep when I got home. How old is she?"

"She is twelve. She is in Ireland with my wife. Or soon-to-be ex-wife." He grunted as he got back up from his crouch.

"Oh. I am so sorry you are going through a divorce. Those are extremely hard. I've had four, and they don't get any easier." I laughed at my extremely lame joke, but Martin didn't have it in him to join in.

"I wouldn't know. This is my first one. Is there anything I can do for you? You were sneaking over here for a reason. Or do you still think I killed the boy?"

"I mean, you saw the notes I had on you. There are rumors you've killed before, and those prison tattoos on your arms don't help. You can't blame an old girl for speculating."

Martin let out a snort through his nose, clearly taken aback by the accusations thrown at him. "Prison tattoos? I've killed before? Where on earth did you hear such nonsense?" Without waiting for my response, he shook his head dismissively. "Never mind. These tattoos are actually inspired by my favorite book, *The Count of Monte Cristo*. They symbolize my belief in justice. You see, I used to be a police officer in Ireland until my ex-wife falsely accused me of threatening her to manipulate our divorce and the custody situation."

Martin paused and took a cleansing breath. "Well, I did express my determination to fight for custody of my daughter, but that's it. Unfortunately, I lost my job, and she cleaned out our joint accounts, leaving me with no choice but to take up these security gigs for quick money. It's tough being away from Maggie, my daughter, but I'm working toward gaining full custody of her, and I have almost everything in place to make it happen."

As Martin spoke, memories of *The Count of Monte Cristo* by Alexandre Dumas flooded back to me. It had been years since I immersed myself in that captivating tale. Examining the intricate tattoos on Martin's arms, I could make out the phrases "Wait and Hope" etched on his wrists, along with the crest symbolizing Cristo's newfound life. They were beautiful and intricate, but I could understand how someone might mistakenly perceive them as prison tattoos. After all, Martin's imposing presence could easily give off such an impression.

"Oh! I wish you the best of luck." I bit my lower lip. "It's just we heard you arguing with someone on the phone in your office, and out of context, it seemed like you were hiding something."

"I was on the phone with my ex's attorney. He is her new slimeball boyfriend, and he is playing dirty. I might have lost my temper, but I'm not a killer."

"There was also someone arguing with Seth in your office. It didn't sound like you, but it was a man. You were the only one who came out with Seth after hearing it."

Martin's face contorted with mixed emotions as my words sank in. He seemed taken aback, and his expression showed a hint of anger. "You shouldn't eavesdrop on other people's conversations," he retorted sharply. "It seems to be a rather nasty habit of yours. Shouldn't you be occupied with knitting, reading, or whatever people your age do? I assure you I have this investigation under control. Please, leave it alone and try to enjoy the rest of your trip." He moved to walk away, but before he could, I reached out and gently touched his arm, seeking to convey my genuine concern.

"I actually have a favor to ask you."

Shock swept across his face. "A favor, eh? What kind of favor? You have been nothing but a pain in the ass this whole trip."

Courtny Bradley

I couldn't blame him for thinking that. We were extraordinarily nosy and persistent in our investigation. Still, I promised Zoe, and I would keep it. "The bartender here? She doesn't deserve to lose her job. Seth attacked her first by grabbing her arm. She told him to let her go, but he wouldn't listen. She only shoved him because she had to. Don't let her one action ruin the rest of her career or her life. We have many people who witnessed this. Could you talk to Gary about keeping her on?"

Martin's gaze softened as he regarded me, surprised by my unexpected request. He paused, taking a moment to process my words. After a thoughtful silence, he finally spoke, his voice carrying a hint of sincerity. "I'll look into it. Your friend is certainly a spirited and diligent individual. I can't make any promises at the moment, but I'll reconsider her situation and see what we can do for her. Thank you for approaching me and showing such genuine concern. Now, please enjoy the rest of your vacation away from my investigation." He turned to walk away again. I should have let the conversation drop, but something was nagging at the back of my mind.

"Um, one more thing. I promise to try to drop this investigation, but did you know that Seth, Robyn, and our steward, Arba, knew each other from the past? They all worked on the same ship together with Robyn's brother, Gray. I'm not sure if Gray is his real name, but he seems to have a lot of pull on the ship."

Whatever I said must have resonated with him because anger and annoyance flooded his face again. "Ms. Mide, I *really* need you to back off of this case. This might seem like a regular whodunit, but someone was killed. Murdered. Strangled to death. They are still on this ship. The more you stick your nose in where it doesn't belong, the less likely I will be able to protect you from the killer. Please drop this. Go back to your friends. Enjoy your time on the boat. I will find out who did this, but I can't do that if you keep sticking your nose where it doesn't belong. Do you understand me?"

A chill ran down my spine, giving me the heebie-jeebies. It hadn't even crossed my mind that the killer might still lurk around every corner of the ship. And who knows what they'd do if they caught wind of our snooping? The ship was like a giant puzzle with secret nooks and crannies where you could stash a body, or it could just disappear into the vast ocean. It was enough to make me break out in a cold sweat.

I gave myself a mental slap on the forehead. What was I thinking, poking my nose in this investigation? It was time to hand the reins over to Martin. If Veronica came up empty-handed, I'd be the first to suggest we drop the whole thing. No more playing detective and risking our lives. We were here to unwind and have a great time, not tangle with a crafty killer.

Taking a deep breath to calm my nerves, I returned to the table where the group was waiting. Now was the time to put the mysteries aside and focus on enjoying each other's company. No more poking our noses where they didn't belong. Martin had the skills and determination to handle this. From now on, we'd leave it to the expert and trust in his abilities to bring justice and keep us safe, as long as Veronica's internet sleuthing came up with nothing more to pursue.

Chapter Twenty-Six

I shook the chills off my body and turned back to the table where all my friends were blatantly staring at me. They had looks of concern on their faces as I approached. Letting me know my face was revealing how scared I was feeling.

"Everything okay, sugar?" Wilma asked as I sat down in between her and Richard.

"I'm not sure. Things aren't adding up. Or aren't adding up the way my scientific brain wants." I explained to them what I overheard Martin and Gary talking about.

"Who is Birdie?" Beverly asked as she took the notebook and pen out of my bag and started taking notes from what I overheard.

"I'm not sure. But Gary knew or knows her."

I turned to Wilma. "Do you remember when Seth was talking to the other person in Martin's office about 'Little Bird'? I think she is on the boat the way they talked about not bothering her or bringing her into this. But that is two people we don't know who they are, so we don't have any more information to add to the list. But you know who I now think we should add to the list?" I asked them as I looked around the table.

"Gary!" They all said at the same time, and I nodded. We needed to find out more information about him.

162

A couple of hours passed since I sent my email to Veronica, and now I found myself leaving Wilma peacefully, meditating on the deck outside our room. As I stepped out, I noticed Charlotte and Beverly making their way to a delightful dessert restaurant, indulging in an afternoon treat. It warmed my heart to witness my friends embracing the relaxation and enjoyment this vacation was meant to offer. I should be immersing myself in a thrilling book, savoring the company of my dear friends, or even opening myself up to new acquaintances. Yet, a persistent feeling tugged at the corners of my mind as though I possessed a piece of vital information that could propel this investigation forward.

Perhaps my age was catching up with me, I pondered. Maybe they released me from my archaeological work just in the nick of time before my forgetful mind led me to contaminate or damage precious artifacts unwittingly. As I entered the computer room, I scanned the area for any sign of other occupants. Finding it deserted, I chose a computer positioned facing the entrance. There was no need to startle myself like last time when Richard managed to sneak up on me, nearly giving me a heart attack.

I logged into my email and saw one title: *Mom? Shouldn't you be relaxing?!*

I laughed at the idea. My daughter knew me, though. She knew I would not be able to sit still or rest until I solved the puzzle in front of me, even if it put me right on the pathway of a psycho.

I opened the email and saw dossiers for everyone. I asked for Martin Wick, Robyn Leed, Seth Shannon, and Arba Chen. Gray was the only person missing, but I wasn't shocked. Veronica was okay with computers, but

I couldn't expect miracles.

Hey, Mom, thanks for being cool about me moving to Kansas. I know it is hard for me to move away, but you could have made it a lot more complicated than you did. I really appreciate you letting me do things on my own and in my own way. You are a wonderful mother and have prepared me for anything and everything that I could possibly have come.

Speaking of being prepared, you know this should be a vacation, right? How did YOU find a body out of all those people on the boat? We deal with hundreds, if not thousands, of years-old corpses and artifacts. Please be careful. I looked into everyone I could, but I couldn't find anyone named Gray Leed. The only Leed, hahaha; see what I did there? The only person with the last name Leed is Robyn, but you should look into her profile; there might be something there.

I'll talk to you later and see you at home. I can't wait to go apartment shopping with you when you get back. Be careful, Mom. Love you.

I started by opening Martin's file, hoping it would confirm his earlier statements and reassure me of his honesty. As I perused the contents, I discovered it aligned perfectly with what he shared. Martin's wife, Patricia, had filed for divorce and sought full custody of their twelve-year-old daughter, Margaret Samantha Wick. The document included a newspaper clipping, frozen in time, capturing their wedding day.

Looking at the snapshot, memories flooded my mind. Martin, the heartthrob of his younger days, standing tall and proud, with no trace of the tattoos or bulging muscles he sported now. He'd been right about Patricia's infidelity and their ongoing battle for custody.

Veronica, as thorough as ever, delved into the depths of her research, unearthing a link between Patricia's new partner and the Irish Mob. I made a mental note to print out this particular piece of information and present it to Martin as a peace offering. After all, we'd been a thorn in his side throughout this entire week, and it was the least I could do.

With a sense of purpose, I clicked the print button, the sound of the printer whirring to life. Armed with this newfound knowledge it will not only provide some solace to Martin but also contribute to unraveling the mysteries surrounding us.

Curiosity piqued, I moved on to Arba's file. Driven by a hunch, I realized there might be more to his connection with Robyn, Seth, and this mysterious figure named Gray. As the file opened, a series of screenshots greeted me—a birth certificate, a visa permit, and a photo capturing a younger Arba holding a radiant, youthful Robyn in his arms. Their love and happiness were palpable, shining through the image.

But what caught my attention was the presence of Seth, standing behind them with his familiar smug expression. His arm casually draped over the shoulders of another young man, who struck a chord of familiarity within me. With his slightly shorter stature, fuller build, and boyish features, he reminded me of someone I couldn't quite place. I leaned in, trying to recall where I'd seen him before.

My gaze shifted to Veronica's note in the corner of the image. According to her findings, this photo sourced from Arba's rarely-used Facebook page. It was his only picture; intriguingly, it carried a caption with AC, RL, SS, and GB initials. As my mind raced, I couldn't help but wonder if GB referred to Gray, the missing piece of this intricate puzzle. The pieces were slowly falling into place, and the interwoven connections between these individuals became more apparent.

I clicked print on the picture and went to open Seth's file when Richard came running into the lab. He was out of breath and sweating. "Lisa! We have to get to the infirmary."

As I closed all the computer windows and signed out of the computer, my heart started pounding, and I grabbed my printouts. "What? Why? What is wrong? Is everyone okay?" It was always scary when we were told we needed to go to the hospital at our age. We were so much more fragile than we gave ourselves credit for.

My grandmother once told me, "I am as young in my mind as I was when I was in my thirties. I only wished my body felt that way." I now knew exactly what she meant. I didn't feel like a day over thirty-five, but I was nearing my seventies at a frighteningly scary speed.

"It's Wilma. She has fallen down the stairs. They are taking her to the infirmary. She had lost consciousness as I turned the corner to come and get you from your room. Before she passed out, she let me know where you were."

"She fell down the stairs? That is ridiculous. Wilma doesn't fall down anything. She isn't clumsy. She is the one who has been telling us to take the stairs to keep up with everything we have been eating. She has been running laps around us. There is no way she fell." I shook my head as we both raced to the nearest elevator. As the door opened and I pressed the button for the lowest floor, I turned to Richard for a response.

"That's the thing, Lisa. Before she passed out, she told me she didn't fall. She was pushed."

Chapter Twenty-Seven

"Excuse me? Pushed?" I uttered in disbelief, my head shaking in dismay. The thought of someone intentionally harming an elderly lady was beyond comprehension. What kind of sick and heartless individual would stoop so low? Perhaps they had a twisted motive, like being in the person's will and eyeing a hefty inheritance. However, none of us onboard the ship had any relatives accompanying us, and apart from maybe Charlotte, none of us possessed fortunes worth killing for.

"That's what she said, Lisa. She claims she was pushed, and then she lost consciousness. The ship's medical staff wheeled her away. I was instructed to fetch you, as she may regain consciousness by the time we reach her room," Richard explained hurriedly, the words spilling from his mouth. I couldn't help but feel that this unfortunate incident was another violent episode he'd been reluctantly dragged into, all because he was stuck among us old gals and our mischievous escapades.

Why did I always meddle in matters that had nothing to do with me? Seth may have been our neighbor, a rather unpleasant one at that, but I never anticipated the possibility of one of us getting hurt. A killer was lurking on this ship, and we should have heeded Martin's advice to enjoy our vacation and let him handle the investigation.

The truth was, we weren't as young and resilient as we liked to believe. A simple fall could result in a broken hip or a shattered wrist for us. The recovery process for someone our age wasn't a walk in the park either. We could be in physical therapy for months, even years, for injuries younger folks would shrug off without much consequence.

The mere thought of Wilma being unable to engage in her beloved goat yoga or conquer new mountains churned my stomach. She wouldn't be able to cope with this ordeal on her own. It was my fault she got hurt. I should have restrained myself from sticking my nose into everyone else's affairs. Who did I think I was, anyway?

I made a firm decision as we rounded the corner toward the medical bay. We were going to drop this case. Enough was enough. Let the younger, more capable individuals handle it. It wasn't our place as old bats to make it about ourselves and try to solve the mystery. We lacked the knowledge, agility, and stamina to keep up with someone who was likely much younger than us and already had a violent streak.

I pushed open the door, ignoring the disapproving gaze of a nurse who seemed poised to challenge my unannounced entry. Taking in the sterile decor and clinical atmosphere, I couldn't help but feel that no matter how they spruced up a hospital, it would never truly lose its somber aura. The scent of sickness hung in the air, and an undeniable sense of mortality lingered, as if staying within those walls for too long might invite the afflictions they aimed to cure.

Only two beds were occupied; one held my lifelong friend, Wilma. She was attached to an array of machines, tubes, and unfamiliar medical contraptions. The room was filled with beeping sounds and the mechanical noises of the devices assisting her breathing. A bandage was wrapped around her head, and her eyes remained shut. I approached her bed, my heart pounding and my mind growing hazy.

Wilma, the embodiment of strength and resilience, appeared fragile and vulnerable before my eyes. It was a stark contrast to her usual indomitable presence. I struggled to find the right words, feeling a whirlwind of emotions swirling within me. The room started to spin, blurring my vision, and leaving me momentarily disoriented.

"Ma'am? Ma'am? I need you to sign in." The nurse followed me to Wilma's bed and handed me a clipboard with a sign-in sheet.

"I'll take that for you, my dear," Richard said in his calming accent, signing us in.

Wilma must have heard our voices because she opened her eyes and met her gaze with mine. "God, Lisa, who died?" She laughed and then coughed.

"Well, it was almost you. What the hell happened?" I rushed to the bedside and grabbed her hand. It felt frail in my own.

"What? This?" She indicated all of the machines, wires, and tubes. "This is a doctor on the ship who sees someone's age before seeing the person. They are overreacting. I am perfectly fine and have asked to remove these multiple times. I'm fine."

"You are most certainly NOT fine," said a young woman about the age of Veronica in a doctor's coat. "You're injured, and I am putting in for some blood tests just in case. You need to be patient with me, Mrs. Point. Let me do my job. You might have been an emergency room nurse before you retired, but that means you know things can seem fine until they aren't. Now, will you introduce me to your friend?" The doctor turned to me and extended her hand out for a handshake.

"Lisa, this is Dr. Maddison. Dr. Maddison, this is one of my longest and dearest friends, Lisa-May Mide. She is my roommate, and the other two should find their way here soon." With an air of resignation, Wilma let out a sigh and allowed the doctor to proceed with the tests. Despite her current condition, her spirit remained unwavering. She turned to me, a smug smile gracing her lips, clearly unyielding in her confidence. It was reassuring to see her maintaining her trademark cockiness even in this challenging situation.

"Wilma, what happened?" I asked again.

"Yes, Mrs. Point, what did happen?" a familiar voice came from behind me at the room's entrance, startling everyone in the room. I glanced towards the entrance and caught sight of Martin, his expression a blend of exasperation and genuine concern.

"Someone pushed me, obviously." Wilma rolled her eyes as though tired of being asked the obvious.

"Yes, I see that, dear," I responded with just as much annoyance in my voice as hers. "What happened leading up to the incident? What were you doing?"

"Well, I had gone back down to our room after going to the spa. I wanted to rinse off, read a book, and relax before you came back from the computer lab. It is just as important to find relaxing time as it is to get exercise." Wilma turned to the doctor to acknowledge her minilecture before returning to us.

"I got to our door and found a note folded on the doorknob. It said we better drop our investigation, or another death would be on deck. I needed to get to Lisa before anything else happened. As I ran up the stairs, I remembered I should probably get the notebook we used and ran back to our room. Before I could go down the last flight of stairs, I felt two hands shove me down, and then I remember waking up to Richard hollering my name and calling for help." Wilma laid her head back on the pillows, waiting for us to respond.

"Another notebook?" Martin asked between gritted teeth. "I believe I'd made it clear. You were supposed to stop putting your nose where it doesn't belong."

"Well, yes. You might have said something along those words. But then I got this email from my daughter, and I thought it wouldn't hurt to do a little poking around about the other people we suspected. No one knew we were looking into it. We didn't see the harm in a little sleuthing. Plus, we are just four old ladies and a British gentleman. Who would be scared of us?"

As I fidgeted with my hands, deliberately avoiding Martin's piercing gaze, I could feel his eyes boring into me like lasers, ready to penetrate my thoughts. His reaction was a mix of grumbling, growling, and exasperated sighing as if battling a whirlwind of emotions, uncertain of which to settle on. Finally, he managed to speak through clenched teeth, his frustration evident. "Another notebook? How is that possible? I took your notebook."

I glanced at Wilma, and we both flinched. "Well, one must always be prepared with multiple items. Just in case."

"Yes! Notepads. Pens. Pencils. Extra reading glasses. Antacid. Tissues. The works," Wilma sitting up a little taller in her bed.

"Where is this notebook?" Martin asked, extending his hand as if expecting me to simply hand it over.

I smirked, playing along with his expectations. "Oh, dear, the exact whereabouts of the notebook elude me. You see, as we age, our minds aren't as sharp and agile as they used to be. Forgetfulness tends to creep in, especially at a certain age." I glanced at Wilma and Richard, their eyes crinkling with amusement as we exaggerated our age for the sake of our argument.

Martin shook his head, not fully buying into my act. "I don't buy it, ma'am. While it's true that there's nothing wrong with your mental faculties, I suppose age catches up with us all. But let's focus on the matter at hand. You mentioned asking your daughter to do some research. Who did you ask her to look into? What did she find?"

I decided to deflect his attention from the missing notebook by offering a tidbit of information. "Ah, yes, the younger generation and their exceptional Googling skills. I simply sent her a few names to verify some people's stories and dig deeper into their backgrounds. You know how it is."

My goal was to divert Martin's scrutiny and buy myself some time, hoping he wouldn't press further about the notebook.

"Oh? Like what?" he asked incredulously.

"How about a possible connection to the Irish Mob for your soon-to-be ex-wife's lawyer? Would that be something interesting to you?" I opened my bag on my shoulder, grabbed the printout of the newspaper Veronica had attached, and handed it over. I had the picture of young Robyn, Seth, Arba, and the stranger in my other hand. I was absentmindedly folding it to make it seem unimportant.

Martin's expression turned serious, and a subtle twitch of his lip caught my attention. I realized discussing this in front of everyone was not the wisest choice. I should have shared this information with him privately. However, my agenda and the pressing need to explore Veronica's email further compelled me to keep him engaged with his matters. I hoped by doing so, he would grant me the breathing room I needed to investigate the picture and gather more information from the computer.

"You had your daughter do a background check on me?" Martin asked while looking at the newsprint in his hand.

"Well, I just wanted to make sure you were who you said you were. Trust but verify, as an old professor told me years ago. I trusted and believed you, but you can't fault an old lady for making sure you weren't lying. Plus, look, Veronica was able to find something that might be able to help you." I motioned to the paper in his hand. "Had your lawyer found that little piece of information?"

I could see Martin's jaw tense. "No. We had a hunch he was a part of the mob, but there wasn't any proof. Someone wiped his slate clean. We couldn't find any newspapers or copies of them. How did your daughter get this?"

"Well, we are researchers. It's in our blood. We are like a hound dog on a rabbit trail. She can find out about anything, and we also have access to databases your lawyer does not. Would you like me to ask her to look more?" Maybe if I could get Martin to see me as beneficial to the investigation, he might give me some more information on his side of the investigation.

As Martin opened his mouth to respond, an unexpected interruption stole the attention of our group. A throat was cleared, and Martin turned around, signaling for everyone to look in the direction of the sound. To our surprise, it was none other than Gary, our cruise director, who'd arrived unannounced.

"Gary? What can I help you with?" Martin inquired.

"I am here to check on our young passenger here." The smarmy grin on Gary's face made me cringe. He was out of breath, as though he used the stairs to get to the med bay, but looking at his physique, I doubt he chose to use the stairs. Perspiration pooled on his top lip, and his hair was disheveled.

"She is doing a lot better, sir," Doctor Maddison replied as she stepped in with her clipboard. "However, visitation is now over, and I need my patient to rest. She will be released after I get her blood results, which come out clean. Ms. Mide, can you come and get Mrs. Point in about three hours?"

"Of course. I'll make sure to do that." I turned to Richard and grabbed his arm. I accidentally dropped the image from Arba's Facebook account on the floor as I moved to adjust my bag, and it fell open. Martin grabbed the photo before I could catch the paper, and Gary looked around his shoulder.

"Something else your daughter sleuthed out?" He looked down and saw the image of Arba, Robyn, Seth, and the unknown man behind them.

"Yes, I hadn't the time to look at it yet."

"Where did you say you got that?" he questioned, his voice trembling slightly.

Gary's voice carried a sense of urgency as he confronted us, his face turning pale and beads of sweat forming on his forehead. Something about his reaction sent a shiver down my spine, but I couldn't quite put my finger on it. His demeanor seemed off as if there was more to his concern than met the eye.

I exchanged a puzzled glance with Martin, sensing Gary's reaction held a deeper meaning. Something about the photograph struck a nerve with him, though it remained a mystery to me.

"This was the only picture on Arba's Facebook page. Why does it concern you?" I pressed, determined to unravel the truth.

A flicker of unease crossed Gary's face as he replied, "I think it's best if you heed Martin's advice. You should refrain from meddling in other people's affairs. Trust me, you don't want to face the consequences. Look what happened to Mrs. Point here."

A chill ran down my spine as he mentioned Mrs. Point, the victim who'd been pushed down the stairs. Gary's words carried a warning as if he knew more than he was letting on. But why would he be adamant about keeping us from the investigation?

Before we could question him further, Gary swiftly grabbed the printed image from Martin's hands, nodded at the doctor, and hurriedly exited the room, leaving us with more questions than answers.

Chapter Twenty-Eight

Richard walked me to my room, and I walked past our door to knock on Charlotte and Beverly's, hoping they would be in. Beverly opened the door as soon as my first knock was finished.

"Where the hell have you been? Where is Wilma?" Beverly looked out into the hall behind Richard and me and looked for Wilma.

"She is in the med bay right now, but we can go and get her in a few hours after all of the tests are done." I indicated that Richard and I wanted to talk in the room.

Charlotte's eyes widened in disbelief as she processed the information. Her hands trembled slightly, revealing her growing concern. "What do you mean the med bay? What tests?" she questioned, her voice filled with urgency. She seemed ready to spring into action, but I quickly shook my head, silently signaling her to stay put.

With Richard by my side, we relayed the events that had unfolded since we last saw Beverly and Charlotte. The gravity of the situation settled upon them, and their faces turned pale with shock and fear. They clutched each other's hands tightly, seeking solace and strength amidst the chaos.

As I reached the edge of Wilma's bed and prepared to sit down, my gaze wandered across the room, catching sight of Charlotte's impromptu makeshift wall adorned with logoed cruise paper. It was a collage of information, meticulously arranged with gum as adhesive. Each piece of paper bore a name, and beside it, meticulously jotted down, was every detail Beverly had recalled. The bubbles and insights we had gathered about Martin Wick, Robyn Leed, Gray Leed, Seth Shannon, and Arba Chen were all there, forming a web of connections and unanswered questions.

The wall served as a visual reminder of the puzzle we desperately tried to solve. It symbolized the tangled threads of our investigation, interwoven with the lives of those around us. It was a stark reminder that we were knee-deep in a mystery that grew more complex by the minute.

I tore my gaze away, not wanting to delve too deeply into the wall's intricacies. Our immediate focus needed to be on Wilma's well-being and the urgency of finding answers to the dangerous events unfolding aboard the ship.

I pointed to Martin Wick's profile. "We can remove Martin. I have solid intel from Veronica that he has been telling the truth about himself. That and our conversations make me believe he isn't our killer. He really is trying to do his job. We might even be able to ask him for a favor with what Veronica could get on his cheating soon-to-be ex-wife and her scum of a mob lawyer boyfriend." I filled in everyone with what Martin was going through with his personal life, and everyone agreed he was no longer a suspect.

Charlotte reached up and took off Martin's profile. She motioned with her other hand. "Do we know anything else about the rest of the Murder Gang up here?"

"Murder Gang?" Richard asked with a hint of humor in his voice.

"Listen, we authors have to put flare somewhere, and we couldn't keep calling them all by name," Charlotte huffed.

"True. I think we can remove Zoe. I didn't even have Veronica look up more information on her. I really think we can take her down. That leaves us with Robyn Leed, Arba Chen, and Gray Leed."

Charlotte carefully removed Zoe's profile from the wall, a solemn expression on her face. Meanwhile, my stomach growled audibly, a reminder it had been a while since I last ate. The combination of hunger and the mounting tension was threatening to push me towards the edge of becoming hangry, as my daughter often teased me.

Searching the bed for a distraction, my gaze landed on a menu conveniently placed nearby. A glimmer of hope flickered within me, knowing that satisfying my hunger could bring some temporary relief. However, my attention quickly shifted as I discovered a flyer nestled amidst the menu's pages. It promoted a limited-time offer: access to the ship's internet services through our phones for only twenty dollars a day.

A surge of excitement coursed through me as I realized the significance of this discovery. It was precisely what we needed to gain access to the remaining information Veronica had sent me about everyone else on board. With the internet at our fingertips, we could uncover crucial details, potentially unraveling the mysteries surrounding our fellow passengers.

While satiating my hunger was a pressing need, the opportunity to delve deeper into the investigation took precedence. I set the menu aside, my appetite momentarily forgotten, and eagerly grabbed for my phone, ready to seize this chance to gather more information and shed light on the enigmatic individuals we had come to know aboard the ship.

"Hey, ladies and gents. How about we call for room service, and then I'll pay the twenty bucks to get the internet on my phone and check the rest of the information? I have an inkling of who Gray might be, but I want to see if Veronica was able to get any information at all."

We were ready to tackle the rest of the email once we all had our burgers, fries, and shakes. Wilma would have been annoyed with us and our unhealthy meal choices. Knowing she would be okay and joining us in a couple of hours made the burger and fries taste much better. I slurped the rest of the chocolate shake from the bottom of my cup and sighed in contentment.

"Alright, ladies and gentlemen. Let's see what else my daughter was able to find out!" I pulled my phone and credit card out and started the process of getting the internet.

"After shelling out thousands of dollars for this cruise and indulging in numerous expensive drinks, you'd think they could at least provide us with a day's worth of internet access. It's outrageous," I grumbled, my frustration evident in my voice.

Without a second thought, I opened my phone, fingers itching to input my credit card details into the system. Skimming through the fine print, terms and conditions briefly crossed my mind, but I quickly dismissed them. Who has the time or patience to read through all that legal jargon? Only the meticulous few, or perhaps the sociopaths among us.

With a rebellious determination, I agreed to the terms and conditions without fully comprehending what I was getting myself into. My desire for information outweighed any concerns about potential risks or hidden charges. After all, this was our chance to delve deeper into the mysteries surrounding our fellow passengers, and I wasn't about to let a little fine print stand in my way.

As the internet connection flickered to life on my phone, a surge of excitement mixed with a hint of guilt. I opened up my email, and my stomach turned. Apparently, I was still on the university's staff email list. An email congratulated my assistant for being hired into my previous position. There wasn't even a mention of me retiring in the email. It made my blood boil. I had to do Lamaze breathing exercises to calm my heart rate as I deleted and blocked the email address from my contact list.

With a swipe of my finger, I scrolled down to find Veronica's email and eagerly clicked on Seth's dossier. As the page loaded, a series of screenshots from his social media accounts appeared before me. My eyes scanned the images, revealing a pattern of deceit and manipulation.

Seth had dabbled in various fraudulent schemes, targeting men's insecurities and toxic masculinity to make a quick buck. His posts were filled with endorsements for questionable products, ranging from erectile pills to testosterone supplements, all promising to enhance masculinity and virility. It was a despicable exploitation of vulnerable individuals seeking validation and confidence.

I couldn't help but shake my head in disgust as I read through the brief explanations provided by Veronica about Seth's past employment opportunities. It was a trail of deceit, weaving a web of lies and false promises to deceive unsuspecting victims. The sheer audacity and lack of moral compass displayed by Seth left me speechless.

This revelation painted a clearer picture of the kind of person Seth truly was. He was not only a mean-spirited neighbor but also someone who preyed on others' insecurities and profited from their vulnerabilities. It was no wonder he had rubbed so many people up the wrong way.

"Sounds like he was a cad," Richard stated. "Surely the men he was trying to sell those to knew they wouldn't really work. Snake oil salesmen are notorious for giving out poison to honest people."

"Sometimes people just need the hope something will work. That is why there are placebo pills in medication testing. You'd be amazed at how much your mind can convince you you feel better or the medicine is working," Beverly responded. "Many times, my husband was offered to have his patients take a position in the trial. Many times, he would say no. He didn't have the option to ensure they were given real medicine. He would always recommend they wait for the medicine to go through the hoops." We all nodded in understanding. Sometimes, just a little hope those medical tests can give is enough and worth it.

Excitement surged through me as I clicked on the newspaper clipping Veronica had uncovered. The article detailed an embezzlement charge against Seth, shedding light on a hidden aspect of his past. As the page loaded,

I scanned the text, eager to uncover the truth.

According to the newspaper, Seth had indeed been involved in an embezzlement scheme, but what intrigued me even more was the mention of a silent partner. The partner, who remained unnamed in the article, had apparently turned in the state's evidence in exchange for a reduced sentence. The article hinted at a familial connection between the partner and Seth's long-time girlfriend, adding another layer of intrigue to the unfolding mystery.

The newspaper clipping indicated Seth had been caught embezzling funds from the cruise line he had worked for. Surprisingly, the punishment seemed relatively light considering the severity of the crime. Seth had served only six months in prison, paid fines, and been sentenced to perform service hours. It was clear he had managed to secure a skilled lawyer who negotiated a relatively lenient outcome.

As I absorbed the information, a flurry of questions raced through my mind. Who was Seth's silent partner? How were they related to his girlfriend, and what role did they play in the embezzlement scheme? Did this past crime have any connection to the events unfolding on the cruise ship?

The more I delved into Seth's background, the clearer it became he was no stranger to deception and criminal activity. The embezzlement charge added another dimension to his character, further fueling suspicions about his involvement in the ongoing incidents during our voyage.

I couldn't help but wonder if Seth's past crimes and associations had caught up with him, intertwining with the web of secrets and intrigue that had enveloped our group. There was much more to Seth than met the eye, and uncovering the truth about his actions could potentially unravel the mystery looming over us.

"There doesn't seem to be much other information in Seth's profile we didn't already know or have learned from others. We only have one more profile. We know that Robyn couldn't have done it. She was on that date, but we might learn who Gray is from her profile."

Before I could open up the last email attachment, there was a knock at the door. We stopped what we were doing, and I turned to the group and indicated with my hand that they should remove the images from the walls before we opened the door. I didn't want Martin to take everything we had been working on for the case. I could feel it in my gut. We were close to figuring out who killed Seth and hurt Wilma.

As the persistent knocking continued, Charlotte and Richard quickly finished organizing our notes and placed them inside Beverly's suitcase. The urgency in Martin's voice hinted at something important happening beyond the closed door.

We gathered ourselves and prepared to face whatever news awaited us. Taking a deep breath, I approached the door and opened it, revealing Martin standing there with a grave expression. "Yes, how can we help you?" I asked, trying to maintain a composed demeanor.

Martin's voice was laced with a mixture of concern and urgency as he replied, "I will need you all to come down to the med bay. The doctor didn't disclose the details of the blood results due to patient privacy regulations, but she believes Mrs. Point shouldn't be left alone."

My heart skipped a beat, and time appeared to slow down around me. The weight of the situation settled heavily upon us. I exchanged glances with Charlotte and Beverly, silently acknowledging the fear and worry we all shared. Wilma, our pillar of strength, the one who had endured so much in her life, couldn't possibly be facing a health crisis. It was inconceivable.

Without exchanging a word, we followed Martin out of the room, descending the medical hallway in a somber procession. Each step was accompanied by a mix of anxiety and hope, praying whatever awaited us in the med bay would have a positive outcome.

The hallway stretched before us, the sterile scent and hushed tones creating an atmosphere of unease. Thoughts raced through my mind, memories of our adventures and the bond we had forged over the years. Wilma's unwavering spirit and infectious optimism had been a guiding light for us all. The idea of her facing a health scare was almost too much to bear.

As we approached the med bay, a sense of apprehension settled over us. The door stood before us, a gateway to the unknown. With a collective breath, we steeled ourselves for whatever lay ahead, ready to support Wilma in her time of need.

Chapter Twenty-Nine

As the doctor opened the door to the med bay, a mix of trepidation and anticipation gripped us all. My heart lodged in my throat, and my stomach churned with nervous energy. We stood at the threshold, uncertain of what awaited us on the other side.

With a gentle gesture, the doctor invited us into the room, and we stepped forward, one by one, crossing the threshold into a space filled with a quiet intensity. The sterile environment amplified the weight of the moment, and our footsteps echoed in the hushed atmosphere.

Wilma lay in the bed, surrounded by medical equipment and monitors. The beeping sounds and soft hum of the machinery filled the room, adding to the tension that hung in the air. Our gazes fixed on her, our dear friend, as we waited anxiously for the doctor to provide us with an update.

The doctor's expression was a mix of professionalism and empathy as she addressed us. Her words were measured and carefully chosen to convey the gravity of the situation. Time stood still, each moment stretching, prolonging the uncertainty that gripped our hearts.

"She said that you all had to be here, whatever the news was. This isn't something that I would normally tell someone on vacation or in front of people who aren't family," Dr. Maddison opened her mouth to continue but was interrupted by Wilma.

"And as I've told you already, they are family. Family doesn't always mean that they have to have the same blood as you. Hell, I know people who are my blood but aren't family. Anything you have to say to me, you can say to them."

I walked around the doctor, careful not to invade her professional space, and positioned myself at the end of Wilma's bed as I looked at her, a faint flush on her cheeks, evidence of her recent passionate outburst. The fire in her eyes, though slightly tempered now, still burned with the same intensity I had known for years. It was a reassuring sight, a testament to her indomitable spirit that had always propelled her. At that moment, I found solace, hoping that whatever the doctor had to say wouldn't be cause for excessive concern.

To Wilma's left, Charlotte and Beverly took their positions, clasping her hands in a gesture of unwavering support. Their presence offered tangible reassurance, a united front against any adversity we might face. Feeling a deep connection to Wilma, I gently placed my hand on her foot, a silent affirmation of our enduring bond.

As we settled into our positions around Wilma's bed, our collective focus shifted to the doctor standing before us.

"Alright, doc. Out with it. What is wrong with me?" Wilma lifted her chin in defiance. This was a look that we all knew well. Something terrible was going to happen, but she wouldn't let it run her over.

Dr. Maddison stood before us, her white coat accentuating the seriousness of the moment. She spoke with a calm yet empathetic tone, her eyes conveying a genuine concern for Wilma's well-being. The sterile scent of the med bay mingled with a faint aroma of antiseptic, creating an atmosphere that amplified the gravity of the news about to be delivered.

"As you know, we performed a routine blood test to ensure everything was fine," Dr. Maddison began, her voice carrying a hint of reassurance. "And for the most part, Wilma, you are one of the healthiest people I've had the pleasure of working with. Even more than some twenty and thirty-year-olds." Her words held a touch of admiration for Wilma's vitality.

"But," the doctor continued, her expression slightly grave, "we found a high level of platelets. This can mean many different things, but you can make an appointment with your primary care physician when we dock." The click of her pen punctuated the statement as she made a note on her clipboard, her focused gaze shifting to Wilma, awaiting her response.

Wilma, a retired nurse, possessed a deep understanding of medical jargon and the implications behind test results. I watched as she absorbed the information, her gaze darting momentarily to the floor before resolutely meeting Dr. Maddison's gaze. It was evident that Wilma's mind was racing, contemplating the possibilities, weighing the potential challenges ahead. She had faced adversity with unwavering strength throughout her life, yet the unfairness of life's relentless obstacles couldn't be ignored.

In that fleeting moment, the med bay held its breath, the beeping monitors and distant murmurs fading into the background. Wilma, a beacon of resilience, stood at the precipice of another daunting journey, her unwavering spirit poised to tackle whatever lay ahead.

"What does that mean?" Charlotte asked.

Beverly and Wilma met each other's gaze. Beverly told Charlotte, "A high level of platelets can often mean that there could be cancer."

I had to give it to Beverly. I could barely hear the quake in her voice as she spoke the "C" word aloud.

Charlotte gasped and put her hand to her mouth while tears threatened to escape. "Cancer?"

Wilma finally snapped out of her momentary daze and let out a sigh; her voice laced with a fragile sense of hope. "Yes, cancer. But there are other reasons for a high platelet count, right, doc? It could not be cancer, right?" Her words hung in the air, tinged with vulnerability and a yearning for reassurance. It was as if she sought solace in the doctor's response, seeking a glimmer of hope akin to a child seeking comfort from their parents.

Dr. Maddison maintained her composed demeanor, understanding the weight of Wilma's question. "Yes," she replied, her voice gentle yet honest. "There could be an infection that your body is fighting against. A medication you are taking could interfere with your blood and other body parts. There are many other reasons why it might be high. This is why you need to follow up with your doctor next week. Do you have any questions for me?"

Wilma's acceptance was evident as she shook her head. "No, I don't. There isn't anything that I can do about this right now. I live a healthy life, and I'm not going to stop now. My only question is, when can I get out of here and drink?" Her determination shone through her words.

Dr. Maddison proceeded to sign the release papers, her gesture signifying that Wilma would be contacted by her doctor with the results that were taken at her medbay.

With a nod of understanding, Wilma took hold of her release papers; her head held high as she walked through the door, refusing to look back. Her resolute stride exemplified her strength, unwilling to let fear consume her.

"Let's go to the bar. Stat!" Wilma called out over her shoulder without turning to check if we were following. At that moment, it was clear that she sought solace in the familiar embrace of friendship and the temporary reprieve that the clinking of glasses and laughter could provide.

Without hesitation, we all hurried to catch up with her, knowing that if Wilma chose to deflect her anxiety with margaritas, it was our duty to support her. Margaritas and a captivating mystery serve as the perfect distractions, momentarily whisking us away from the weight of uncertainty. There was so much we needed to share with Wilma, a convergence of secrets and revelations, intertwining the allure of the unknown with the steadfast bond of friendship.

Chapter Thirty

We walked into the Below Deck Pub and were eager to find a place to sit and chat. The world had shifted and changed, yet everyone around us was laughing, telling jokes, and having a grand old time. To them, the world hadn't changed. To us, our world was tilted, and to Wilma, it was spinning out of control.

"You, ladies, find us a seat. I'm going to see if we can get a pitcher of margaritas and some menus. We need to eat. Fuel for the brain. We have a mystery to solve and a killer to catch." I started walking to the bar and recognized a friendly face.

I waved and smiled as I walked up to the bar. "Hey, stranger! Good to see you here. I hope you don't have too much grudge against an old lady."

Zoe gave me a genuine smile that reached all the way to her eyes as she wiped the counter down and started stacking glasses on the bar in front of her. "I hear I have you to thank for keeping my job. Your old lady wiles got them to give me another chance. Thank you. Drinks are on me for you and the Cruisin' Crew." She lifted her chin in the direction of my childhood friends. I turned, and they snagged the corner table I was starting to consider ours.

"The Cruisin' Crew?" Confused, I creased my brows. "How in the world would you know that name?"

"That's what everyone is calling you ladies now. We

191

have bets going on who is going to solve the murder first. The favor is high with you all. So, what will you ladies have?"

I asked her for a pitcher and some menus and leaned against the bar as she made our margaritas and stacked a serving tray with glasses. "So, have you heard anything around the ship? You know, about 'the death.' " I looked around the room to see if anyone was watching me watching them.

"I haven't heard much because I've been worried about what I might have to do if I was stuck on our next stop. But I found out something about the higher-ups wanting this to disappear."

"Oh? What higher-ups?" I hoped she would confirm some of my inklings about who I believed was involved in this mystery.

"Our cruise director, Gary, for one. He keeps pulling the managers aside and telling them he better not hear us gossiping about this with each other. That the guests don't need to overhear us talking." She shrugged as she motioned that she would walk me and our drinks to the table and take our orders.

"The thing is, scuttlebutt is our lifeblood on the ship. We don't have much else to do. We only get so much internet and phone calls allowed to us workers. The rest is for our guests. Trading gossip passes the time, and something like murder is too juicy not to talk about, you know?"

I nodded, understanding. "So, Gary is really trying to keep this hush-hush?"

Zoe nodded as we approached our table, the anticipation evident in her eyes. Taking my seat, I instinctively reached for the frosty glasses adorned with a perfect rim of salt, ready to embark on this temporary escape from our worries. Pouring each of us a drink, I carefully distributed the refreshing concoctions, a tangible symbol of camaraderie and shared moments.

Gathering everyone's attention, I relayed the information Zoe entrusted me with; their ears perked with curiosity.

"We never got to finish looking at Veronica's email. Maybe there is something we are missing?" Charlotte's voice carried a note of determination, her gaze scanning the table for confirmation from the rest of us.

"Agreed," I concurred, my gaze meeting Charlotte's. "I have a feeling Gary knows something." With a slight pause, I proceeded to share with my companions the peculiar reaction Gary exhibited upon seeing a particular photo Veronica uncovered on Arba's Facebook page. He recognized someone in the image, someone that eluded my grasp. The mystery hung in the air, intertwining with the fragrant aromas of the drinks Zoe had just served us. We ordered our lunch, and the table descended into silence.

Wilma's voice broke through as we sipped our drinks, contemplating the possibilities that lie before us. Her determination was undeterred by the uncertainties looming over her health. "Alright, everyone. Stop the moping. We don't know if I have cancer, and I'm not letting this put a downer on our first vacation together in years. Now, Lisa, open the last email attachment, and let's figure out what is happening."

Eyes filled with renewed resolve and shared purpose, we all nodded in agreement. My fingers brushed against the touchscreen of my phone as I opened the final dossier, delving into Robyn's story. Our collective focus sharpened as we dissected each piece of information, carefully weighing the evidence against our growing list of suspects, while we couldn't dismiss Robyn entirely, the possibility of her involvement as an accomplice.

Veronica's thorough research on Robyn yielded a detailed and extensive attachment that was significantly longer than the profiles of the other individuals we examined. Robyn was highly active on various social media platforms, leaving a digital trail for us to follow. She maintained accounts on Facebook, Instagram, and LinkedIn, showcasing her talents as a skilled makeup artist and demonstrating a genuine passion for her clients. The glowing five-star reviews on her business pages attested to her expertise and dedication.

However, Robyn's approach to online privacy was either lacking or nonchalant. Her Facebook profile was entirely open, granting access to anyone who stumbled upon it. Filled with numerous pictures capturing her and Seth's journey to the cruise, along with love-themed poems, and what my daughter would refer to as "vague-booking" statuses.

Recalling my own experience with social media during Veronica's high school years, I couldn't help but reflect on the tendency of people to post cryptic updates, inviting others to inquire about their issues while simultaneously feigning reluctance to discuss them. To me, it seemed childish and draining. I silently expressed gratitude that social media and the internet hadn't existed during my own youth. I could only imagine the potentially embarrassing and trivial things we might have posted, things that time had mercifully allowed us to forget.

A Facebook memory status came up as I scrolled. It read: *Just a Little Bird and her Gray. I love you, brother. Family doesn't always mean blood.* Below the caption was a more recent picture taken that couldn't have been more than a few years ago.

We finally figured out who Gray was. We were looking straight into the face of Gary, our cruise director. He had his arm around Robyn, smiling. The pose seemed familiar. I opened up the picture Veronica sent from Arba's Facebook.

It was him, alright. Younger, fifty pounds lighter, and more hair. But Gray was most certainly Gary. Family might not always be blood, but was Gary willing to spill some for someone he considered his sister?

A palpable tension filled the air as we absorbed the implications of our findings. The silence, unusual for our chatty group, lingered until Wilma broke it with her astute observation.

"Did you see how scared Gary was when you dropped the picture from Arba's Facebook? It was as if he'd seen a ghost," she remarked, her voice carrying a mixture of concern and curiosity.

We all nodded in agreement, our minds processing the significance of Gary's reaction. He seemed acutely aware that we were on the brink of uncovering the truth about his identity. Wilma's insight struck a nerve, amplifying our determination to unravel the web of secrets.

"I can't help but wonder if the cruise line owners are aware they have an ex-felon on their payroll," Charlotte mused, her tone laced with suspicion and concern. It was a valid question, given Seth's shady history and the possibility Gary might be involved in illicit activities.

Joining the conversation, I expressed my own thoughts. "Considering Seth's reputation as a swindler, it's plausible that he may have used Robyn as a means to get to Gary. I think Gary might have been the whistle-blower who put Seth behind bars. But what strikes me is the gaps in Robyn's timeline. It's as though she deliberately removed or concealed certain posts, or perhaps she took a hiatus from social media altogether."

"Lisa, you should email Veronica again and ask her to dive deeper into Gary. We need to figure out his last name if he doesn't share the same one as Robyn." Beverly drank her margarita, and it looked like something caught her attention.

"Agreed. She did write, 'Family doesn't always mean blood.' " A sentiment all of us felt toward each other. I could feel the weight of the quote settling onto each of our shoulders.

"This could mean they have different parents or aren't family by marriage," Wilma said before grabbing the pitcher and pouring another round. No one objected to more liquid courage.

I remember Arba talking about how Robyn was in the system. Maybe Gary and Robyn were in the foster system together. But before I could bring it up, I looked at the entrance, and Martin walked in. His gaze caught mine, and he started heading toward our table.

"Hello ladies, Wilma, seeing you up and about is nice. I'm glad your tumble won't affect your vacation too much." Martin had a genuine look of concern on his face. I think he was getting more attached to us than he wanted to let on.

We all turned to each other and looked at Wilma. It wasn't our business to tell her story if she didn't want anyone to know about her results and the magnitude to which it could affect her life.

"Hello, Martin. It wasn't a tumble. I did not fall or trip. I take Pilates, yoga, and barre. I have fantastic balance. I was shoved. Someone intentionally pushed me down the stairs. Now, I know you are trying to solve a murder, but have you been able to look at the cameras in that staircase and get the culprit?" Wilma's voice was filled with frustration and a desperate need for answers.

Martin's ears turned red, and he looked visibly embarrassed. After clearing his throat, he finally responded. "We had a glitch in our system during that time. Our cameras for that area of the ship were off for twenty minutes. My team didn't catch it because they were dealing with something else on the ship, and there were hundreds of cameras throughout the ship. It is hard to figure out what happened. Some tech guys think it was an internet drop or a power surge."

Charlotte, surprising us with her knowledge of surveillance cameras and the internet, asked, "If it was a glitch, were any other cameras affected? Or was there a drop in the internet connection in the computer lab?"

We turned, taken aback by Charlotte's unexpected expertise. She explained, "I am in the middle of researching a new book, and I needed to know about surveillance cameras and how they are connected to other networks. It's fascinating." She took a deliberate sip of her drink, clearing her throat.

Martin, recognizing the significance of Charlotte's questions, pulled out his notebook and diligently wrote down every detail she provided. "I actually didn't ask or know to ask. This is the first time we've had anything like this happen on the ship. But, Wilma, I promise you we will find the culprit." He made a slight turn to leave but paused when I caught his attention.

"Martin, can you answer us one more question?"

"It depends. I can't talk about an ongoing investigation. We will dock in Cozumel tomorrow morning and hand the investigation to the proper authorities."

"We totally understand. We all want the perpetrator to be caught and served justice. We just want to know Gary's last name."

Martin's eyes squinted in suspicion. "Why do you want Gary's last name? He is the cruise director. We don't need to be pointing fingers at random people."

"That is correct, Martin. We don't. We just want to find out a little more about him. He acted strangely yesterday and today. Either you can tell us his name and lift our curiosity, or we can find out ourselves and get into more trouble. It is up to you." I smirked.

He sighed. He knew I was right. It was better for him to give in to a frustratingly stubborn woman like myself. He rubbed his temples with his fingers. "Baggs."

"Pardon me?" I asked.

"His last name is Baggs. Gary Baggs. Now, if that is all, I will reach out to our tech guys and see if they can pinpoint when or if the servers or internet service went down."

He went to turn away but paused mid-step and turned back around. There was a kindness in his eyes I hadn't seen before. "Ladies, if you are correct, and Wilma was shoved, this means the killer is getting more reckless. They have killed before. They won't hesitate to do it again. I would recommend you all do a buddy system. None of you should be alone. You have put yourself into this investigation, and the killer seems to know that. Please be careful." Martin walked away, and we all turned to each other.

"All for one," Wilma said.

"One for all," the rest of us chorused as we clanked our glasses together.

We weren't about to let someone bully us. We did one summer and lost someone because of it. Granted, we were children, but we aren't now. We were going to catch a killer.

Chapter Thirty-One

After walking outside the elevators, we made our way to our respective rooms to prepare for the final dining night aboard the boat. The upcoming meals would be a departure from the usual restaurant setting, with cafeteria-style options on the Lido Deck or meals enjoyed on our beach excursions. Given the revelation about Gary's true identity, I took it upon myself to email Veronica, urging her to conduct another thorough investigation into Gary's background. There was an undeniable sense of unease surrounding him, and we needed concrete evidence before jumping to conclusions.

Upon entering our room, I couldn't help but notice Wilma's usual vibrant energy seemed slightly subdued. I could only imagine the weight of uncertainty she was carrying. The fear of not knowing—whether she would fall ill, if her life would be consumed by the relentless battle against cancer, or what the future held.

However, knowing Wilma's resilient spirit, I was confident she would put on a brave face and find joy in every moment. She wouldn't let cancer dampen her exuberance. In fact, she would bring smiles to the faces of everyone she encountered at the hospital. Yet, in this private moment, she was allowed to grapple with her own fears and anxieties. Despite it all, I reassured myself she would be fine and planning her next adventure like rock climbing the following weekend. We simply had to wait until we returned home to find the answers plaguing her and all of us.

Wilma could sense my thoughts. Having spent so much time together, we developed an uncanny ability almost to anticipate each other's thinking.

"Listen, Lisa, we don't know if anything is actually wrong with me. Until I get more testing from my doctor and can interpret the results myself, I am choosing to believe I am perfectly healthy," Wilma asserted, determination shining in her eyes. "I feel great. In fact, this is the best I've felt in my entire life. I am free from burdens and family obligations, and I am finally able to breathe. Right now, all I want is to dress in an age-defying outfit that makes me feel alive and enjoy another drink. Oh, and of course, let's not forget about catching a killer. That's not too much to ask for, is it?"

As Wilma's gaze met mine, I detected a hint of sadness and a plea I'd never seen before. She was asking for permission to be selfish, but the truth was, she never needed my consent to be her authentic self. It dawned on me that Wilma always harbored a fear of disappointing others despite her trailblazing nature and willingness to break barriers. Now, she was ready to fully embrace and love herself, a step many, including myself, often struggled to take.

Smiling warmly, I reassured her. "It's definitely not too much to ask, my dear. Now, tell me, what sexy ensemble did you pack that will leave these gentlemen drooling?"

Wilma laughed and turned towards her luggage, playfully teasing, "Oh, Lisa, just you wait. By the time I step out of the bathroom, you might even be tempted to hit on me." With a chuckle, she closed the bathroom door, hiding her garment bag from view.

As for myself, I opted for a lovely green slip dress accompanied by black strappy heeled sandals, a birthday gift from Veronica a couple of years ago. I styled my silver hair into a messy bun, intentionally letting a few strands frame my face. I added soft curls to those strands and adorned my neck with my favorite gold pendant necklace featuring an intricately embossed tulip. Diamond stud earrings completed the look, and with a light touch of blush, mascara, and lip balm, I felt ready for our final extravagant dining experience. Little did I know the lasting impact this evening would have on me.

Richard stood at the glass front doors of the dining hall, exuding his usual charm and dashing appearance. Whether in khaki shorts and a polo shirt, or a well-tailored suit and tie, he always managed to look impeccable. As we approached him, a rush of warmth flushed my cheeks, and I couldn't help but feel a flutter of anticipation. Richard gracefully bowed and planted kisses on each of our cheeks, lingering just a bit longer on mine. Or perhaps I imagined it, caught up in wishful thinking.

Uncertain of what was happening to me, I couldn't deny a romantic entanglement was the last thing I needed after everything I'd been through in the past month. I glanced over at Wilma, who was laughing heartily at Richard's playful banter, and she looked absolutely stunning. True to her word, she'd chosen a tea-length dinner dress made of black silk-like fabric. The neckline featured a teasing teardrop-shaped cutout over her décolletage, while the back plunged into a deep V shape, secured with delicate lace tied at the nape of her neck.

She completed her ensemble with open-toed black lace heels that would have brought me to my knees had I attempted to walk in them.

Witnessing my friends enjoying themselves radiating confidence was a breath of fresh air, . Beverly caught my eye, adorned in a floral A-line dress with intricate embroidered mesh detailing. Paired with satin Mary Jane shoes, the outfit perfectly matched her vibrant and distinctive personality. She had a way of making you feel like you were in the presence of the world's best grandma—someone you wanted to cuddle up with.

Charlotte, on the other hand, embraced her unique sense of style with a 1950s vintage green knee-length plaid swing dress. The outfit, paired with heeled Mary Janes, transformed her into the embodiment of a perfect 1950s librarian. Sometimes, I couldn't help but feel Charlotte was born in the wrong era, but she'd found her place in her career and life. I admired her unwavering authenticity and her refusal to seek fulfillment from others. There was much I could learn from her.

Richard gallantly pulled out chairs for everyone as we approached the table, ensuring the last remaining seat was beside me. Our attentive waitress, Rachelle, promptly arrived to take our drink orders, and we perused the menu to explore the tantalizing options for the evening. My choices included a classic Caesar salad to start, followed by the delectable chicken Milanese as the main course. For dessert, I couldn't resist the temptation of the baked alaska; its warm and sweet allure beckoning me.

The ambiance of the dining area exuded elegance, with soft lighting casting a warm glow upon the tastefully decorated tables. The clinking of cutlery and the pleasant hum of conversations filled the air as guests savored their meals and relished themselves in the company of their loved ones.

As we eagerly awaited our appetizers, to our surprise, Gary Baggs and none other than Robyn entered the dining hall together. Their arrival seemed more like a romantic outing than siblings joining for a meal. I couldn't help but feel a wave of revulsion as I observed the way Gary's gaze hungrily roamed up and down Robyn's figure. It was a display that left me thoroughly disgusted. Sensing our table growing quiet and our gazes fixed upon him, Gary turned to Robyn and motioned in our direction, prompting them to make their way toward us. Uncertainty filled the air as we exchanged glances, unsure what to expect when they finally reached our table.

"Good evening, ladies and sir," Gary greeted us with a nod. "I hope you're enjoying a delightful and relaxing trip thus far. Once again, Mrs. Point, I am sincerely sorry to hear about your unfortunate incident, and I hope your recovery is progressing well. Please allow me to treat you all to drinks this evening." Gary's smile suggested a few beverages would be enough to placate us, hoping we would cease our inquiries into what truly transpired.

I cleared my throat and spoke up for the table. "Thank you so much, Mr. Baggs." I let him know we knew who he was. "I just wanted to give you my condolences about Seth. I now know you and Robyn were close to him, and I am sorry for your loss." The blood drained from Robyn and Gary's faces as they floundered, trying to find a response.

"Thank you, Lisa," Robyn responded, looking down at her hands, clutching Gary's arm like a vice grip.

Gary cleared his throat, attempting to assert his authority. "We appreciate your concern," he said, his voice laced with condescension. "But let's be realistic here. We are soon arriving in Cozumel, and it's time for you ladies to redirect your focus. Leave the investigation to the professionals. You can go back to your knitting circles, book clubs, or whatever women of your age occupy themselves with."

I could feel a collective surge of indignation among our group. Gary's attempt to belittle and dismiss us only fueled our determination. We were not about to be patronized and underestimated. Wilma leaned forward, her gaze blazing with resolve.

"Mr. Baggs," she said, her voice steady but laced with a hint of defiance. "We understand the police have a role to play, but we have a personal stake in finding the truth. We won't simply sit idly by and let others handle it. We are strong, capable women, and we'll pursue justice with every ounce of our being."

The air crackled with determination as the rest of us nodded in agreement. Gary's illusion of control began to waver, realizing he was facing a group of fierce and relentless women. He would soon discover that underestimating us was a grave mistake. We were united in our resolve to uncover the killer and the person responsible for Wilma's fall, and nothing would stand in our way.

"I know I'd love to go back to our everyday lives. Wouldn't you ladies?" Wilma continued. "Just as soon as the authorities arrest the person who was craven enough to push an elderly woman down the stairs."

"Craven?" Robyn's face twisted into confusion, but Gary's vocabulary was a little more robust than Robyn's due to the fire in his gaze.

"Ah. Yes, dear. Craven. You know, coward? Yellowbelly? Wuss? Fraidy-Cat? Wimp?" Charlotte started spouting synonyms at an incredible speed. Having an author at the table made the conversation a little more robust.

With every new synonym Charlotte spouted, Gary's face grew increasingly rigid, and the warmth that once colored his cheeks spread down his neck. His discomfort was evident as his expression tightened, resembling a piece of lumber, rigid and unyielding. He grimaced begrudgingly, his resentment palpable as he glanced at the table and took hold of Robyn's hand.

"Come on, dear," he said curtly, his voice strained. "We mustn't keep these guests from their last meal. We have things to discuss. Have a good evening, everyone. We shall see you soon."

Robyn's pained expression revealed her discomfort at Gary's forceful grip on her hand. It was evident she had no desire to engage in discussions with him, but that concern was overshadowed by a sense of unease settling over our table. Gary's words felt more like a thinly veiled threat than a casual farewell. I was disheartened to witness Robyn exchanging one controlling figure in her life for another. My disappointment was tinged with worry for her well-being.

"What did he mean by our last meal?" I mumbled to myself, my voice barely audible amidst the resumed chatter at the table.

Richard, sitting next to me, overheard my question and turned to me with a concerned look on his face. Taking a bite of his buttered bread, he nodded understandingly. "You felt the threat in that as well, eh?"

he remarked, his voice lowered.

Nodding in agreement, I continued to tear apart a piece of bread on my plate, my mind working to connect the scattered puzzle pieces. "It felt like he was talking about a final meal like a prisoner would have before they walked down to the execution room," I said, the gravity of the situation sinking in.

Beverly, who'd been engaged in her own conversation, now joined in, her voice filled with unease. "I agree. It sounded like an ominous threat," she said, her eyes scanning the faces of our group.

Wilma and Charlotte, who'd paused their own side conversation, tuned in to our discussion and offered their input. Wilma shook her head in disgust, her expression reflecting her disdain. "I think he didn't like looking like a chump in front of Robyn. I have a feeling that, since they are not actually related by blood, Gary's feelings for her are more than platonic," she speculated.

Charlotte's frustration was evident as she voiced her thoughts. "Why can't some people get a clue? I feel horrible for Robyn. She goes from one man trying to control her life and hurting her to Gary, who also wants to control her," she lamented, her concern evident in her tone.

The table fell into a momentary silence as we all contemplated the tangled web of relationships and potential threats that surrounded us. It was clear our suspicions about Gary were deepening, and we were more determined than ever to uncover the truth and protect Robyn from any harm.

"A person who has been abused most of their life will be pulled into that world no matter what. In Robyn's mind, she might see this as a step up. At least Gary isn't hitting her. Mental abuse is just as bad, but the bruises aren't on the outside," Richard added as Rachelle approached with our meals, and we all started eating in thoughtful silence.

Curiosity piqued; I couldn't help but wonder about the depth of Richard's knowledge on the subject of abuse. From his outward appearance, he seemed untouched by the scars of pain and suffering. Yet, appearances can be deceiving. I found myself increasingly intrigued by this enigmatic British man. What lay beneath his extraordinary face, flawless hair, and impeccable fashion sense? There had to be more than meets the eye, and I was determined to find out.

Chapter Thirty-Two

My phone buzzed in my clutch on my lap as dinner finished up. The only notification I set to send was for my email. This had to be the research update from Veronica on Gary.

"Ladies and Richard! It looks like Veronica has come in 'clutch.' " I put air quotes around the clutch. This was a word Veronica used the last time we'd gone shopping together. It didn't refer to my purse in my lap, either. Everyone stopped what they were doing or took the last bite of their baked alaska, as was Beverly's right. It was pretty delicious.

"Well, open it!" Wilma demanded impatiently.

I gazed at my phone screen, my heart racing with anticipation and trepidation. This email held the potential to unravel the mystery that had consumed our attention for days. It was a bittersweet realization, for as much as I relished the exhilaration and camaraderie this adventure brought us, it also left one of our own injured and in need of justice. We needed answers, and Veronica's email promised to provide some much-needed clarity.

With a trembling finger, I tapped the email icon, revealing two messages awaiting my attention. As I'd anticipated, the first was indeed from Veronica, but the second caught me off guard—a message from the Board of Education at a local community college. My curiosity was piqued, but for the moment, I set it aside, knowing Veronica's email held the key to our current quest. Taking a deep breath, I clicked open Veronica's email, the contents unfurling before my eyes.

Mom, I don't know what you are up to, but I hope you and the aunties are staying safe. This guy really doesn't look good. You said that he was the cruise director of your ship? If you ask me, you might want to get off and find another way home. Here is everything that I could find on "Gary Baggs." I do hope that you are trying to stay safe and are having fun. You mean the world to me, and I would be devastated if anything happened to you.

Love you!

Veronica

Excitement coursed through my veins as I delved into the attachments accompanying Veronica's email. Financial records, Department of Human Services documents, and an email from the higher-ups at the cruise line awaited my eager scrutiny. I clicked open the financial document with a sense of purpose, eager to uncover the truth hidden within its digital pages.

As the spreadsheet unfolded before my eyes, I couldn't believe what I was seeing. Gary, it seemed, was drowning in a sea of debt. Multiple entries from quick loan companies indicated he owed over half a million dollars. The weight of his financial burden was staggering, painting a picture of desperation and an insidious motive. It became clear someone in such dire straits would be driven to steal from an employer or involve themselves in whatever illicit activities Seth might have been involved in.

Without hesitation, I shared the shocking revelation

with the rest of the group, presenting the evidence and voicing my thoughts. The collective gasp and furrowed brows mirrored my own astonishment. It was undeniable—this discovery had the potential to turn anyone, especially someone who'd been given a second chance by the company, against their benefactors. And if Gary had a gambling problem, the cruise ship's lavish casino would provide ample opportunity to dig himself even deeper into financial ruin.

"Open the DHS file next. I wonder how Veronica got a hold of that one. Those are supposed to stay buttoned up pretty tightly," Wilma said.

Beverly nodded and added, "There were many times when a DHS report would have helped at the office when we had patients from the foster system."

I opened the file attached to the email and a picture filled my screen. A photograph capturing a young and vulnerable Gary, his teenage frame projecting an air of fragility and sadness. My heart ached at the sight, contemplating the countless children who suffer due to circumstances beyond their control. It stirred within me a profound desire to provide love and care to every child needing a nurturing home.

As I read aloud from the file, the details of Gary's troubled childhood unfolded before us. After the tragic car accident that claimed his mother's life, he was left without any immediate family to care for him. From that moment, he became a nomad within the foster care system, bouncing from one home to another. It was evident that most prospective parents sought infants they could shape and mold according to their own values, leaving older children like Gary overlooked and deprived of the stable environment they desperately needed.

While this glimpse into Gary's past shed light on the hardships he endured, it did not excuse any potential wrongdoings he may have committed aboard the ship or the harm he may have inflicted on others. In fact, this revelation only heightened our suspicions and cast a more ominous shadow over his actions. It became clear the scars of his tumultuous upbringing could have left a lasting impact, influencing his behavior in ways we were yet to uncover.

We all agreed Gary was someone to look out for, but we couldn't accuse someone of murder when we didn't have hard facts to back up our feelings. We could talk to Martin about this tomorrow morning before we dock. Maybe something Veronica came up with, and we'd seen, would help Martin get closer to the killer and whoever attacked Wilma. I felt in my gut it was the same person.

Everyone took one more drink or bite of their meal and got up to leave. As we started for the doors, Richard grabbed my hand, and I stopped and turned.

"My dear, it is such a wonderful night. You look stunning. And well, I'm dressed sharply as well. Could we take a long walk around the boat and chat? To get to know each other a little bit more. I will walk you back to your room." Richard's eyes held a vulnerability I'd only gotten glimpses of throughout the trip.

I turned to the ladies and could tell they were trying to keep their snickering to a lower level. Wilma locked eyes with me and smiled a genuine, full smile. The first since we all found out she might be sick. I felt like I owed it to her to try. If I was being more honest with myself, I wanted to go. I wanted to have the flame ignite in my bosom again. Some people don't need a companion, but in my time on Earth, I find life much more enjoyable when you have someone to spend it with.

"I'd enjoy that very much, Richard."

As I watched the ladies stepping into the elevator, a knowing grin danced across my lips. I could already predict the topic of their conversation for the rest of the night, and I knew I would be asked to spill the juicy details in the days to come. Let them gossip to their heart's content. After all, they're well aware I'm not one to spill the beans. A lady never kisses and tells.

Ah, the thrill of a kiss. It's been quite some time since I've experienced the flutter of butterflies in my stomach

"So, where to, Richard?" I asked.

"That would be the bow of the ship. I think it is quiet this time of the evening and has lovely benches where we can talk and get to know each other a little more. Wilma has mentioned some things about you, but I'd love to learn it firsthand." He offered his arm, and I put my left arm through his. Our heights matched perfectly. I didn't have to look up too much to meet his gaze while we chatted.

"What would you like to know about me?" I inquired, feeling the gentle breeze tousle my hair as I inhaled deeply. The salty tang of the ocean air filled my lungs, expelling the stress that'd been building inside me ever since we discovered Seth's lifeless body on the Lido Deck.

"Well, I want to know everything about you. But let's start with something easy. What is your favorite book?" he inquired.

I couldn't help but tease him in response, a playful

glint in my eyes. "Oh, you said you'd start with something easy, huh? Asking me to pick a favorite book is like asking me to choose a favorite child." I chuckled. The mental catalog of books raced through my mind, each holding a special place in my heart. *Pride and Prejudice* by Jane Austen, *The Help* by Kathryn Stockett, and *The Shell Seekers* by Rosamunde Pilcher all clamored for attention, but I couldn't simply pick one. Each book had its own profound meaning to me, and I told him as much.

"Alright, what about your favorite child? You wouldn't have too much issue with that one. You only have one. Veronica, right?" He turned his smile up a notch, catching my breath in my throat.

"That's right," I replied, pride and wistfulness evident in my voice. "She's in her thirties now, following the same career path as me. The travel bug has bitten her too, and she's eager to dig her hands into the Earth and uncover its hidden treasures."

Watching Veronica grow up and forge her path so closely aligned with mine was a bittersweet feeling. There were times when I stumbled along the way, and it wasn't always smooth sailing. But I knew she needed to navigate her own journey and make her own decisions. I would be there to offer guidance and advice, but ultimately, she had to discover the secrets of the world and learn how to thrive within them on her own.

"Ah! I bet she is as vibrant and full of life as you." Richard's genuine tone didn't go unnoticed. It was clear he was a man who spoke his mind and meant what he said. That kind of authenticity was a rare find, and it intrigued me.

Curiosity sparked within me, and I couldn't help but

Death on Deck

inquire about his own life. "Do you have any children of your own?" I asked, genuinely interested.

He let out a sigh, and a hint of sadness crept into his voice. "No, I wasn't fortunate enough to meet someone with whom I wanted to share my life and have children. I've been married once, but it wasn't meant to be."

His response struck a chord, and a sense of empathy washed over me. "What happened with your last marriage? And if it makes you feel any better, I've been married and divorced four times myself," I admitted with a wry smile. "Marriage wasn't my cup of tea, or perhaps I wasn't theirs."

I took a moment to collect my thoughts, realizing that in the presence of Richard, I had opened up more than I'd intended. But there was something about being on this ship that created a different reality, where inhibitions were momentarily set aside, and genuine connections could be formed.

The world outside faded away as we embarked on this journey. The rules and expectations of everyday life were put on hold, allowing us to be our true selves. This was a refreshing change to be seen and known by Richard for who I am now rather than the person I once was.

There was a certain sweetness in the lifelong friendships I had with the girls. They witnessed my growth, transformations, and even the less flattering aspects of my past. They knew me better than anyone else. The memories of our shared experiences made me cringe at times, but they also reminded me of the bonds we forged over the years.

Glancing over the ship's railing, I was met with a sight that evoked awe and trepidation. The world beyond the ship appeared enveloped in darkness like a vast abyss swallowing everything in its path. It created an illusion that we were the sole survivors in this secluded realm, granting us a sense of freedom and limitless possibilities. But deep down, my rational mind reminded me that actions always have consequences. The world kept a record of our deeds, both good and bad, and would eventually demand its due.

"Not at all. I married a con artist, it seems. She knew of my family, and my worth, if you will. She was twenty years my junior. I should have considered that, but you can't blame an old champ for hoping someone could love him, can you?" He didn't wait for my response. "That decision will always haunt me, but let's talk of happier things."

We made our way to the ship's bow, which reminded me of the movie Titanic. It was going to come up at some point in my mind. I felt the overwhelming itch to go to the front of the ship and stand up there. This time, I could be the "Queen of the World." We didn't need any more kings.

Richard and I strolled toward the benches, a gentle breeze caressing my skin and sending a shiver down my spine. The sun began its descent, taking its warmth with it, leaving a chill in the air. Ever the gentleman, Richard shrugged off his jacket and draped it across my shoulders, a gesture that warmed my heart as much as it did my body.

"Thank you." I snuggled into the warmth of the jacket. "I'm so sorry that you had to go through that. Some of my ex-husbands would not feel so kindly to me. But I only have to stay in touch with Veronica's dad, which is less and less as she ages."

"I am glad about that for you." Richard stared off into the night, lost in the distractions of his mind.

I sensed the shift in our conversation's tone and decided to redirect it toward lighter subjects. "But yes, let's change the subject. What are you most looking forward to when we disembark tomorrow? Any excursions planned?" I inquired, curious about Richard's plans for his time ashore. Considering his combination of business meetings and leisurely activities, I wondered if his trip was a mix of both.

Richard's eyes lit up with enthusiasm as he responded, "Ah, yes! This is my first cruise, and I've heard about the wide range of exciting excursions available. I'm particularly interested in swimming with dolphins and diving. How about you?"

Chuckling, I shared our usual routine. "Well, we girls tend to stick together. We find a beautiful beach, claim our chairs, and seek out a spot with unlimited beverages. It has always been a foolproof plan for us. After all the excitement in my life, sometimes it's nice to relax. However, I'd be thrilled to show you around Cozumel. I've been there a few times before."

"Oh? I'd love that. I think it would be splendid," he responded, leaning closer to me. I could feel the electricity in the air. The anticipation of his kiss sent shivers down my spine, and my heart pounded in my chest. Was I really about to let a man I barely knew kiss me?

Just as our lips were about to meet, a throat cleared, interrupting the moment. "I am so sorry to be interrupting. Mr. Taylor, we have a bit of an emergency in your room. There has been a burst pipe, and we need you to change rooms and check your belongings," a staff member explained, breaking the spell.

I could sense Richard's annoyance, his teeth grinding together, mirroring my own feelings. It was frustrating and amusing to be interrupted at such a crucial moment. He looked down at me with a ravishing smile and said, "Until next time, Lisa? Would you like me to walk you to your room first?"

Smiling back, I replied, "No, this seems important. I can make my way back to my room. There are still a lot of people around. There shouldn't be any issues. I'll see you tomorrow. I hope all of your things are okay. I can't imagine having all my belongings water-logged." Little did I know my journey back to the room would take longer than anticipated, filled with unexpected twists and turns.

Chapter Thirty-Three

While I knew a killer was aboard the ship, it was lovely to be alone for a little while. I was one of those people Veronica called an introverted extrovert. Although I love being around people and getting energized around my friends and family, it takes a lot from me. I have to have my downtime and be alone to recharge. I need time to spend on my thoughts. I hadn't realized until now that I hadn't had a lot of downtime since this vacation started.

Of course, that was part of the plan, wasn't it? I was trying to distract myself from life's troubles. And what was the best way to do that? To have my best friends around me twenty-four seven on a ship in the middle of nowhere, of course! Who knew we'd also throw in a murder and an assault on one of us? We liked to keep things active and exciting, didn't we?

I sat on the bench, basking in the warmth lingering from our stolen moment of intimacy. With my eyes closed, I let the gentle sea breeze caress my face, carrying the faint scent of salt and adventure. As the ship continued its voyage, the vast and seemingly endless ocean stretched before us, its deep, almost black expanse meeting the horizon in a seamless union. The rhythmic sound of waves breaking against the hull resonated in my ears, a constant reminder of our journey toward distant lands and elusive destinations.

Lost in my thoughts, I allowed myself to surrender to the peaceful solitude of the moment. Time blurred as I contemplated the mysteries unfolding on this voyage, both within and beyond the ship's confines.

Eventually, a playful chuckle escaped my lips as I imagined the assumptions my friends might have made about my whereabouts. I could almost picture their mischievous smiles and raised eyebrows, convinced I ventured to Richard's cabin to embark on a passionate escapade. Oh, the tales they would be weaving in their minds.

With a contented sigh, I gathered my resolve and rose from the bench, casting a final glance at the serene surroundings. The groups that had once populated the bow had dispersed, leaving behind an eerily quiet space. Determined to find my way back to the familiar corridors, I scanned the area and spotted an entrance to an elevator that had eluded my notice. It appeared to be a service elevator, but it didn't matter—it was an elevator, and it would take me to our floor, no matter the purpose it served.

I pressed the down button and went inside as the doors opened. This was indeed a service elevator. There were marks on the walls, probably from laundry carts and food carts, and footprints from people mopping the deck and tracking in dirt and grime.

It didn't have the nice carpet like the guest elevators, and there weren't any mirrors on the walls. I liked it a bit better, actually. No one needs to see their reflection so much once they hit a certain age. Or at least I didn't. I knew more and more lines were popping up daily on my face, around my eyes and mouth. I frowned, thinking I should really stop frowning so much.

The elevator doors slid open, revealing the familiar corridor of my designated floor. However, an unusual silence greeted me as I stepped into the hallway. The usual signs of late-night revelry and the occasional tipsy passengers vanished. It was as if an eerie stillness swallowed the entire floor.

I glanced around, noticing the absence of any fellow cruisers. The anticipation of the upcoming dock day lingered in the air, suggesting many guests opted for a night of rest to ensure a fun-filled adventure ashore. It made perfect sense, yet a subtle unease crept up within me.

Turning the corner, I continued down the hallway to my room, passing several doors along the way. It struck me that my room was situated quite a distance from the elevator, a fact that hadn't bothered me until now. The solitude of the empty corridor amplified the sense of isolation, heightening my awareness of the unfolding mystery on board.

Just as I was about to reach my room, a faint sound caught my attention—a whimper or a muted cry emanating from a nearby service stair entrance to my left. The rational part of me reminded me it wasn't my responsibility; we were facing a potential killer among us, and Martin had emphasized the importance of the buddy system for our safety.

But my compassionate and somewhat nosy nature urged me to investigate, unable to ignore the sound of distress. Curiosity mingled with caution as I hesitated, considering the risks involved. The tension between curiosity and self-preservation was palpable, like a taut wire ready to snap.

At that moment, I made a choice, setting aside the

logical concerns momentarily. The allure of uncovering the truth and extending a helping hand proved too strong. I cautiously approached the service stair entrance, my senses heightened, and prepared for any unforeseen twist or turn that awaited me within.

I slipped off my heeled sandals, realizing their impracticality in the dimly lit stairwell. The door creaked eerily as I pushed it open, sending a chill down my spine. The whimpering abruptly ceased, only to resume after a brief pause. I stood still, allowing my eyes to adjust to the darkness shrouding the hallway. To my dismay, the safety light that should have illuminated the area was inexplicably out, plunging the surroundings into deeper obscurity. Fumbling in my pocket, I retrieved my phone and activated its flashlight to guide me down the stairs.

As I descended into the service stairwell, I couldn't help but notice its remarkable cleanliness and meticulous organization, a stark contrast to my preconceived notion of such utility spaces. There were no leaking pipes or haphazardly strewn debris; everything seemed to be in its proper place. Casting a glance toward the attached hallway on the next level, I observed four doors within my line of sight. Three stood closed, while the one at the far end remained slightly ajar. The whimpering grew more distinct with each step, urging me forward.

With silent determination, I approached the partially open door, my heart pounding in anticipation. Peering cautiously into the room, my eyes widened in shock at the sight before me. There, bound and currently being gagged, was Robyn Leed—the last person I expected to find in such a distressing state.

Chapter Thirty-Four

A gasp escaped my lips before I could stifle it, reverberating through the eerie silence of the stairwell. It bounced off the walls, returning to me amplified, a chilling reminder of my recklessness. Despite my countless nights engrossed in cozy mysteries and glued to crime shows like NCIS, the weight of that knowledge offered no leverage at this moment. None of it had truly sunk in. I should have quietly retreated, sought help, and emerged as the hero in the end. But fate had other plans for me, far removed from the realm of heroism.

My gasp had been louder than anticipated, drawing the attention of the person responsible for Robyn's torment. As they turned to inspect the source of the sound, a surge of regret coursed through me. It was Gary, the cruise director himself. His gaze locked with mine, seething with a mixture of hatred and anger. Instinctively, I took a step back, my pulse quickening at the danger of crossing paths with a man who, until now, had seemed nothing more than an out-of-shape, balding figure perpetually drenched in sweat. Yet, in that chilling moment, he appeared more menacing than I'd ever imagined.

"YOU!?" Gary snarled as he shoved Robyn back onto the concrete floor and approached me slowly. The classic bad guy slow walk every killer in every horror movie had taken. I finally regained my legs and started running back toward the stairs. I leaped up the stairs as fast as my varicose veined legs let me. Gary lunged after me, but I had longer legs. He almost caught me as I turned the corner to go up one more flight to the door I'd initially entered.

I finally remembered having my heels in my hand and took a second to turn and throw one at him. The spike of the heel hit him in the temple as he turned to follow me up the stairs. He yelped in pain, but I didn't turn back to see if he stopped. I reached for the handle of the door. I could feel the blood circulating and pumping in my veins. My hands were sweaty and shaking. I turned the doorknob for freedom and opened it. I was about to run out when a strong hand gripped my neck and choked me. I dropped my other heel and started clawing the hand at my neck.

"You really thought you'd get away, you bitch?" Gary's breath assaulted my nose with alcohol and stale cigarettes..

I could feel my body shutting down from the lack of oxygen in my bloodstream. My eyes started to darken into tunnel vision. He picked me up in a bride-carrying hold, and the last thing I saw was my high heel propping the door to freedom open. It was my only lifeline.

Pain coursed through my body as I jolted awake, my tailbone protesting the rough impact against the unforgiving concrete floor. I winced, knowing the discomfort would linger, assuming I survived this ordeal. With wide eyes, I took in the grim surroundings from my new vantage point. Gary loomed above us, his heavy breaths betraying the strain of carrying my slight frame.

"You really should hit the gym more, Gary. It's great for your overall well-being. Although, where you're headed, I doubt there'll be much besides reading and working out to occupy your time," I quipped, mustering a hint of sarcasm. It was a feeble attempt, drawing inspiration from countless movies and TV shows, but I figured I might try my hand at the sardonic banter. If I managed to escape this predicament, I had room for improvement in my repertoire.

"Don't concern yourself with me. I'll be sending both you and Robyn to a watery grave. Tomorrow morning, I'll disembark this wretched existence and find my way to paradise," Gary sneered, his satisfaction palpable as he bound my wrists together with the same rope restraining Robyn, ensuring we were tethered together.

"You're planning to kill Robyn, too? But why?" I pressed, buying time for both of us. My friends would soon realize I was missing. Wilma, in particular, would be anxiously waiting, eager to catch up on all the gossip. She knew me well enough to expect a call if I stayed out late or ended up sleeping over on a first date, just to spare her needless worry.

Gary's gaze shifted to Robyn, who was helpless, her hands tightly bound, and her voice silenced by the gag. Tears welled in her eyes, a mixture of fear and betrayal evident in her expression. Memories of the pictures I'd seen on her Facebook flashed through my mind. The images portrayed a cheerful, trusting dynamic between Robyn, Seth, and Gary. But now, reality shattered the illusion I'd formed. This is a stark reminder that what we see online is merely a carefully curated version of someone's life, not an accurate representation of their true experiences or the world they live in.

"This is on her!" He directed his resentment toward

Robyn, kicking her legs callously as he paced towards the door, his eyes burning with fury. "She chose the wrong man to love. The wrong man to back up. I told her to stick with me from the beginning, and she'd go far. But no, she had to go with The Charmer. The Manipulator. The Destroyer of People." Gary's rage and frustration reverberated through the room. His voice filled with a mix of desperation and anger.

I took a moment to glance at Robyn. Her face, etched with fear and pain, trembled under his gaze.

I couldn't bear to witness such injustice and cruelty. The boiling anger within me surged to the surface, pushing aside any lingering fear. "Are you telling me that you would kill her because she doesn't reciprocate your feelings?" I challenged, my voice quivering with a blend of anger and disbelief.

"SHE COULD HAVE HAD EVERYTHING! I WOULD HAVE GIVEN HER EVERYTHING! BUT I WASN'T ENOUGH!." Gary turned toward me, his face contorted with anguish.

Tears streamed down his cheeks as he unleashed his pent-up emotions, his words laced with a toxic mix of sadness and resentment. His outburst echoed in the room, and I hoped desperately someone, somewhere on the ship, overheard his confession. The ship couldn't be completely devoid of life; there had to be a night crew, a vigilant ear that caught even a fraction of his words.

"That is not your place, Gary. I can tell that Robyn loves you. She cares for you. But you cannot control the ways of the heart." I slowly scooted closer to Robyn so I could try untying her hands. Gary wasn't paying attention to me. He was too wrapped up in his own world and twisted thoughts to be paying me any attention at that moment.

"You could have learned to love me. You would have wanted for nothing. But if I can't have you, no one can." Gary approached us; his gaze darted around the room, searching for something specific. His gaze landed on a rolling laundry basket that seemed out of place amidst the cluttered inventory overflow room. Boxes filled with toiletries, towels, and laundry detergent were scattered haphazardly, revealing the utilitarian nature of the space. It became evident this room served as a storage area for housekeeping supplies.

I couldn't help but notice the stark contrast in Gary's appearance. Gone were his usual flamboyant, tropical-themed shirts and extravagant attire. Instead, he wore a plain steward uniform, blending in with the ship's staff. He hurriedly placed a hat on his balding head, effectively disguising himself. Reluctantly, his disguise worked surprisingly well.

The rolling laundry basket stood prominently in the room; its sturdy steel frame and thick linen basket made it capable of accommodating a person or two. It was a familiar sight, often used by the housekeeping staff to transport fresh bedding and towels between rooms. Realization dawned on me—this would be our means of escape, a method of leaving undetected. It was a clever choice, considering the ship's vast number of rooms and the constant need for laundry services. An individual maneuvering a laundry basket at this late hour wouldn't raise suspicion in the bustling corridors.

"Both of you, stand up. You are going in this basket, and you will remain quiet if you know what is good for you." He raised a pipe that was sporting an inch-long crack at the far end of it.

Robyn and I managed to help each other off the floor. With our hands tied at the wrist, getting the leverage to stand was challenging. Gary pushed both of us in the back with the pipe to get us moving toward the laundry basket. I recoiled at the idea of getting into the basket and being unable to control my surroundings.

"I am not great in tight spaces, young man. You can still stop what you are doing. You haven't done much damage to us yet. You could let us go and run. You know this ship better than most people. I'm sure you could hide and get off in the morning. Disappear. We wouldn't say anything, would we, Robyn?" I looked for confirmation; even though she was gagged, she could still move her head. Her gaze met mine, and she started nodding enthusiastically.

"Nice try, hag. Martin is on to me. I think I have you to blame for that. He knows this ship as well as I do. He will figure out I cut the wires to the hallway camera, pushed your nosy friend down the stairs, and killed Seth. Nothing and no one will get in my way this time." Gary pushed me again harder with the pipe. I'd have a circle-shaped bruise on my back in the morning if I lived that long.

As the reality of our escape plan sank in, my heart pounded in my chest, and a cold sweat broke out on my palms. The mere thought of climbing into the laundry basket sent shivers down my spine. The room constricted around me, the air growing stale and suffocating. Panic welled up inside me, and I couldn't shake off the feeling of impending darkness closing in.

Overwhelmed by fear, I pushed away from the laundry basket, desperate to escape this suffocating space. I turned to run, but before I could take more than a few steps, a searing pain erupted at the back of my head. The world spun around me, and as my vision blurred, everything faded into darkness.

Chapter Thirty-Five

I found myself abruptly awakened in a place I hadn't laid eyes on in four decades. I was back in Cabin Four at Camp Cimarron. I couldn't fathom how I ended up here again, but everything looked exactly as it did during that first summer. With a surge of determination, I pushed myself up from the bed and glanced around the familiar surroundings. The five beds in the tiny cabin stood empty, meticulously made. The walls beside them were adorned with photographs, drawings, and personal mementos of everyone who once occupied these bunks. My gaze settled on the bed labeled "Diane." A sudden pang shot through my head, momentarily blurring my vision. I shook off the discomfort and clarity returned.

As I rubbed my eyes, I looked down at my hands. They were youthful, devoid of age spots and wrinkles. It couldn't be real. I couldn't possibly be here again. I made my way toward the cabin's front door, passing by a full-length mirror fixed to the wall. And there, reflecting back at me, was a fifteen-year-old version of myself. The lines etched by laughter, grief, and the trials of life vanished, replaced by smooth, unblemished skin that hadn't yet weathered the storm of existence. I was me, but not me—a teenager's body inhabited by an adult mind. To some, it might have been a dream come true.

The windows were open, inviting a gentle breeze and making the curtains dance in the sunlight. The sounds of birds and nature filled the air. Everyone must be outside, waiting for me. This could be a fresh start, a chance to make things right. But the dream soon transformed into a haunting nightmare, dredging up my deepest fears.

As I approached the door, a scream pierced the air, sending a chilling sense of déjà vu down my spine. I had heard that scream in my nightmares every night since I was fifteen. This time, I believed I could prevent the impending catastrophe. I sprinted out into the fading daylight, the sun retreating behind darkening clouds. Moonlight filtered through the gaps in the trees, casting eerie shadows.

The scream echoed once more, followed by sounds of struggle. Determination fueled my steps, driving me closer to the source of the anguish. But before I could reach the edge of the woods, a pair of hands seized me from behind, muffling my cries with a grimy palm.

Not again! I thought, fighting against the assailant's grip. I had to succeed this time.

"Listen, girl. This isn't about you," a gruff voice hissed in my ear, tainted by the stench of alcohol. "No one's here tonight. They're all at the bonfire, where you should be. Now, let's get you secured. I'll be back for you once I'm done."

Thrust backward, pain seared through my leg as I tumbled onto the dirt floor. I glanced down, my fingers touching a wound, dark fluid staining my fingertips. I needed help and soon. Searching frantically, I discovered a shovel and rake nearby. I was trapped in a tool shed, one of two wooden structures on the camp's property. This one was rarely used due to its inconvenient location. In this desolate place, I could scream for help all I wanted, but no one would hear. I had to rely on myself to escape.

But before I could begin attacking the rotting door, a scream—a familiar voice that resonated deeper than my own—reached my ears. "Please, don't! Don't touch me! I'll do anything! Stop! NO!"

It was Diane. I knew it.

Chapter Thirty-Six

After a long while, my surroundings were moving, and I was covered by blankets and towels when I opened my eyes. There was another body next to mine. As I turned away from the blankets on top of me, my gaze met with Robyn. Her eyes were bloodshot and wide. Her mouth was still gagged, and I suddenly realized mine was also. I'd been knocked out twice in one night. If I made it until the morning, my head wouldn't be thanking me. If I made it, it would be the biggest question.

I brought my hands to my mouth to remove the gag, but it was too tightly tied, and with my hands tied to Robyn's, there was no way I would be able to remove it.

Outside of the cart sounded quiet. It was late, and most passengers had already returned to their bedrooms or were on their way. The cart paused, and I heard the elevator ding. We were pushed through the opening as I listened to the wheels on the cart click on the gap between the floor and the elevator. The doors started closing when I heard someone holler, "Wait! Hold the door for me!" My heart started beating in anticipation of being found and freed.

"Sorry! Get the next one!" Gary said in a deeper Australian -accented voice as I heard him quickly press what I assumed was the close door button. Gary's voice sent a shiver down my spine, instantly recognizable from when Seth was taken into Martin's office. The memory flooded back, mixing with the current reality, intensifying the fear gripping me. The door closed, sealing us in, and the towels covering our faces were yanked away. The air was thick with menace as Gary taunted us.

"I bet you girls thought you would get rescued, eh?" His words dripped with smugness, igniting a seething anger deep within me. The taste of bile rose in my throat, burning with the intensity of my fury.

I strained against my restraints, desperate to lunge at Gary, to unleash the pent-up rage coursing through my veins. But I knew, deep down, our chances of escape were slim, and the impending threat of death loomed ominously. Helplessness washed over me once again, reminiscent of that dreadful day when Diane was taken.

In that moment, I confronted the harsh reality that our lives hung in the balance, and there was little I could do to change our fate.

"You're never going to get away. You can stop struggling." Gary chortled as we waited for the elevator to reach its destination.

The elevator dinged, and the cart pushed over the threshold again. If one of us didn't do something, we would be overboard and gone before anyone else would miss us. It was now or never to make a scene. Gary was going to kill us either way. The least I could do was go out of my way and not give him the satisfaction of having the last laugh at this old lady.

Locked in our silence, I turned to Robyn, our eyes communicating the desperate plan taking shape in my mind. Pantomiming my intentions, I swayed my body back and forth, urging her to join me. If we could both disrupt the stability of the cart, it might throw Gary off balance or even topple the whole contraption.

With synchronized determination, we began swaying within the confines of our restraints. The rusted wheels of the cart, worn down by the constant exposure to sea air and moisture, emitted piercing squeaks reverberating in my ears, drowning out all other sounds. The cacophony was almost deafening, a symphony of defiance echoing through the confined space. The loud noise must have reached far, alerting anyone within earshot.

I heard Gary's frustrated expletives as the cart jolted to a sudden halt. One of the wheels had given way, caught in its deteriorated state. Our makeshift rebellion had momentarily disrupted his control, offering a glimmer of hope in the midst of our dire circumstances.

Gary pushed into my back as he tried to physically re-adjust the wheel. With all of our weight in the cart, adjusting it was turning out to be tricky, but there was no way the basket would move now. A sudden pain spread throughout my shoulder when Gary hit the side of the cart with what I assumed was the metal pipe.

"Move your weight off this back wheel and slide forward." Gary's grunts filled the air as he attempted to overpower me, pushing me forward in an effort to relieve the weight on the stuck wheel. But I resisted with all my might, defying his intentions. Instead, I exerted pressure onto that very wheel, using my feet to anchor myself in the opposite corner, gaining the advantage of leverage.

The wheel groaned in protest, its metal frame straining under the force I applied. Gary's efforts to push me in the opposite direction proved futile against my determined resistance. And then, without warning, the corner of the cart against which my back was pressed creaked ominously, giving way under strain. In an instant, the cart lurched downward, causing my rear end to meet the unforgiving surface below—concrete, I surmised.

"Damn it!" Gary groaned as he pulled off the towels and blankets from Robyn's and my head.

I glanced up at Gary, my gaze locking with his as he stood over me, his face drenched in sweat. The droplets cascaded down his flushed face, trickling along his neck before disappearing into the fabric of his shirt. His visage seemed even more deranged and frantic than before, reflecting his escalating desperation.

There was a wildness in his eyes, a glint betraying the depths of his disturbed state of mind. The intensity in his gaze sent a chill down my spine, a stark reminder of the danger we were facing.

"This is YOUR fault!" he screamed. "You shouldn't have stuck your nose where it wasn't needed. Get out! Both of you! We are going to walk down the hall to the disposal room. We have a slight change of plans."

Gary's voice was getting hysterical and high-pitched. He grabbed Robyn's arm and yanked her to stand. "Now, don't think you can run," Gary sneered as he reached for his pocket and pulled out a knife. "I will use this. I have nothing else to lose." I believed him. He wasn't thinking logically or rationally. He would stab us without thinking twice about it. Robyn and I needed the upper hand soon before he finally lost the last bit of self-control.

Gary reached into the basket and yanked my arm hard, forcing me to stand and get out of the crashed basket. I looked around and noticed deck number three labeling the hallway. We'd actually gone further down in the ship than I had ever been . How anyone was going to find us, I'd yet to learn.

Chapter Thirty-Seven

The dimly lit corridor on this lower level of the ship
exuded an eerie stillness as if time slowed to a crawl. The
absence of people amplified the sense of desolation,
indicating it must be approaching midnight. Only those
unfortunate enough to be assigned the night shift would
travel into this part of the ship so late at night.

As we rounded the corner, hushed whispers reached
our ears, prompting Gary to seize handfuls of our hair,
yanking us forcefully to a halt. The sharp pain of my hair
being wrenched from its carefully arranged updo pierced
through me, leaving behind a lingering sting. It had taken
considerable effort to fashion my hair into an elegant
style just a few hours ago. How swiftly the tides turned
since then, plunging us into a nightmarish reality that felt
like an eternity in the making.

The distant voices gradually faded into the night,
retreating in the opposite direction, carrying with them
any flicker of hope igniting within me. Their diminishing
footsteps were a stark reminder of our isolation, leaving
us to navigate this treacherous path alone.

Continuing our journey, we walked past several
more rooms. Seizing Gary's distractedness, I covertly
wriggled my ring off my trembling right hand, allowing
it to slip onto the cold floor. I masked the faint clatter
with a cough, hoping to conceal any evidence of my act
of defiance. In response, Gary shoved me with a force

exceeding necessity, a vicious retribution for my inadvertent noise.

Finally, we entered the next room, only to be greeted by a nauseating stench permeating the air. The putrid odor invaded my senses, causing my stomach to churn and threatening to expel the dinner I'd consumed earlier. Gagging uncontrollably, I turned to Robyn, and her expression mirrored the discomfort I felt deep within.

As my eyes adjusted to the room's dimness, I could see many barrels with warning labels on them. Waste, biohazard signs, and other symbols read like a foreign language. Some machines radiated heat, and others had tags about the type of water: gray, black, and bilge. All of these were foreign to me, but we shouldn't be in this room if I had to guess.

Gary motioned us forward, closed the door quietly, and turned the light on. He moved toward the barrels in the corner labeled biohazard and prized two of the lids open. He peered inside and smiled.

"Welcome to the last home you will ever know." He took a step towards Robyn, and she started crying. The closer he came to us, the more her cries started escalating into hysterical sobs. She gasped for air, her breathing becoming increasingly labored. Suddenly, she collapsed to the floor, her body convulsing uncontrollably. Gary's gaze widened in alarm, torn between his initial intentions and the sight of Robyn in agonizing pain, her vulnerability piercing through his hardened demeanor.

"Help her!" he bellowed at me, his voice trembling with uncertainty. I raised my hand, gesturing towards the gag that silenced me, attempting to convey I was willing to assist but entirely dependent on his mercy. With hesitant urgency, he approached me and seized my hands, clumsily wielding his knife to free me from the constricting ropes.

"Don't try anything! Just make her shut up," he growled, his voice laden with a mixture of desperation and menace, as he propelled me toward Robyn. Keeping a cautious eye on the door, he cracked it open slightly, checking for any signs of approaching footsteps or eavesdropping ears.

"May I remove her gag? She's hyperventilating. Taking it off will help her regain control of her breathing," I asked, employing the soothing tone of a seasoned teacher. Years of experience dealing with students and distressed parents had honed this voice, granting me a semblance of authority in this dire situation.

"Fine! But do it quickly. I have other things I need to tend to." He responded as though killing us was just something he had to mark off his checklist, not homicide.

I leaned into Robyn and tried to sound as calm as I could under the circumstances. "We are going to be okay," I said, unsure if I actually believed it, but we were still alive.

Gary's unease was palpable as he witnessed Robyn's struggle with hyperventilation. The prospect of taking her life seemed to weigh heavily on him, and I dared to hope his remaining shreds of humanity would overpower his sinister intentions, prompting him to flee instead. This was a glimmer of possibility amidst the darkness enveloping us.

Robyn's nod indicated her agreement, her breathing gradually steadying as the absence of the gag provided her with some relief. I tenderly ran my hand down her back, offering solace, and began softly humming the familiar tune of "You Are My Sunshine." This comforting melody had been a cherished song in my family, and I had sung it to Veronica when she was little.

The resonance of my humming reverberated through the room, filling the air with a gentle vibration. Robyn, still shaken from the recent trauma, started swaying back and forth, seeking solace in the rhythm. Her breaths grew more regular, and the flow of tears subsided. Leaning down, I pressed a gentle kiss to her forehead and brushed her hair away from her dampened face. The combination of sweat and tears caused strands of her hair to adhere to her temples and cheeks.

Her eyes were swollen from how much crying she'd done tonight. Blood vessels had burst around her eyes and cheeks. She wasn't speaking to me, and her eyes were shut tight. If we made it through this, there would be a lot of therapy Robyn would need. That, along with a support system, will help guide her through this experience. I would be willing to help her get through this shared experience, but she would need someone else to depend on.

"Well?! Is she finished having a fit?" Gary turned with a mixture of hatred and worry in his gaze. His body language told me he was way over his head and wasn't sure what to do next. It looked like he was having an inner war with himself. He had cared for and loved Robyn for so long that he wanted to come and comfort her, but his hatred and victim-blaming self won over. He wasn't going to change his plan for anyone. Even the person he claimed he loved and wanted to spend the rest of his life with.

"She is starting to calm down, but I think the trauma of all of this has greatly impacted her mentally, emotionally, and physically." I tried to keep his focus on Robyn. The person he had feelings for. If only one person made it through this, I wanted it to be her.

Gary paced back and forth, his internal struggle evident in his restless movements. Sensing an opportunity, I mustered the courage to ask the burning question that plagued many victims in the presence of their abusers. "Why are you doing this, Gary? You had a chance to start over." Transparency was key at this point, and I laid all my cards on the metaphorical table.

Gary's gaze flickered in my direction, and he halted his pacing. "Why? You want to know why?" Without waiting for my response, the words spilled out of his mouth in a rush, fueled by pent-up emotions. He leaned against the door, peering into the depths of his memories. "You know Robyn and I were in the system together, right?"

I nodded silently, fearful of speaking aloud in his presence.

"We ended up in the same foster home when we were seventeen," Gary continued. "We were considered too old to be wanted by a loving family but too young to be deemed adults and left to our own devices. They threw kids like us into homes filled with castoffs. Those people only cared about the financial benefits we allowed them. They didn't care where we ended up, who we lived with, or what became of us." His gaze drifted past my shoulder, lost in the recollection of his tumultuous adolescence.

I turned to look at Robyn, realizing she, too, was fixated on Gary's words, unshed tears shimmering in her eyes. They were both reliving the pain of that time, and my heart ached for them. The thought of growing up without a supportive family was unimaginable.

"Robyn and I made a pact then and there," Gary continued, his attention shifting back to Robyn. "We decided to be the family we needed for each other. I promised to take care of her." He paused, locking his intense gaze with Robyn's. "And I kept that promise, didn't I, Birdie?"

Robyn shrank back under his gaze but nodded in confirmation. "But it wasn't enough for you. It was supposed to be us against the world. When we turned eighteen, we left. I found us jobs on a cruise ship, a chance to see the world and have everything we never had as kids. We were going to do it together. That was until…" Gary's voice trailed off, and he hurriedly moved to squat in front of Robyn.

Clearing my throat, I completed his unfinished sentence, my voice laced with curiosity and concern. "That was until you met Arba and Seth?"

Gary's piercing glare shifted toward me, filled with hostility. "Yes. Arba was never a threat to my relationship with Robyn. He was harmless. I knew he could never replace me."

"But…" I urged him to continue, to reveal the missing piece of the puzzle.

"Seth and I had become close friends. Or so I thought," Gary confessed, his tone tinged with bitterness. "We both knew the cruise line didn't pay us what we deserved, so we devised a plan to claim our rightful share. Everything was going according to plan until Seth set his sights on Robyn. My Robyn. My Birdie." He paused, the weight of his words hanging in the air.

I furrowed my brow, showing my confusion. "Why

is your nickname Gray?"

"Robyn is dyslexic," Gary explained, his voice thick with emotion. "She often switches numbers and letters when she reads. That's one of the reasons she became a makeup artist. You can't really mess up makeup, can you? Anyway, she misread my name as Gray instead of Gary. I found it endearing at first until people started mocking my supposed 'gray personality' or how dreary I am." Anger, temporarily quelled, surged within him once more, and he violently shoved Robyn, causing her head to collide with the nearby barrel.

"She needs to see a doctor!" I hollered as I reached for her.

"She isn't going to be needing a doctor. Not where you and she are going. No amount of modern medicine will be able to bring you back. Now I'm going to need you to stand up and walk toward that barrel over there. It has your name on it." Just as Gary started walking my way, there was a bang in the hallway outside the door. Someone was out there.

Gary jolted and turned back to the door, mumbling some choice words. Apparently, this wasn't going as well as he'd planned in his demented head. He turned back to both of us and growled a non-human sound.

"You two stay where you are. I'm going to see what is going on. Do not move. If you do, more things will be done to you before you go into your barrel." He left what those things would be to the imagination. He moved towards the door and opened it more to peer outside. Whatever he saw had piqued his interest as he threw us a threatening glance before stepping out into the hall and shutting the door firmly behind him. I knew it was only a matter of time before he would return to finish his job.

A wave of gratitude washed over me as I reflected on my life. I'd been blessed with a rich and fulfilling journey filled with remarkable experiences and cherished memories. From the exhilaration of my first plane ride to the wonders of my archaeological expeditions, from the joys of love to the profound happiness of becoming a mother, I had lived a life that resonated with purpose.

As danger loomed before us in this critical moment, I realized I had no regrets. I'd lived fully and authentically, embracing every opportunity that came my way. The weight of my past accomplishments and the love I'd shared with others fueled my resolve.

With a serene smile gracing my lips, I made a silent vow to protect Robyn, the young woman whose life was just beginning to unfold. She deserved the chance to experience all the wonders and joys ahead. If sacrificing myself could grant her that precious gift, then it was a sacrifice I was willing to make.

A calm determination settled within me. I would face whatever challenges lay ahead with unwavering courage and unwavering love. My heart, free from regret, beat in harmony with the conviction that this act of selflessness was the truest testament to a life well lived.

With a renewed sense of purpose, I steadied myself, ready to confront the danger awaiting us. There would be no hesitation, no second-guessing.

Chapter Thirty-Eight

I gently turned to Robyn and grasped her face in my hands. "Everything will be okay. When I stand up, I am going to need you to move and hide behind some of the machinery. Nod your head if you understand me." I whispered into Robyn's ear. She must not have been as far gone as I thought because she could give me a slight nod. That was good enough for me.

As I stood up, Robyn finally opened her eyes. She looked around in panic, but there was strength in the set of her jaw and the way she stood up. I moved to untie her hands and gave her the rope. I motioned to her with my head to go and hide. Her eyes filled with tears as she lunged at me and hugged me. I patted her back, kissed her forehead, and pushed her in the direction of the machines behind us.

I waited for her to hide before looking around the room for a weapon. I may be going down, but I wouldn't go down without a fight. The room was very well organized, no matter the smell. There was a small closet beside the door Gary left through. I tried my luck at turning the handle, and apparently, the gods were with me. As I turned the knob to the right, the door was unlatched, and what waited beyond the door was none other than a broom and mopping equipment.

As I stood in the closet, my mind wandered to a familiar holiday movie my daughter adored: *Home*

Alone. The tale of a clever and resourceful young boy defending his home against intruders played vividly in my thoughts. I'd once dismissed the boy's antics as implausible and fantastical, but now, in this dire situation, his ingenuity sparked a glimmer of inspiration within me.

Time was of the essence. Gary's absence provided a fleeting opportunity, but it wouldn't last long. With a sense of urgency, I scanned the closet's contents, searching for any useful tools or items. And then, my gaze settled upon the mopping fluid and the mop.

A plan started taking shape in my mind, borrowing a page from the young protagonist's playbook. If the boy in the movie could create a series of elaborate booby traps using household objects, surely I could devise a simpler but effective defense strategy with the limited resources at hand.

Without hesitation, I seized the mopping fluid and the trusty mop, envisioning their potential. The slippery nature of the fluid could serve as a clever obstacle, hindering Gary's movements and buying us precious time. This was a small but significant step toward turning the tide in our favor.

I dumped all the liquid on the floor in front of the door and made a slippery path within the first ten feet of the entrance. If he didn't fall right when he walked in, he might as he tried to find us girls. I took a deep breath and readied myself behind the door with the mop handle in my hand. I may not be as strong as I was when I was younger, but I could swing a mop and hit someone. I let all the air release from my lungs and stilled my body. I was only going to get one shot at this. Armed with a mop and a reservoir of determination, I readied myself to face the impending danger. The echoes of *Home Alone* lingered in my mind, reminding me that sometimes, even the most improbable solutions could be the key to survival. I needed to make this swing count for everything in my life. I put all of my anger towards this man, toward all men who treated women as trophies to be owned, into my hands. I was ready. I was going to give it all I had.

I didn't have to wait long before I heard Gary outside the door. "Thanks, Arba! I appreciate you going above and beyond for our crew and guests. I left my walkie-talkie in here, but I'll be following shortly behind you!" Gary sounded his usual "Aussie" self. Very happy-go-lucky. A shiver went down my spine as I realized how easy it was for him to turn on and off the charm. No one should be that artful at lying.

"No problem, Mr. Baggs. See you in the morning!" Arba said as I heard his footsteps starting to walk away. My heart broke a little as our last hope of freedom walked back to his quarters. But I needed to focus my energy back on the plan at hand.

As Gary cautiously stepped into the room, unaware of our absence, I observed him intently. The anticipation of his reaction heightened my senses, and I relished the thought of defying his expectations. No one had ever labeled me a "good girl," and I had no intentions of conforming to his twisted desires.

A hushed whisper escaped his lips as he muttered, "What the hell? Where are you?" His confusion was palpable, evident in his tone as he closed the door behind him. I couldn't help but feel a tinge of disappointment he didn't slip on the slippery floor I'd prepared. After all, one cannot expect the same results as a resourceful ten-year-old boy with a movie budget.

However, I had my own plan in motion. Positioning myself stealthily behind Gary, I tightly gripped the mop, ready to strike. Inhaling deeply, I steadied my nerves, channeling a surge of determination.

With a forceful exhale, I swung the mop downward, aiming for the crown of Gary's head. My intention was to incapacitate him, but the reality fell short of my expectations. His scream pierced through the air, echoing off the walls much louder than I'd anticipated. Disappointed and taken aback, I realized reality diverged from the often sensationalized portrayals of violence in murder shows.

Nevertheless, I maintained my composure, refusing to let the setback deter me. The thrill of defiance coursed through my veins, fueling my resolve to protect myself and Robyn at any cost.

"You bitch!" Gary screamed as he turned toward me. I'd done some damage because I could see drips of blood falling on his shirt and getting in his eyes. It must have hurt, but he lunged toward me anyway. That was the moment that *Home Alone* didn't disappoint. Gary couldn't gain purchase on the floor and started to fall forward as he ran toward me.

As Gary lay on the floor, struggling to regain his footing, I seized the opportunity to strike him once more, aiming another blow at his head. This time, it had the desired effect as he ceased his attempts to move or rise. I cautiously approached, leaning down to ensure he was still breathing. However, just as I neared him, he unexpectedly lunged forward, snatching my wrist and twisting it with a sickening snap. The pain surged through my arm, and a scream escaped my lips, causing me to drop the mop in agony. Just like in the scary movies, the villain always manages to rise again.

But in that pivotal moment, Robyn burst out of nowhere, seizing the opportunity to retaliate against our captor. With a swift leap onto Gary's back, she retrieved the rope he'd used to bind her, swiftly wrapping it around his neck and pulling it taut. Gary, desperate to free himself from the grip of the rope, released my injured wrist, struggling to loosen the noose around his throat. Robyn's eyes blazed with a mixture of anger and accumulated pain; her determination evident as she refused to let go. I couldn't help but recognize if given the chance, she might have taken his life at that moment.

Yet, as Gary's hands dropped from his throat, his body succumbing to unconsciousness, the maintenance door abruptly swung open, revealing the unexpected arrival of Martin, Wilma, Charlotte, and Beverly. They entered the room, their presence a timely intervention in this chaotic scene.

"Well, it does seem you get to have all the fun," Wilma scoffed as all my friends ran toward me to envelop me in a gut-wrenching hug. We all cried and laughed as we realized how close we were to losing each other. I was never going to let this happen again. I had a new lease of life and wasn't about to let it go so easily.

Chapter Thirty-Nine

The next morning, I awoke in the med bay, finding myself all too familiar with this part of the ship. This was becoming a recurring pattern that needed to be broken for the remainder of our journey. My arm was encased in a cast, and while the pain was bearable, I opted to stick with Tylenol rather than anything stronger, heeding the doctor's advice. I wanted to keep my mind clear, alert, and present.

With Gary now in custody and Robyn resting in her room, both of us nursing physical bumps and bruises that would heal over time, our emotional wounds ran deeper and would require more time to mend. After delving into the depths of our past during this harrowing ordeal, I realized the importance of seeking professional help to address the lingering trauma. The past wasn't the only thing haunting me; I also had present traumas to confront. I would rely on Veronica to assist me in finding a trustworthy therapist, someone with whom I could share my experiences and begin the healing process.

Shifting on my bed, I adjusted the pillows beneath my head and turned my gaze towards the row of chairs around me. Beverly, Wilma, and Char steadfastly refused to sleep in their own rooms last night, instead choosing to keep watch over me. Martin, ever the caring presence, had his team bring in additional chairs and blankets to ensure their comfort. I couldn't help but feel a growing fondness for him, appreciating his support and presence throughout this ordeal. As we prepared to depart the ship, I would miss having him around, even though the rest of the Cruising Crew might not reciprocate the feeling.

I chuckled and shook my head at the ridiculousness of our team. They looked so uncomfortable in the chairs wrapped in the blankets. But they were my family. My chosen family. I could feel my heart swell with love and pride for them and what they did to find me. They went through hell to make sure I was okay, and I loved them even more for it. I recalled their tale as a nurse wrapped my arm last night.

"How did you all find us?" I asked, grimacing from the sharp pains as the nurse moved my arm around to get the gauze on.

"Well, first, it was your shoe. It was left outside the door. I woke up and needed some ice water. You know how much I despise room-temperature water," Charlotte responded. "I thought it was strange you just left it out there. But maybe you and Richard were in a passionate embrace. He flung you into the stairwell and took you like the young maiden you are. You know how my mind goes when my imagination gets a story. So, I picked it up, returned it to your room, and gave it to Wilma.

Wilma took over then. "I was confused about why you'd left it. So, I called Richard's room to make sure you knew I had it. I also hoped you were having a love affair and was shocked when Richard answered the phone. He told me about his room being flooded and how you decided to go back to our room." Wilma grabbed my other hand, which wasn't fractured. She squeezed it so tightly that I might have needed the nurse to wrap it if

Beverly hadn't cleared her throat to alert Wilma to my discomfort.

"I just knew something had happened to you. So, I called the girls, and we all left to find Martin. He was in such a fuss because he had a break in the case and didn't have time for us. Of course, we insisted he help us find you. We even made him do an all-call on the ship's speaker system, but no one called." Wilma's eyes filled with worry and tears.

Beverly continued. "We were told to return to our rooms and wait for Martin. He would send a team to look for you. He was trying to find Gary, but he wasn't in his room or office. We returned to our rooms and found Arba outside Robyn's room. He told us he'd been trying to find Robyn to apologize, but she wasn't answering the door, and no one had seen her for a while. We all remembered that the last time we saw Robyn was in the dining hall with Gary."

"We convinced Arba to open Robyn's room, and what we found was a lot of broken items and no Robyn. It was much of a coincidence that you and Robyn were missing, and Gary couldn't be found," Charlotte added.

"Arba took it upon himself to start searching the crew areas while Beverly and Charlotte found Martin. I stayed at our door with the promise that someone would come and get me if they found you," Wilma said. She let go of my hand but rested the hand on my leg. She needed to touch me to feel grounded and see I was really here.

"But how did you all find us? I was only able to get my one shoe and ring off. There wasn't a lot we could do." The nurse started on the plaster of my cast, and the protection felt much more secure, and I could feel the pain lessening.

Beverly cleared her throat to continue. "Well, that's the thing. Apparently, Gary wasn't being as stealthy as he thought, and he didn't know the maintenance crew's schedules. Quite a few people saw him in the stairway with Robyn. When he had the laundry basket, he made a lot of noise, and a crew member tried to use the elevator that Gary shut on him. He knew that area was not meant for laundry as it was the disposal area for more unsavory things like chemicals and waste. Arba found your ring on the bottom level, though he had no idea where you all were," Beverly explained.

"It wasn't until Gary stepped out of the room that he suspected anything. Gary didn't normally allow himself to slum it in the bottom decks of the ship. He felt like that was beneath him. When Gary tried to shoo him away by being a little too nice, Arba started getting suspicious," Charlotte said, continuing to untangle the events of the night.

"When did you guys start making your way down?" I asked.

Martin and Arba walked into the med bay, I'm assuming, to check on me and get my statement.

"I knew something was wrong, and I found your ring. I remembered you wearing it before, and with Robyn missing too, I thought something had happened. I called him on the walkie-talkie. We were the only ones on the channel, so even if Gary had his walkie-talkie on him, he wouldn't have heard it unless he was on the same channel as us," Arba said shyly.

Martin nodded and then cleared his throat. "Yes. The ladies and I met Wilma at your room and went below deck where Arba said he saw Gary. And you sort of know the rest of the story. I'm very impressed with how you handled yourself in saving Robyn and your lives." Martin tilted his head as though he was wearing a cowboy hat.

"But I would have rather you kept your nose out of this investigation. You and Wilma might not have gotten hurt," he finished.

"But Robyn could be dead, and Gary could have left at the docking point, and you would have been none the wiser. You should be grateful to us older ladies for putting our heads together to solve this for you," I answered with a lilt of anger in my voice. Yes, I knew what we'd done was reckless and dangerous, but we'd done it with compassion in our hearts, saved someone, and locked up a killer.

"I will give credit where it is due. Your daughter's online sleuthing is impressive and helped me access the needed files to ensure I could put Mr. Baggs in the brig. Authorities will be waiting for us at the dock. They will probably want statements from all of you," Martin said. "I have more paperwork to do, but I hope you ladies will enjoy the next few days to yourself and try not to get into any more murder investigations. No matter how good you think you are at solving them." He winked and motioned for Arba to join him.

I raised my hand for them to stop. "Before you leave, Arba, I just want to say how thankful I am that you pushed past yourself to help Robyn and me last night. You are the true hero. We might not have made it without your interference and allowing me time to put a trap together for Gary. Thank you." I could feel my voice shake as I finished, but he needed to know he was the hero. My hero.

Epilogue

For the rest of the vacation, we found solace and camaraderie among ourselves. Richard, guilt-ridden for leaving me alone, visited the med bay after Martin and Arba left. He apologized profusely, revealing that Gary sabotaged the bathroom pipes in Richard's room to ensure his absence during the ordeal. This was a chilling realization that Gary intended to dispose of me later, wielding the very pipe he'd threatened us with when forcing us into the laundry basket. Martin informed us Gary planned to keep it as a twisted memento.

With a renewed sense of determination, we all agreed to make the most of the remaining time on the ship. We indulged in adult beverages, danced with abandon, and soaked in the hot tub, relishing the freedom we'd fought to reclaim. Wilma, finally shaken by her own mortality after the fall, let go of her insistence on morning walks. Upon returning home, she would have her own battles, but knew she wouldn't face them alone. We promised to stand by her every step of the way.

Upon docking, Richard and I exchanged contact information and addresses, vowing to stay in touch. He had matters to attend to back in Europe but assured me he would reach out. Before he departed, he kissed me passionately, eliciting cheers and applause from our friends. As I walked toward the car, I opened my phone and found an email from a community college inquiring about an adjunct position for the upcoming fall semester. The fire within me ignited, fueling a desire to continue seeking new experiences and perhaps embark on another adventure.

This trip taught me that while I may not be young in years, the depth of my life experiences held value. I realized there was still so much to embrace, explore, and contribute to the world. And with that realization, I embarked on the next chapter of my life, ready to seize the opportunities awaiting me.

A word about the author…

Meet Courtny Bradley, affectionately known as Courtagonist in the cozy mystery realm. An educator with over a decade of experience, Courtny has been unraveling cozy mysteries online since 2017. Married to her best friend, she juggles the delightful chaos of parenting two rambunctious toddlers in the heart of Oklahoma. Courtny's cozy expertise shines as she guides fellow mystery enthusiasts through the charming world of whodunits, a journey seasoned with warmth, wit, and a touch of Oklahoma flair. www.courtagonist.com

Printed in the USA
CPSIA information can be obtained
at www.ICGtesting.com
LVHW021821071024
793118LV00001B/218

9 781509 257577